He was MW00475497 twenty years old, no more, taller than average but not excessively so, and dressed more casually than was the current style: fading green trousers, a grubby white T shirt and white running shoes. There was a lean and hungry look about him that reminded the guide of an ancient legend she had been read by her mother as a child. It was something about men being dangerous when they have that look . . .

Also available in Target Books by the same author:

The Blake's 7 Programme Guide
Blake's 7 – Afterlife

The Companions of Doctor Who

TURLOUGH AND THE EARTHLINK DILEMMA

Tony Attwood

By arrangement with the
British Broadcasting Corporation.

A TARGET BOOK

published by
the Paperback Division of
W.H. Allen & Co. PLC

A Target Book
Published in 1986
by the Paperback Division of
W.H. Allen & Co. PLC
44 Hill Street, London W1X 8LB,
by arrangement with the British Broadcasting Corporation.

Copyright © Tony Attwood, 1986

Printed in Great Britain by
Hunt Barnard Printing Ltd, Aylesbury, Bucks.

ISBN 0 426 202368

This book is sold subject to the condition that it shall not,
by way of trade or otherwise, be lent, re-sold, hired out or
otherwise circulated without the publisher's prior consent in
any other form of binding or cover other than that in which it
is published and without a similar condition including this
condition being imposed upon the subsequent purchaser.

Contents

'Philosophers merely explain the world. The thing however is to change it.'

INTRODUCTION

Dear Readers,

I imagine that most of you about to embark on *Turlough And The Earthlink Dilemma* will have seen my portrayal of the character on BBC TV – be prepared for a surprise!

One of the problems of being a companion on *Doctor Who* is that you would really, of course, like to be playing the Doctor, but within the context of a 25 minute episode there just isn't time for everyone to play a leading part, or to have their character developed as fully as you might wish . . . You may have noticed that Turlough spent a great deal of time kept captive in various states of bondage. It was always a disappointment to me that there seemed to be no getting around this problem. The novel puts no such limitations on the writer, and Tony Attwood comes out with creative guns blazing.

I first met Tony eighteen months ago when he was doing research for the book, since when he has constantly been in touch, but the end result of his labours surpasses even my expectations. Here Turlough arrives for the first time with three dimensions: he has warmth, depth, a sense of humour (believe it or not!) and, dare I say, a 'humanity', which leads to a romantic side to his nature, which, as a confirmed romantic myself, was especially nice to see – hanky-panky was a definite no-go area in the TARDIS!

For one who lives without answerphone, video machine or computer, and whose only concessions to modern gadgetry are an ancient black and white television and a food mixer, some of the scientific jargon was a little difficult to understand – you may have noticed me having the occasional problem getting round the words on *Doctor Who* sometimes – but the story kept my attention throughout as I'm sure it will you.

I shall tell no secrets to give the game away, but leave you to discover the real Turlough for yourselves; suffice it to say, be assured that the wretched shining cube does *not* make an appearance – I made sure of that!

Best Wishes,

Mark Strickson (and Turlough)

00: PROLOGUE

For over nine thousand years the Clans had ruled Trion and the Triic colonies. Initially the regime had been harsh, even dictatorial as Clansmen and women set about formulating the mould that was to last through the millenia. That regime could be summarised in two words: science and technology.

To the Clans, scientific research and development, combined with its application into all technological fields, was the centre of their philosophy; the heart and soul of their existence. Everything was secondary to the maximising of scientific achievement; from the development of science all good would flow, life would be better, richer, freer.

And in many ways they were right. After the early days of Ykstort I and Nilatis IV the Clans began to settle down. The good things of life became more plentiful, shortages were of the past and the vast mass of the populace (who were not of the Clans) were left to get on with their own lives, organising themselves as they best pleased. If they chose war and savagery, as they did from time to time, that was their affair. The Clans did not interfere.

The empire expanded. Everyone recognised Clan supremacy, and in return for that recognition the Imperial Clans, as they became known, were happy to pass on the fruits of their research. Some ideas caught on at once—the one thousand kilometres a minute Vacuum Transport system, for example, revolutionised travel overnight. But the development of cold fusion power waited four hundred years before a non-Clansman realised it made for smaller, more efficient, faster space ships. The Clans had known this all along, but somehow never got round to telling anyone.

9

Yet despite all their work certain problems were never solved. On the practical front the key question of time-travel remained beyond reach, although several great minds almost resolved the issue, only to have their final experiments fail – deliberately sabotaged by Time Lords, according to popular rumour. And in the field of pure theory the last outstanding issue was the total comprehension of the way in which the four fundamental forces that link the Universe combine. That too seemed eternally out of reach.

Such difficulties did not worry the Clans overmuch. Freedom and plenty (for them at least) were assured, and secure in their remote citadels deep in the forests of Trion they could look ahead to another nine thousand years of science.

Except for one thing. Being so far removed from the bulk of the population they failed to notice a change – a new development in everyday politics on the planet, a development tht finally brought about a revolution which overthrew the Clans and exiled the Imperial Clansmen and women to old, now deserted colonies and uncivilised planets far away from Triic influence.

The revolution, backed by a significant section of the populace, nevertheless made many uneasy, for although the Clans had remained autocratic and aloof they had not actually hurt anyone for thousands of years, and had certainly given much in return for recognition as the nominal rulers of Trion.

Yet as the mutterings of discontent grew following the revolution, so too did the control of the revolution by one person, the aging but forceful Rehctaht, the most dominant unforgiving woman Trion had ever known.

Her rule lasted a mere seven years, and during that time virtually all Clansmen were exiled. According to Rehctaht, the Clans could now learn the error of their arrogant ways. Their rule would be broken forever.

Among the exiles was one Vislor Turlough. Young, barely more than a boy, he found himself sent to Earth, where the local Rehctaht agent gained him a place in a minor public school in southern England. Desperate to escape, the boy allowed himself to be used by the alien Black Guardian as a pawn in an attempt to kill the Doctor. The plan failed, and

10

Turlough found his escape from Earth travelling with the Time Lord around the galaxy in that space and time ship called the TARDIS. But then an emergency call led Turlough back to a Triic colony, and the young Clansman realised it was time to give up running and face the rest of his exile.

Rehctaht, meanwhile, was having troubles of her own. She had promised liberty from Clan rule, and the chance to develop new Trion technology through this supposed new freedom. But the developments failed, and the promised liberty proved to be a myth. As the economy declined so Rehctaht was turned upon and a second uprising brought in the counter-revolutionary Committee of Public Safety. Exile orders were rescinded and Clansmen were encouraged to return. At last Turlough could walk on the Home Planet a free man.

In common with all those who did make it back he was treated as a hero, and implored to aid the return to the old ways. This most Clansmen readily agreed to do, although they knew the days of splendid isolation were over. From now on the Clans would live more closely with everyone else . . .

01: ACE

Turning, the guide reviewed her party. There was little to distinguish the group from any other she took round the site three times a day, two hundred days a year. Tourists waiting to be shocked, men trying to impress with their (invariably erroneous) academic knowledge, children anxiously waiting to get into the underground caverns (and children scared witless who had just come out), and the occasional professor seeing for himself after years of lecturing students on the subject of the early ruins of the planet.

Yet despite her initial dismissal of the group there was one distinguishing feature. And if the woman in the blue one-piece jumpsuit had not asked a ridiculous question about the wall inscriptions the guide would never have noticed. He (that is the factor that distinguished this group from any other) was bending low, peering intently at a set of excavations which revealed one of the layout diagrams discovered during the first dig. It was, the guide knew, a significant find, for without it the archeologists could never have made such an excellent job of the site as a whole. The diagrams not only told them *where* to look, they also told the excavating team *what* they were looking for. Not that these tourists would appreciate that. It if didn't move, or better still frighten, they weren't interested.

Except this man. She recognised the face, the ginger-blond (or should that be sandy brown?) hair, cut short just touching the ears, the slightly pointed chin, the deep set, cold blue-grey eyes . . .

A movement in the party brought the guide back to reality. She removed her eyes from the man and led the way down a steep slope into the fifth chamber, returning to her script.

'Who the builders were,' she droned in a voice made monotonous by the endless repepititions of uninspired prose, 'is unknown. Most of the buildings in this complex seem to have been built about 240,000 years ago, suggesting a short period of construction followed by a period of exploration of not more than ten thousand years, and then departure. We don't know why they came, what they found, or why they went. We can only surmise facts about them from what they left behind.'

Still speaking, the guide once more sought out the sandy hair and clear eyes. She nearly missed them, until she spotted the man once more bent double studying an inscription on the wall; a set of characters which were elevated above the surrounding symbols seemed to fascinate him particularly. He was young, barely more than a boy, perhaps twenty years old, no more; taller than average but not excessively so, and dressed more casually than was the current style, fading green trousers, a grubby white T shirt and white running shoes. There was a lean hungry look about him that reminded the guide of an ancient legend she had been read by her mother as a child. It was something about men being dangerous when they have that look . . .

He was the only member of the party who was obviously not with a friend, as well as being the only one not carrying either a camera or a monitoring unit. For that one fact her heart went out to him. The monitoring units were programmed to put the official guide-talk on the screen to match whatever the unit was pointing at. With a real live guide and an active monitoring unit one had total redundancy of one unit. And after fourteen hundred trips round the ruins the live guide knew which unit she felt was redundant.

Turning once more the guide drove her party on. 'The most obvious fact to be deduced from these ruins,' she announced moving into a new chamber, 'is that these buildings were constructed by beings of similar physical appearance to ourselves, although possibly slightly taller. The door height allows us comfortably in, and we could imagine living, although in a rather cramped way, in any of these quarters. This is not so of the ruins in Mhacha, Connall or Bricriu. The

14

people, beings, entities or whatever they were that built Mhacha were at least twice as tall as us, those at Connall left rubbish tips which are not found at Mhacha and Bricriu, and were only found to a limited extent here, and we can be sure that the beings at Bricriu were also exceptionally interested in wide spaces and luxurious conditions for their living accommodation. Indeed, unlike the builders here we may also imagine that they had problems coping with our gravity. In fact, it may be said that our builders here seemed to be almost able to ignore gravity.'

The guide turned to move on, but a question held her back. 'What was in the waste tips?'

A regular question. It was from a sixteen-year-old boy. 'At Connall the tips contained building materials and samples of rock, plants and anything else moveable that had presumably been taken across the planet for study at that base. At Connall we even find remnants that probably came from the settlement here, which almost certainly predates Connall by ten thousand years.'

'And here?' He spoke. It was the man she had been watching. He had been peering carefully at the floor and now straightened up to catch the reply. She wondered why he asked. She wished he hadn't.

'Animal bones, small alloy containers . . .'

'Anything else?'

'Excrement.'

'Which showed what the inhabitants ate?'

'Yes'

'What did they eat?'

'Our ancestors.'

There was a stir among the tourists. It wasn't that visitors were not allowed to know what the beings who had built this complex had lived on, it was just that the news was never broadcast. The owners of the land (who gained most from the tourist trade) knew perfectly well what stories were good for business and which ones were not. After all, they argued (and as the guide suggested in her officially approved speech), their planet had been visited at least five times in its history, and apparently each time by a totally different race of creatures. It

15

just so happened that they owned the land on which were to be found the ruins of the race that did the most unspeakable thing.

'And it was about a quarter of a million years ago you say?' It was clear he was not letting go of whatever it was he was chasing.

She nodded dumbly, her face just discernable in the half-light thrown up from the deliberately feeble torches attached to the walls.

'So our ancestors were us. I mean they had developed into us. There's been no genetic development in the past quarter of a million years has there?'

At last rescue came. No one actually spoke, but several of the party had started to head towards the next chamber. They had paid good money to see the Giants' Drop and they weren't going to be held back by unpleasant debates about the diets of beings from other planets. As she pushed her way to the front of the party, the guide heard a deep eastern accent tell the man not to upset the young lady so. She was grateful.

From then on he said nothing, but continued his detailed examination of wall markings, roof heights, holographics, in fact everything the guide mentioned and quite a few findings she didn't. At the Giants'Drop he did what everyone else did, pushing his head against the magnetic barrier, straining to see as far down into the depths below as he possibly could. 'The Drop is not natural, but carved out of the rock,' the guide informed the party. 'The pathway we are walking continues uninterrupted on the other side. The distance to the bottom of the Drop is in exact ratio to the distance across as the distance of Cu Chulainn to our planet, and our planet to Cu Roi. However such astronomical exactitudes seem meaningless since the builders did not bother to excavate upwards and clear the small amount of earth above their heads so that they could see the satellites and the sun.'

There was a slight coughing sound. One of the more nervous members of the party was going to try and ask a question in a desperate attempt to delay, or perhaps abandon having to walk across the Drop. But the guide knew the ploy well, and before the portly gentleman in regimental clothing who was already

16

trembling profusely could put any queries she pushed on. 'The bottom of the Drop has been fully examined. It is unnaturally smooth and covered in a silvery metallic alloy several metres thick. There are no markings and no indications of use other than that of a floor covering.' She pressed a contact point set into the rock. Red lights appeared where the magnetic barrier had been, clearing at one point to indicate where the force lines of the magnetic field would support the little party as they made their way across the Drop. This was what they had paid for. From now on there would just be a combination of fear and sweat on the tourists faces:no more no less.

To all intents and purposes it seemed as if they were to travel across thin air. Below was nothing. The Tourist Board had removed the illuminations at the bottom of the Drop long ago, after the guides had complained that it was not their job to deal with symptoms ranging from heart attack to violent vomiting. Now it looked as if one was walking across a dark hole, and that in itself was not too unusual. It gave people a scare because in their minds they knew how deep the Drop was. But they no longer saw that alien polished floor below, and that made all the difference.

As always the guide went across first. Reaching the other side she looked back at the mystery man. A smile grew on her lips. Now she had him – he was standing on the far side pretending to study some markings, just as he had done throughout the tour. Except she had seen it all before; the pretence at interest, the sudden desire to study rock patterns, anything to save having to face that walk across the Drop. How appropriate that this enigmatic figure who had embarassed her with his questions should be the one to flunk the walk this time round.

Yet even as she thought of the joy she would have in calling up the Guard Attendant to escort him back to the surface via the emergency staircase on his side of the Drop, the man half rose, and with little more than a cursory glimpse over his shoulder walked backwards onto the magnetic bridge. The guide couldn't believe her eyes. He was still stooping, still peering at the walls as if trying to measure angles, check dimensions, evaluate structures. He got to the other side and didn't even notice he'd been across one of the Five Wonders of the World.

After the Giants' Drop the rest of the ruins represented for the average tourist nothing more than distraction – obstacles in the way of getting out to the fresh air above. The Drop was what they had paid to cross and they had done it. Now they could return and tell relatives and friends they had walked across the deepest hole in the Home System.

The guide, knowing the mood from long experience, moved rapidly, taking in the remaining wonders at full speed, passing in seconds over discoveries that had only been revealed after years of painstaking work, structures that had taken decades to put back together, moving through chambers that themselves appeared to be constructed thousands of years apart – despite what the guide had said (with, it must again be acknowledged, official backing.) And then suddenly they were up and out in the open air. The red hues of Major, the dominant star, mixing with the blues of Minor, the dwarf companion, giving the landscape of tall elegant buildings standing amidst the golden corn colours a shading unknown on worlds served by only one sun.

During those final moments the guide had all but forgotten her mysterious visitor with his deep interests and awkward questions. Now she remembered, and mechanically acknowledging the thanks (and tips) of the tourists searched him out. But search as she might, he was not to be found. Reluctantly the guide moved back down the exit stairs onto the final chamber – the ruin museum. As she had expected he was there peering at inscriptions on the plates and cups neatly arranged on the display shelves. It was the only place that such markings could be found. Not only here on the Home Planet but in fact in the whole planetary system of eight worlds and thirty-seven satellites. He looked up at the sound of her footsteps.

'These markings are different,' he announced. 'Yet you didn't mention them.'

The guide shrugged and put her hands on hips. 'Not part of my speech,' she replied. 'The commentary for guides is written by the curator. Deviations are not encouraged.' She paused looking for a reaction but found none. There was an intensity about the man that was unnerving, giving the feeling that nothing would get in his way. 'But that's what you're doing,' she continued. 'Deviating. The tour is over. You should be outside.'

'If you don't want people looking at the relics, why build the museum?' he asked reasonably. She looked back at the stranger but said nothing. With a single movement he pushed past her in the narrow tunnel and headed for the outside. She followed, with but the slightest glance at the markings that had fascinated the man, reaching the surface just seconds behind him, and only just in time to catch a shout.

'Turlough!' It was a young woman. Long dark hair, very pretty, probably about the same age, with none of the intenseness about the face, yet certainly sharing with the man in terms of bearing and style. However, she combined that with the open friendly look that was more typical of natives of the Home Planet. The man looked up and clearly recognised the girl, but gave little sign of being glad to see her. Instead, he took a path away from her, forcing the woman to run across the grass to intercept him before he entered the nearby corn field. As she reached him she began to speak.

Strain as she might the conversation was lost to the guide, but it caused her no concern. The man was Turlough, that was enough. Knowing that one fact she would now have the attention of every friend, half-friend and acquaintance for the next month with the story. The feeling that she was at last to be a celebrity in her own little circle, if only by passing association, put all thoughts of the motives of the man out of her head. She had shown the famous Vislor Turlough round the ruins of Charlottenlund.

To the woman who had called Turlough's name however a passing meeting was far from enough. Finding him unwilling to stop and talk, she was forced to put her questions whilst trying to keep up with a very fit young man intent on marching at full speed. 'During the past week,' she called gasping for breath, 'you have visited over half the museums of alien life on the planet.' As he kept walking she grabbed his arm and finally slowed the man down. 'What are you going to do now?'

'If you must know,' he replied angrily, turning to face her, 'I shall be visiting the Museum of Natural History at Efnisien, if you will allow me to get there before closing time. And tomorrow I shall be on the Njordr Nerthus shuttle to Fodla base to examine the ruins there. Now if you will let me continue . . .'

He pulled his hand free and pushed forward, but the girl would not be put off. 'Turlough,' she called again. 'Let me ask you one question.'

Something in the woman's voice made him relent. He stopped and turned, looking her straight in the face. They had reached a clearing where the crop gave way to gravel in a no man's land between agriculture and industry, between food growing and food processing.

'One question,' he said.

The woman's response was simple. 'Why?'

He gave no reply, and turned as if to continue walking, but she was not to be put off. 'Turlough, you are an established citizen. Very few Clansmen survived exile – hardly anyone escaped. When you came back we all thought you were returning to rule, to lead, to help. But all you've done since you've been back is traipse around the ruins alongside packs of schoolchildren and tourists with not enough imagination to find anything better to do.'

For a moment it looked as if Turlough was going to offer an explanation, but it passed and he remained silent.

'Turlough, do you know who I am?'

'You are Juras Maateh.'

'Is that all?'

'What do you mean?' He seemed genuinely perplexed.

'Before you were forced to leave by Rehctaht you promised you'd return.'

'And I did.'

'But you promised you would return to *me*.'

In a second the confidence of the man slipped away. He lowered his head and put a hand on the woman's shoulder. 'I'm sorry,' he said. 'Something has come up. Something that I need to work on.'

20

'Something that takes up all your time? Something that stops us seeing each other when we've already been separated two years?'

'For the moment, yes.'

'Before you left, Turlough, you were a strong forthright Imperial Clansman of the Home Planet, taking your duties and life seriously – and that included finding time for an Imperial Clanswoman – me. You shared your thoughts and ideals with me. I also felt I had sme contribution to make. Now . . .'

'Now is different. Besides you have your own life. What have you been doing whilst I was away? Haven't you organised in some way?'

Juras looked at Turlough in despair. It was no use arguing with the man. She would need less direct methods if she were to be successful in her quest.

Without a word she turned away, back towards the museum, leaving Turlough free to march rapidly to the VT station. With luck he thought the Vacuum Tube would get him to Efnisien with an hour to go before closing time.

The National Museum of Natural History of the Home Planet had changed little since Turlough had last visited it, although that visit was now some eight years in the past. Indeed, its location on the single continent that dominated the largely unpopulated northern hemisphere of the planet was a major contributory factor to this lack of change. The law prohibiting any building or enlargement of existing structures within one thousand kilometres of the museum simply ratified what was already the case, for no one in their right mind would dream of building anywhere near the Sacred Temple and its even more sacred Mobile Castle.

The name of the latter, of course, was illogical. Castles, no matter how sacred they might be in the dominant religion of the planet, did not move. And if that were not to be proven (since it was always possible to argue that out there, somewhere, someone would someday discover a castle that did move), what could be said for sure was that throughout recorded history the Mobile Castle had not moved one millimetre, not even when the ground around the Sacred Temple had been shaken by a series of unexpected quakes in the forty-second century.

The Vacuum Tube delivered Turlough to the main gate entrance of the Temple grounds. In front of him, a series of steps led up the side of a thirty metre high wall, into a tunnel and then out again before finally, and for no apparent reason, leading back down to the pink ground below. After all that it was no more than a few seconds stroll through the Temple grounds before reaching the square building of the also thirty metre high Mobile Castle. Blue vines, which emitted a singularly tasty but foul-smelling yellow slime, covered the walls at all points except one – a door kept open through a gravity shield located underground. That shield was also a mystery. It worked, but no one knew how. Many had wanted to dismantle it and find out, but being on sacred ground such interference was forbidden. The vine, needing gravity to grow, shunned the free fall area at the edge of the shield and allowed the visitor to walk through.

Despite his long absence from the museum Turlough knew exactly where he wanted to go. Marching briskly past the surprised receptionist he passed through four rooms until he stood in a long corridor bedecked on either side with bones, reconstructed in the supposed image of the Laima, first of the five sets of aliens thought to have visited the Home Planet. Getting as close to the bones as he dared without setting off every alarm system in the building Turlough peered intently at the joints, skull, teeth, eye sockets, and later, charts of imagined blood circulation, hand movements, and even clothing.

The Laima appeared to have been of slightly greater stature and build than the present occupiers of the planet, although with much more developed foreheads, and, as every schoolchild pointed out, incredibly long fingers and toes. From the fragments of records and oddments that they left behind (they had left no buildings – at least none that had survived, unless the ruins at Charlottenlund were theirs) it was supposed that they had great mental powers, power enough it was said, to control all life on the planet, vegetable and animal. Some myths even had it that the Laima were able to control the minerals in the ground – even the very ground itself, although those scientists who considered themselves part of the more serious contemporary school would have nothing to do with such thoughts. Indeed many rejected even the concept that the Laima actually existed, largely because the name was so closely related to the ancient word *laimee*, meaning happiness. As Turlough would have admitted had the thought crossed his mind, any species which had total mental control of the planet and non-stop happiness had a lot going for it.

Next was another supposed creature from the same period – a kind of giant mollusc, although here again there was great debate as to whether anthropologists had actually reconstructed the being correctly. Certainly it looked cumbersome and huge – big enough to flatten even the strongest Trion if it took it into its head to slide that way.

Turlough was still peering at the recreated skeletons when the Sub Curator came and found him an hour later. Being forced to spend his time in this isolated spot, and hence having more time for the public media than the better paid museum guide at Charlottenlund, the curator recognised Turlough at once.

'Don't get so many visitors these days,' he announced leading the way back to the main door. At least not as many as distinguished as you.'

'Distinguished?' Turlough looked around uneasily. Then as the implication of the remark sank in he coughed nervously and nodded.

'Is there anything I can help you with?' the Curator persisted, not to be fobbed off.

'No, nothing, thank you,' the young Clansman replied automatically. Then he changed his mind. 'Yes, there is one thing. Did the Laima build the Mobile Castle?'

'Some say they did, sir, but who really knows? The evidence, where it exists, is contradictory. Geologists say the rocks that built it are not to be found on this planet – and never have been. The structural engineers say it looks as if the castle suddenly arrived here from another planet. The historical engineers suggest it happened only yesterday – but that of course is impossible.'

'Then what came first? The Sacred Temple outside, or the Mobile Castle inside?.

'The Temple and Castle are undoubtedly the same age, sir.'

Turlough changed track. 'The Laima look like Slots to me,' he said.

The Sub Curator smiled but said nothing. Seeing he had got all he could from the man, Turlough marched through the door and into the florid undergrowth that endlessly threatened to overrun the buuildings.

Not surprisingly, given the remoteness of his location and the lateness of the hour, the VT terminal was empty. A chair was waiting for him on the platform and without pausing he sat down and punched up the co-ordinates for the nearest aerodrome. The move would effectively by-pass Juras. Having been told where he was going she would be waiting near the main spaceport hoping to intercept him before he made it onto a scheduled flight.

Taking a ship from the remote provincial port of Reyer to Fodla base meant that Turlough's trip to Njordr Nerthus, most distant but largest of the Home Planet's three moons would take six hours instead of three as it would on the regular passenger ships that left from the capital. But Turlough needed sleep – and time to think – and the trip he knew would give him an opportunity for both. Certainly by the time he arrived on Njordr Nerthus he felt happier in his plans, and more able to deal with Juras Maateh whenever and where ever she might next catch up with him.

02: DUO

At a distance of some twenty-three million kilometres from the Home Planet Njordr Nerthus was the sort of world that the Tourist Guides and Vidisplays called 'interesting', which by and large meant they could find precious little to say about the place. With its two rivals far closer to the Home Planet and hence reachable in under an hour the moon's owners were always going to be pressed to find any reason to attract people. A distinct lack of minerals, and an apparently total lack of native life forms of even the lowest nature was combined with a thoroughly poisonous atmosphere, which meant that, not only did one have to wear a spacesuit, one did not even get the totally clear atmosphere-free view of the skies that the much smaller inner moons had on offer. It all spelt bad news for the owners.

Only two things had ever given the managers of the Njordr Nerthus economy some slight degree of hope that their forsaken world might begin to earn some credit exchange. The first was a strange (and totally unfounded) rumour which originated some fifty years previously that the girls born on the satellite were the most beautiful within this zone of the Galaxy.

The second was the publishing of a vidisplay programme which claimed that despite all the evidence of alien visitors having come direct to the Home Planet during the past million or so years, and despite the fact that not a single alien ruin, bone or artifact had ever been discovered on Njordr Nerthus, it was in fact this moon in the midst of nowhere that had been the main settlement for those various visiting races.

Naturally, when the work had first been published it had

met with total derision by scientists, archeologists, historians and everyone else who had ever felt the need to pronounce on the early populations of the Home Planet. But largely because of its reversal of all known facts the theory had caught on with the general public, and the tourist trade had followed. The President of the Central Museum on the moon hadn't been best 'pleased of course. His tiny collection of volcanic rocks, and glass cages of specimens which had been bred specifically to exist in the hostile atmosphere looked even more unexciting than usual once the visitors from the Home Planet started working their way through the catalogue of recent discoveries (or inventions depending on your point of view) of Njordr Nerthus.

As Turlough stepped out of the ancient and deteriorating spaceship and through the connecting gangways into the reception lounge he took his first glance at his fellow passengers. A number of them were looking closely at him, some inevitably knowing his face but not being able to recall if he were famous as an explorer, politician, criminal or sportsman. Others, however, had worked it out and were busy telling their fellow travellers just who it was they had journeyed with. Speculation as to what such a famous Clansman was doing travelling on such a slow trip to such an isolated place was reaching fever pitch as Turlough turned his back on the crowd, showed his documentation to the entry guard, gained a very smart salute once his name had been revealed, and made his way to the least crowded of the tour operators' concession stands that faced him.

The booking clerk, her mind stupified through arranging the same trip for hundreds of people day after day failed to look up as Turlough stated that he wanted to take in the entire gamut of alien sights. Only when he put his account card in the desk slot and the hard copy print out came through did a slight smile pass her face. 'A famous name,' said the clerk, pressing the computer terminals which would automatically double check that Turlough's account could take the cost. 'I expect everyone says . . .' She left her sentence unfinished as she finally looked up and recognised her customer. Turlough heard her mutter some words of apology as he took the ticket, perhaps a little too hastily, and made for the departure lounge.

In all, Turlough visited eighteen sights. Some were so ludicrous he forgot them as soon as he was back in the surface buggy, spacesuit removed. Others, fakes and frauds as they were, stuck longer in his mind. The 'ten thousand-year-old' giant head sculpture looked nothing like the alien the guide book suggested, and was clearly suffering from the atmosphere. Yet in the vidguide picture taken just four years before there was no decay. It was a typical fake. The carvings of beings from the Quasar Galaxy were almost certainly copies from the rock engravings on the Home Planet made not by aliens but by the actual inhabitants of the planet – ancestors of the current population – about twelve thousand years before. The 'map' of the rivers that flowed on Njordr Nerthus carved on a cave roof was not 'remarkably accurate' but little more than a random collection of scratches almost certainly made by one of the many animals the Old Regime had transported to the satellite in a vague hope that somehow they might rapidly mutate into beings that could live naturally in the atmosphere. (None of them had.) As such the date didn't particularly matter. It was all a hoax.

Knowing that Juras Maateh would not let him slip by a second time Turlough took the rapidtransit ship back to the Home Planet and was, as expected, met at the aerodrome. He was disconcerted however to face not a barrage of questions and admonitions but instead a very quiet Juras who seemed satisfied to fall in step alongside him as he walked across the aerodrome concourse to the VT terminal. In the end he felt obliged to speak. 'My home,' he said, indicating the destination location he had typed into the departure control board. Still she said nothing. 'Will you come?'

Juras smiled and nodded, and climbed in the compartment next to him.

Turlough's house, still the same one that he had occupied before his exile, was situated deep in one of the many forests that spanned the latitude of fifty degrees north, in the heart of Clan territory. Even in the height of summer it stayed cool, and in the depths of winter had a freshness about the place, which the regular snowfalls only made more picturesque.

The Vacuum Tube deposited the couple in the basement, leaving them free to take the thrust lift to the second floor where Turlough spent most of his time when at home. The 400 kilometre journey from aerodrome to house had taken under five minutes. The silence between the two remained.

Once in the house Turlough brought drinks and sat down opposite his erstwhile friend. He hoped she was still his friend, and would remain so during the difficult times to come. He had a lot of feeling for the woman, but could find no way to express it. Most particularly he hopéd she was still the same Juras Maateh. There was however something different about her. A certain reserve that had not been there before . . .

'Are we still speaking?' he asked. His voice was kind, his face more friendly than previously.

'That's up to you.' The girl was clearly bursting with questions, but holding herself back.

'Then what do we say?' Turlough knew it would be difficult. He had no clear notion of where to begin.

'Tell me what you are doing'.

He stood up and shrugged. Immediately he found himself on the defensive, but could do little to change the inevitable course of the conversation. His eyes narrowed. 'You know,' he said. He was lying and they both knew it.

'I know what you *appear* to have been doing,' replied Juras. 'And I know what people are starting to make of it. Do you know that within an hour of your arrival at that bunch of frauds and fakes on Njordr Nerthus the Tourist Board there had pictures of you all over the southern hemisphere advertising the fact that one of the first things you have done since returning to the Home Planet is visit their so-called monuments? You don't believe that rubbish up there, do you?'

Turlough was cross. He strode across the room. 'Of course I don't believe it,' he answered angrily. 'I just needed to see.'

'Why? Don't you realise what your exile has done to you? You are a public figure. It was the main news for two days when they announced that you had been found and were coming home. You're a grade one folk hero. A real live

28

Clansman who survived exile, and since the revolution there aren't many of those left. If you stand in the upcoming Council elections you'll get in unopposed as a Clan representative. No one would dare to be seen to fight you. If you want a seat in Congress there are twenty Congressmen and women who would consider their own careers advanced by giving up a seat to you. And if you want Parliament the same would apply. You went into exile because you continued to believe in the Imperial Clans, and you stood up to Rehctaht. You were hounded out for your beliefs in the rights of the Clanspeople living in the Home System. Now you come back and power is there for the asking. Yet all you do is spend your time trotting around the system visiting ruins.'

'I have things I must work out.'

'Then hire a secretary and a team of researchers and let them do the dogwork.'

'No.' Turlough was at his most emphatic. 'What I am seeking is too delicate, too important to share.'

'Too delicate to share with me?' She was gentle, almost child-like. She knew such a pose put him at his weakest.

Turlough softened at once. 'For the moment, yes. But when the time is right, I'll tell you first.'

'So now you don't even trust me. What happened to you during your exile, can't you even tell me that?'

Turlough took a long sip of his drink. 'I met a Time Lord called the Doctor. I've no idea what his real name was – like many Gallifreyans he just uses the title, nothing else. I learned a lot . . .'

'About time-travel?;' Juras Maateh's eyes were bright. If Turlough knew about temporal manoeuvering that would revolutionise everything. No wonder he was being secretive.

'About that and other things. I made some discoveries.' He paused for a moment and then plunged on, changing his resolve not to reveal any of his plans. 'I also found the trail of the Gardsormr.'

Juras was unimpressed. 'The Gardsormr signed a treaty with us two months ago. If you were back in politics you would know that. We have our territories and our trade routes, they have theirs, with no competition. Neither side could benefit from either a war of conquest or an economic war. They are helping us rebuild.'

'I know of the treaty,' replied Turlough caustically and working hard now to justify his actions. 'But when I found the Gardsormr they were working in collusion with the Rehctaht Regime on the Home Planet. I intercepted a host of messages from them to the Regime's HQ, and some of them were directly to Rehctaht herself.'

'But Rehctaht is dead and the Revolutionary Regime dispersed. When the end came it became quite clear that Rehctaht was the revolution. Even most of her senior officers didn't really believe in what was going on under her rule. So t..e Regime collapsed and now we have a government elected by the people, and a general recognition that the Imperial Clans were actually useful after all. Isn't that enough for you?'

'No! If the Gardsormr were working with the Revolutionary Regime why suddenly change and offer a deal with a counter-revolutionary government? For all the peace and tranquility there now seems to be on the Home Planet, it doesn't feel right to me.'

'You have more evidence?'

'Some yes, but circumstantial. The Doctor had a fascination with a strange planet far out in one of the spiral arms; the place I was exiled to. In fact the Doctor spent a lot of his time being involved in the affairs of one island on that planet.' Speaking faster now, Turlough warmed to his theme. 'The strange thing is that this backwater of a place has no significance in Galactic affairs – not surprising because the natives haven't even discovered interstellar travel. And yet, they seem to play a strangely important part in Galactic history – and the Galactic future if the Doctor's autologs are to be believed. It was in his logs that I found all the references to the Gardsormr.'

'But what has this backward planet got to do with you throwing away a career in politics which is sitting there waiting for you to take it?'

'Whilst I was stuck on the Earth, as they call it, I spent some time learning about the planet – its cultures, histories and that sort of thing. And deeply rooted in its myths is the story of the Gardsormr – only they call it the Midgardsormr. It is a story about how a monster will arise during a time of anarchy after the sun and moon have been eaten up, and the stars fallen.'

Now it was Juras Maateh's turn to express impatience. 'This sort of rubbish,' she stated emphatically, 'belongs on Njordr Nerthus, not on the Home Planet. And I must say I'm glad you're not saying it all in public. Your mind has been warped by four years away Turlough! I was wrong to suggest you return to politics straight away. You need a rest – a long period of quiet. At least I presume you've finished running around the ancient monuments of the system.'

'Just one more to go.'

'Where?' Juras haa a resigned look on her face. She felt it would be best to accompany Turlough to stop him talking in public, if nothing else.

'The Slotsruins.'

The girl said nothing and sat back down on the sofa with a very solid bump. She opened her mouth , and closed it again. In the end she said simply, 'You're mad.'

'Possibly,' agreed Turlough disconcertingly. 'But this is my problem and I'm seeing it through.'

'You'll certainly see it through,' agreed Juras. 'And the Slots will see you through. If you come back, you'll come back dead.'

'I doubt it. The Slots may be different from us but they live on the Home Planet and they are subject to the law of the Clans, just as we all are.'

'Only because they've never bothered to pull out, and they've not done that because no one ever bothers them. You'll be the only non-Slot on the island.'

'Then you won't feel embarassed about anything I do.'

'Are you seriously going?' she asked. Turlough nodded. 'Then I'll come too.'

'No – I have a way in and out for me. But two people will arouse suspicion.'

'But what have the Slots got to do with a backward planet, the Gardsormr, and all the other places you've been visiting?'

'If I knew that I wouldn't have to go.'

Juras Maateh softened in the face of Turlough's determination. 'How long will you be gone?'

'Two or three hours. You can wait for me here.'

'You're taking a Vacuum Tube, right into the Slotsruin?'

'And out again. Like I said, I won't be long.' And with that the young Clansman turned to the elevator and disappeared from sight.

There were probably very few people on the Home Planet who realised that it was possible to take a Vacuum Tube to the isolated island set in the centre of the massive ocean that dominated the eastern hemisphere: the home of the Slots. And of those few who did know the island was served by the public transport system, certainly only a handful would ever have considered using the VT Terminal built by the Clans three thousand years ago following a request by the Trions to 'put an end-point in every inhabited spot.' As Turlough had pointed out, the Slots occupied land that was part of the Home Planet, and the mere fact that no one ever went there was not enough to put him off. He had, however, had the forsight to make contact with the self-governing council of the Autonomous Republic (as it was officially designated) and requested that he be allowed to visit. The application had been accepted by the Slots' Council without question or comment.

The Slotsisland VT terminal looked from the inside exactly the same as every other station. Only when Turlough emerged into the daylight did the total strangeness of the landscape finally hit. He stepped out onto a beach of yellow white sand. All around were signs of life – grey shell-like creatures carrying dull red spikes dominated, with smaller pointed molluscs of similar colours sprinkling the background. A few metres ahead the sand gave way to a deep blue lake – an inlet of a greater stretch of water that could be seen in the distance. More sand on the far side, followed by thick jungle.

A sound to his right made Turlough step backwards. A Slot representative came forward. Like all of his race he was tall – a clear head higher than Turlough. His eyes were narrow, his skin dark, his hair long, thick and jet black. In his hand he carried a weapon of some kind – Turlough opted not to enquire what kind.

'You are Turlough,' announced the Slot. His accent was

32

thick and difficult to follow, even when speaking just three words.

Turlough acknowledged: 'You are kind to allow me to visit your island.'

To his dismay, the Slot burst into a deep raucous laugh. 'Do not seek to mock me with your false modesty, Turlough,' he replied. 'You are a proud Clansman and you know what is good for you. You asked permission even though it was not needed, because you knew it would increase your chances of getting what you want. The island is part of your empire. Trion rules the Slots.'

The last word was said almost as if it were Schlootz. Had Turlough's kind done these beings the ultimate indignity of simplifying their name just to make it easier to say? Turlough kept his thoughts to himself.

'You want to see the Slotsruin,' continued the emissary. 'Come this way, see what you need to see, and then leave us in peace.'

Turlough followed, eyeing the weapon nervously. As they walked along the beach he caught sight of animals peering through the undergrowth on the far side of the inlet. Long-necked, long-nosed blue and brown creatures nibbling leaves, owl-like beings that could have been half-plant with huge mouths which captured passing insects, and in the background the ceaseless rustle of undoubtedly far larger and more dangerous species. He caught glimpses of multi-coloured six-legged eagles hovering above the trees, armour-plated birds with thick black beaks on white heads that flew just above ground level, flattening anything that got in their way, and even the swish of the tail of some vast reptile long extinct elsewhere on the planet. Turlough realised that his Slot guide's weapon was probably the least of his worries. Five minutes on the far side of the inlet and he wouldn't have a care in the world.

Suddenly they turned inland; within seconds the landscape changed. The beach had gone, and with it all thoughts of the jungle on the far side of the water. A few paces on and they had moved onto rocky soil reaching the edge of a cliff. Below, the Slotsruins.

How could they exist so many hundreds of metres below sea level and yet be so close to the inlet Turlough could not imagine. What forces had worked the landscape were equally hard to conceive, but the questions went to the back of Turlough's mind as he contemplated the extraordinary scene before him. He was looking down a ravine with the rock face on either side used in every way imaginable as a starting point for buildings, buildings hewn from the dark red rock, structures which undoubtedly continued deep into the rock face itself. Why the Slots of old should choose to dig themselves into the rock face and then abandon the location was not apparent but they clearly had, for the centre of the ravine, which must have been at least three hundred metres deep and two hundred metres wide, was totally devoid of all forms of activity. Yet in the centre of the ravine was the most unexpected object of all: a tower rising to exactly the same height as the cliff on which he was standing. It appeared to be made of the mineral as everything else on the landscape, but had no openings or markings to indicate any use.

'That,' said the guide, pointing at the monument and the buildings around, 'is what you call the Slotsruin.' And then to ensure there was no confusion he added, 'You are permitted to see the ruins from up here and you can walk along the central roadway. But that is all. The buildings are ours. We built them, or our ancestors did. But that,' this time he pointed specifically to the central monument, 'is the oldest part of all.'

'Can you get inside?' Turlough asked.

'It is solid, and not made from the rock that we now use. It is built from materials not available on our island. Perhaps not even available on the planet. It is very old."

'How old?'

'A hundred thousand years? Five hundred thousand? Who knows?'

'Can I go down and touch it?

'You can try, but there is a field surrounding it which repels all objects. You can never make contact.'

'I'd like to try.'

Without a word the guide led Turlough back to the vacuum station, down the thrust tube and out onto the floor of the great ravine. On both sides of him now the rock towered up, cut into left and right to make an endless series of doors, windows, levels. High above the ravine a few birds squealed but it was impossible to make them out at that height. And in front was the monument. The sensation on approaching the edifice was exactly as the Slot had suggested; a push back which became stronger the closer one got until it physically forced Turlough to stand no closer than half a metre from the object. Engraved on one side was a picture of an animal – a long snail-like creature with a huge repulsive head and enormous thick legs.

His guide answered his questions succinctly. There was no knowledge as to how the thing was powered, no knowledge as to how deep the power source went, but attempts to dig under it had consistently failed. The object had no other operations, and no apparent function. It just sat there, predating all existing civilisation on the planet.

And that was all there was to say. Turlough thanked his guide, was escorted back to the VT terminal and made the sort of hasty departure which he felt obligatory under the gaze of the Slot. As he sat in the carriage he realised he had seen no other Slot at all during his brief visit, other than his guide. As the carriage door closed the Slot had said, 'We shall meet again.' To Turlough it seemed highly unlikely.

Back at his house ten minutes later he removed the recorder woven inside his coat and replayed the data. As he was doing so he checked the house for the presence of Juras Maateh but as he had half expected she had given up the wait and left.

The data replay showed clearly that the source of the energy powering the monument in the centre of the Slotsruins was inside the monument itself, and that the buildings in the cliffs were as deserted as they had appeared. It also seemed that the obelisk stretched as far underground as it did into the air, although why that should be remained totally unclear.

Turlough put the recording away in his living room vault, sealed the door and took the lift to the basement connection with the VT terminal. From there he took a chair to the industrial aerodrome two hundred kilometres away and finally made his way on foot to a modest looking four-person craft waiting unattended in one of the outer loading bays.

During the next four days as he supervised service and modification work on the ship the thought that Juras had not returned since being left in the house nagged at him, but it was a thought constantly pushed to the back of his mind by the work in hand. Only when the modifications and servicing were complete did the issue resurface, and Turlough put in a call from the ship to the Clanswomans' house. There was no reply. He tried the few friends from the olden days with whom he had re-established some fleeting contact since his return from exile, but none had seen Juras for a week or more. In the end Turlough decided to leave a message on her vidfone telling her that he had to leave for a short while but that he'd be back. When he returned, he said, he would explain all. It didn't sound convincing, but it was the best he could manage.

The message completed he packed the few personal belongings he had brought from the house, and applied to the control tower for immediate take-off. The automatic controller logged the flight and gave clearance and safety checks in the same grave and insistent manner used by machines throughout the galaxy. The audio channel however was there merely as as a psychological reassurance for the pilot. In reality the key information was passed not to him but the autopilot systems in intense computer code. Their responses had been checked, processed, double-checked and cleared long before the voice channel had got half way through its laborious catalogue of safety instructions. As Turlough munched thoughtfully on a sandwich he had made up yesterday but forgotten to eat, the ship eased itself through the atmosphere, tilted at ninety degrees to the inclination of the planet and made its way out of the Home System.

It was, Turlough felt, a relief to be back in space, alone. Before his exile he had never been a particularly gregarious young man, and although his period of forced exclusion had given him a sense of grievance which had grown through the years of wandering with the Doctor, he had also developed a taste for the periods alone which deep space travel bought. Certainly he knew that on this flight there was going to be no time to get bored. Although most of the modifications had been installed before take-off, Turlough had considered it a far too risky affair to give the systems a proper trial.

The key question, as he had told himself repeatedly before take-off, was whether he had fully understood the temporal control mechanisms at the heart of the Doctor's TARDIS. Not that he had a fraction of one per cent of the information necessary to build a machine as sophisticated as the Type Forty with its totally different internal and external dimensions, plus its ability to travel virtually anywhen anywhere in almost no time at all. Instead during his two years with the Doctor, Turlough had concentrated his attention on just one feature – the central temporal control, the one function above all others that made time-travel possible. Of course there was much he had never seen, and what he had discovered of the TARDIS was largely controlled by which sections had broken down during his time on board. There were whole areas of the mechanism which had worked perfectly during his time with the Doctor and which he had therefore never been able to get close to.

Thus much of Turlough's work had been from scratch, often invoking new principles quite seperate from those on which the TARDIS was based. Only a Clansman, the inheritor of nine thousand years continuous scientific research and technological application, could have done it. Now, if he had got it right he had just built himself a ship which once in the correct physical location could travel forwards and backwards in time. Not as comfortable, not as varied and certainly not as sophisticated as a TARDIS, but nevertheless a crude time-machine, and the first one for the Home Planet.

It was while still munching on his half-stale food and pondering the deeper implications of what he had done, and what he had yet to do, that Turlough first heard a noise. In a perfectly quiet ship the sound stood out like a sore thumb. It took only a couple of seconds to indentify the source and open up a vidlink.'Come up to the control room,' he called with a resigned voice. Partly he wanted to express himself, to have a strong arguement, to tell Juras Maateh how foolish and selfish she had been. But he knew it would be pointless.

He had two options – to return the ship to base and put the woman off, or to continue to tell her the details of his research, and what he was planning to do about it. And since he had no idea how much she'd seen on the ship already it was, on reflection, probably easier to have the girl on board than risk telling her suspicions to all and sundry back on Home Planet.

Entering the control room Juras looked tired and dirty, dressed in a one-piece black and white overall used by supervisory technical staff at the aerodrome. Turlough's feelings went out to her. She had probably been camped in the engine room for three or four days once she had discovered that Turlough was equipping a ship for a long flight. And that was a risky thing to do, for any stowaways who didn't get out of the red zone within fifty seconds of engine start-up would not only find themselves covered in a lethal dose of radiation but would also find the doors locked in place. Fifty seconds was the compromise time. The ship manufacturers and owners wanted zero. Since no one should be in the engine room, no one should be given time to get out, they argued. A well-announced change to zero time, they said, would stop all stowaways once and for all. On the other hand more liberal elements among the government's safety control committee argued for one hour. However since every minute on the departure apron was liable to cost a ship owner a sizeable chunk of potential profits that target was never going to be accepted. Fifty seconds was all you got.

'There are safer places,' said Turlough as his passenger sat in the co-pilot's seat. The drive control room was large enough to house both of them comfortably, as long as they didn't want to do anything other than sit down in front of the control panels. He offered her a sandwich.

'And you'd have discovered me, and thrown me off the ship,' replied Juras, accepting the food gladly.

'Yes,' agreed Turlough, 'but your life wouldn't have been endangered. However, now you are here, why don't you clean yourself and get some rest? I have some work to do, and then we can talk.'

'And then perhaps you can explain what all this is,' (she

waved her arms around the modified control panels, knocking several contacts as she did) 'has to do with the Slots, all the ruins and fakes you've visited and this obscure planet on the other side of the Galaxy that you've found.'

Turlough agreed to the request, and without a further word Juras left her seat to install herself in a cabin, whilst Turlough turned his attention to the screens. Everything was proceeding normally – indded the surprise would have been if the automatic controls had allowed anything abnormal to happen. Now he had to try and link the temporal unit into the rest of the ship. If he succeeded they would be able to travel in time. If he failed, the time unit itself could well disappear into the past or future leaving a gaping hole in the ship where it had once been. And that would do little to aid the safety of the rest of the ship, or its crew of two.

All in all, Turlough reflected as he made his way to the converted store room that housed the temporal unit, the risk was probably not one that he needed to share with Juras Maateh. What he really had to do before he showed her anything on the ship was to work out whose side the woman was on. But how he could achieve that in the present circumstances, he had no idea.

One hour later Turlough looked at an image of the woman on the screen, trying to read something into her face, but still without any clear idea of how he was to proceed. She was atrractive indeed. He had remembered her as a beautiful girl, warm and loving. Now she seemed to have blossomed into a woman far bayond his memories. But physical concerns were not at the centre of his thoughts. She was becoming well know throughout the civilised system not for her traditional Clannish good looks, but for her brilliance as an engineer. For a while Turlough and Juras had studied together, before their interests had led them to different institutes – he had to study astro-physics and she to physical engineering. Yet the separation of studying thousands of kilometres apart had done nothing to stop them seeing each other – after all it often took longer to walk out of the VT terminal and travel in the lift to Juras's house than it took to travel across continents by the planet-wide transit system.

So they had remained good friends until politics had reared its head. Like all Clanspeople of their time, both were committed to the established system which allowed them to devote their lives to science and technology unhindered by any other thoughts.

When the Old Regime had fallen it had taken both of them, along with all their families and friends, totally by surprise. Yet they had reacted in different ways. Turlough had made his feelings for the supposed egalitarianism of Rehctaht well known. He disliked her belief in greater personal freedoms. When pressed he clearly said that he believed in the historic activities of the Clans in providing advancement for ordinary Trions. The Clans were superior, and it was right that the rest of Trion could benefit from their superiority in return for leaving them in peace. The outsiders should look after themselves, care for their sick and elderly, and work out their own survival. The Clans wanted to know nothing of such problems.

Such talk ran directly counter to the Revolutionary Regime's demand that everyone on the planet should be subject to the same rules and regulations, be they Imperial Clansmen, regular Trions, or Slots (although Turlough noticed with others that an invasion of the Slotsisland was always put off for another day, whilst attacks on the Clans became regular sport). And so Turlough, making no secret of his views, was exiled for ten years to a suitably backward planet where he would learn humility and the error of his ways.

Juras had been more cautious in her statements, and Rehctaht, aware that she had to have some science advisors had willingly seized on the girl as a potential ally. Inevitably however, the promise of further study facilities was forgotten as Juras became involved in new areas of work which those in the Revolutionary Regime saw fit to keep secret from almost everyone in the system. Indeed, even now, Juras had no idea what most of those people who had worked with her had been doing each day whilst she poured over analyses and test runs.

After the counter-revolution removed Rehctaht from power Juras had been faced with an awkward choice – one that she by no means relished. The Law of the Imperial Clans was quite clear. All knowledge, all innovation, all discovery, was to be distributed freely. Secrecy was not permitted. And having been brought up on that belief, when she first encountered the fanatical secrecy of Rehctaht's regime she had found it a cloying ache that pulled endlessly at her brain. Yet as time had past the notion that some things were better off for being kept quiet began to make some kind of sense, and it was this feeling that stayed with her when the counter-revolution came. Working for the newly formed Committee of Public Safety which was overseeing the transition away from the revolution Juras still felt that there were certain matters she had discovered which even now were best not revealed in full to her new employers. The New Regime, she argued to herself, was still young. It needed time to grow before it could be fully trusted with the most sensitive information.

Something of the unease of her position came through to Turlough. He had expected change in the girl, but not his extra edge to her personality. Soon after his return home he had run a request for a resumé on her activities. Such information, previously freely available under the Old Regime of the Imperial Clans was now highly restricted. The individual had the right to privacy, he had been told, when he pressed his enquiry. Privacy, he had replied angrily, meant having something to hide. He knew all about privacy himself, when he had kept his real intentions from the Doctor.

But he did manage to get some information on Juras and discovered just what a senior job she had gained. And that knowledge played on his mind now. He was giving up a lot by making this trip into space – power, prestige, friends, influence. But the prize was ultimate knowledge – if this wasn't worth a sacrifice, nothing was. And Juras, in stowing away, was giving up just as much. But why would she do that unless she knew what he was up to? Could she really be leaving everything just for undeclared love? It seemed unlikely.

To Juras, the knowledge that Turlough had been with a Time Lord, and had travelled in a TARDIS, was enough to convince her that the decision to make the journey had been correct, even without the hints he had so recently dropped about his next move. She was a good engineer – a brilliant engineer many would say, but that had not stopped her spending some time looking into the work going on in other fields. Turlough himself had been highly regarded before his disappearance, and his time spent with the Gallifreyan would not have been wasted. And she knew, with a total certainty that comes from a complete mastery of one's own field, that if she had been able to work closely with an astrophysicist during her time under Rehctaht, her special research problem would have been solved.

Turlough left the control desk and walked through the cramped ship to the tiny recreation room. He was unsure what recreation could possibly take place in such an environment – the room would more properly have been described as a cupboard. But at least there it was possible for the couple to sit and face each other, and for each to decide just how far the other could be trusted.'

Moments later the girl came in, refreshed and cleaned up. They both selected food from the auto dispenser – the recreation room was also the galley. Juras ate greedily. Turlough munched more thoughtfully, and remained quiet. At last Juras spoke.

'The Time Lord's ship – the TARDIS – was it really as big as the legends say?'

'Virtually infinite,' replied Turlough. She had started talking about the one thing that most interested her professionally, as he knew she would. It confirmed his suspicions. 'I doubt if I ever saw more than one percent of the place. I spent most of my time either in the control room or galavanting about on some planet or other trying to keep the Doctor under control.' Turlough had not lost his ability to boast even when it was not necessary.

'You didn't explore the TARDIS?'

'There was no point. We travelled the galaxy. We could have travelled the Universe if we'd had a mind to. Why spend time running around inside a machine rather than real worlds?'

'And you learnt how it works?'

'Only Time Lords know that – you know that is true.'

'And I also know you, Turlough. You have a mind that

42

collects information, that turns it, twists it, deals with it, analyses it and finally uses it.'

'As do you, Juras.'

'So maybe we are similar and should work for the same ends,' she countered. 'Tell me what you are up to and let me help, instead of forcing me to run around in circles chasing you.'

'What do you want to know?'

'Everything of course, but we can start with some details about where we're going, why we are going there, who we are going to see, and what the point of it all is.' She dialed numbers. Food appeared. She resumed eating.

Turlough remained quiet for a few seconds as if examining the possibilites, before he began his explanation. 'As to where we are going, we are heading back to what you called that "insignificant little planet" on the other side of the galaxy. As to why, because when I escaped from exile on that dreadful place I left in something of a hurry, and with other things on my mind. Among the many items left behind were a set of electronotes which I had smuggled onto the planet at the start of my exile. They relate to our New Regime's friends, the Gardsormr. They contain dates, times, and other details of Gardsormr sightings which indicate (and possibly prove) that those creatures, whatever they are, should not be allies of the New Regime.'

'You'll have a few problems convincing the government that is true,' Juras told him. 'You may have a high reputation on the Home Planet, but even so you can't just march in and state that the first set of allies the New Regime teams up with are actually the enemy in the midst,'

Turlough sighed but said nothing. Juras seemed annoyed. 'You're not politically ignorant Turlough,' she continued. 'You know as well as I do that even if what you say is true and can be proven, people now in power won't agree, because it will be tantamount to declaring that the very first thing that they ever did on gaining control was a total error. People never admit they are wrong – they'll go on making the same mistakes over and over rather than agree they were mistaken in the first place. So then what will you do?'

'If necessary work to overthrow the New Regime as I did to overthrow Rehctaht. And before you ask, I'll risk exile again. There are some interesting exciting places around the Galaxy, many of which I would like to explore more fully, but I still have a desire to see the Imperial Clans back in their rightful position on the Home Planet. We deserve no less. Doesn't that seem reasonable to you?'

'You know I share your feelings, Turlough,' she said unconvincingly. 'And maybe on Earth you can give me the evidence to show me that the Gardsormr are not our allies. If you are right, that is going to cause more chaos on Trion – and perhaps yet another revolution. Is that what you really want? Or are you involved in something else too? Have you told me everything you are up to?'

'Isn't what I've told you enough?'

'For most people yes, but you are not most people.'

He smiled. 'There is more to the Gardsormr – and what you say about it raising questions is certainly true. My notes show that the Gardsormr concentrate their attentions on a small number of worlds. They have a very sophisticated, very fast, but apparently very small fleet, and yet they keep hanging around just a tiny number of locations, all of which seem to have no real significance in Galactic terms.'

'What do they want? Minerals, or control of trade routes?'

'I've thought about those things and neither applies. They have just chosen three planets and they keep a really close watch on them.'

'Which planets for example?'

'Earth, and the Home Planet, to give you just two. The third is totally remote – at the very edge of the Galaxy. Earth is a backwater, and our system, for all its advances, is no different from any one of a thousand other systems, each with more minerals and better transport facilites. And if they are after Imperial Clan science and technology they can simply come along and ask for it.'

'So we go to Earth, and we collect evidence that the Gardsormr are a menace. And we try to figure out why the aliens like the three planets in particular. What else?'

'In reality it's not just the Gardsormr who like Earth,'

44

admitted Turlough. 'The Doctor has a strange fascination with the planet too. But I could never find out why; he just seem to like the inhabitants. Yet I'm sure there was something under the surface, something extra. It was as if he knew something: there is a link between the Doctor and that planet, I am certain. There is also a link between Trion and Earth – the Gardsormr prove that. And therefore it is not too outrageous of me to suggest that there might be a link between Trion and the Time Lords. But what the link is . . . Like you I'm a scientist, not a logician. I'm entering new fields.'

'So it's a hunt for information. Good. And what else?'

'What else what?' That's it.' Turlough was emphatic.

Juras got up, nearly banging her head against the lockers that jutted out into the tiny room. She put hands on hips and stood facing Turlough. 'You are a great Clansman, Vislor Turlough, a brilliant physicist – and a terrible liar. This is a Style 976 interseller Hawk. 976 Hawks are fast, small to the point of being cramped, economical, totally automated, and just the sort of thing you would choose to fly across the Galaxy to Earth.'

'You've read *Ships of the Line* too. I'm impressed.'

'And you will also know that in *Ships of the Line* there are pictures, diagrams and a vast array of illustrations. 976 Hawks carry a single storage room for picking up minerals or whatever.'

'So does this one.'

'And the storage room is locked. Added to that, you have spent more time in that room than anywhere else since coming aboard.'

'So you didn't spend all your time in the engine room.'

'I came out enough to watch you personally carrying endless streams of equipment onto the ship and into the hold. And I stayed out enough to realise that there are plenty of dock workers around, not to mention androids, who would happily have carried it all for you. So, Turlough, I now use what we both learnt during the compulsory six months primary logic course at the first grade school, and suggest that you have been building something in the hold. It is something that contains delicate machinery. I also know that you have spent some time with the Doctor, and so now I jump to the outlandish conclusion that you have built a time-machine and it is sitting in the hold of this ship. Right or wrong?'

Turlough stayed seated. He looked away from the woman. What he had to sat next was going to be a problem.

'Before the counter revolution, after I had gone into exile, you worked on a special research project,' he said at last. Juras nodded. 'That project was so secret that even your fellow workers didn't know exactly what you were up to.' Still she remained quiet. 'Yet you had to report. You reported direct to Rehctaht herself.' He looked up at her. 'I'm not worried that you worked for that madwoman. Some people had to stay when most of us were exiled, just to keep the planet running. What I would like to know is what it could have been that kept you at it for so long with an insane idiot breathing down your neck.'

'It was secret research,' said Juras simply.

'Secret, yes – but like you said, we both spent six months on the same logic course. You got to solve the problems of my actions easily, because the trail was open. I have to do just a little more work in discovering what you were up to. But still it is possible. What work could be so secret and sensitive that not only did Rehctaht not want anyone to know about it, but also after the counter revolution came either you, or your new bosses, all supposedly dedicated to a return to open government, also decided to keep it secret? Whatever this thing was you enjoyed working on it – otherwise you wouldn't have stood that proximity with the lunatics of the Rehctaht regime. What could it be?' He looked at her with a grin, but it was slowly turning into a snear. 'What would that woman have wanted beyond anything else? Time-travel? No, I think not. Everyone knows that that is the secure province of the Time Lords. So what? There is only one candidate I think: Gravity theory.' Turlough looked up. To her imense relief Juras saw he had changed his expression and was now grinning. He had found her out just as easily as she had him. They both had secrets and both needed the other.

'Did you complete the work?' asked Turlough.

'Not yet,' admitted Juras, 'And you?'

'In the next hour or two we shall find out,' he said. And with that he led her into the depths of the ship, where he ceremoniously unlocked the door and revealed his prototype time unit for the first time.

Yet having unlocked it, Turlough did not immediately enter the hold. Instead he stood in front of the door and waited. The magic eye beam scanned him, recognised his face and allowed him through into the room. Juras followed, as he held the beam at bay. It was noticeable however that he did not offer to set the beam to recognise Juras. Diplomatically she made no comment on the omission.

Inside the room, the unit looked remarkably small considering all that it was supposed to do. Turlough watched with some pride as Juras walked around it. 'Does it look like you expected?' he asked. It was an irrelevant and somewhat silly question, but in his pride he sought to extend this moment of revelation as long as possible.

'No,' she said honestly. 'I expected something neater.' Little could be seen of the machinery itself – Turlough had taken the precaution of covering it in a protective wall of steel, which made it look like a rather unexciting grey blue box about one metre square. On one side was a control panel, fourteen items each controlled by a slider. On top was a screen, itself about half as high and half as wide as the main unit.

'Two sets of connections to go,' Turlough explained, 'one to the main control room and the other direct into the power supply. I am fairly happy with the structure of the unit itself. What I don't know is if it will actually carry the ship with it when it moves. If the unit does move in time without us it is likely to leave a massive rupture in space, and I don't think we shall survive.'

'How much like a TARDIS is this?' asked Juras, taking the whole scene in.

'In effect it's just one fraction. It moves forward and back with power speed controls. The faster you go in time, the faster you are able to go. It increases power by the square of its own power over unit time.'

'Which means you have to have a good breaking system!'

said Juras. 'What about movement in other dimensions?'

'I'm relying on the ship to do that.'

'So you pilot the ship to the space you want and then hop in time?'

Turlough nodded. 'Messy, I know, but the relative dimension stabilisers on the TARDIS were in terrible chaos – the Doctor was always tinkering with them which meant I got a lot of close looks but never had the faintest chance to actually find out how they were supposed to work.'

For the next two hours the couple exchanged notes, ideas and thoughts, Juras putting in her own views of how the engineering functions of a temporal unit should work, based on three years of uninterrupted research in the laboratories of Rehctaht. She had had every piece of equipment, every resource she needed, for her research into gravity waves, but without a working model on which to base her research she had been infinitely more hampered than Turlough. That she had made any progress at all on the subject was a testimony to her genius. That she failed to reveal just how far she had got with her work showed that Turlough's mistrust in the girl was possibly not misplaced.

Only once did Juras call attention to an aspect of Turlough's work: the constant relativity balance. Still working, Turlough shouted his recognition of the problem over his shoulder. 'The TARDIS took no consideration of gravity waves,' he said. 'It sailed space as if they didn't exist. So either that means that if you travel in time they don't exist, or there was a mechanism that automatically compensated for the waves which I never found.'

'But the ship must have been affected by gravity itself,' protested Juras.

'All the time, but it would move through the centre of the Galaxy as if relativity itself played no part of its existence. The faster you move the slower you experience time. But does that mean that if you move in time but attempt to physically stand still you actually move in space despite your efforts? If so, will you move faster in space as you travel faster in time? And if that is so how do gravity waves affect the whole movement?'

Juras looked at the mechanism that Turlough had created.

Helpfully he typed up the representative diagram on the screen above the unit. Juras studied it carefully. 'You have assumed that relativity works in all dimensions,' she said.

Turlough stopped working and turned to look at her. 'It is all I *can* assume. If it is untrue then I just switch out sections 76 and 77, and the compensation stops.'

'The only problem then is if you don't decompensate in time,' said Juras. 'If you add a circuit loop the system will be able to judge if it is needed, and, if not, cut itself out.'

'If you can do it,' said Turlough gratefully, 'then please do.' And with that he returned to his work. Juras looked at the problem and rolled up her sleeves. As she said a little later whilst still working, given their overwhelming lack of knowledge, they were probably about to take the biggest risk they could ever imagine.

03: TRIO

In common with most travellers of their planet Juras and
Turlough retained the convention of adopting the standard
time of home even when in space. By their ship's master clock
it was gone midnight when they finally stopped modifying and
installing the time unit, and returned to the control room. The
ship, acting under the instructions given by Turlough before
take-off had moved into interstellar drive, heading up and out
of the plane of the Galaxy. In another six hours it would have
cleared the drift of stars that made up the main segment of the
cluster, and allowed the ship to begin its journey across the
Galactic periphery towards Earth. The journey, almost twice
as long as a straight line route, would nevertheless take far less
time than if they had tried the more direct trip. That way
would have meant an endless set of navigations between the
star groups, restricting travel to little more than one light year
per hour. This way, once the maneouvering was over, they
could travel far faster.

Both Turlough and Juras were tired and needed rest as they
contemplated the finished control panel, squeezed in among
the other main drive instrumentation in the navigation section
at the front of the ship. It was quite possible to control the
time-travel unit from within the hold, but they also needed to
see exactly what was happening to every other instrument as
they made their first move. And anyway, with an untried and
untested machine it somehow felt a little safer to be at this sort
of distance, however much they knew that the safety thus
gained was totally imaginary.

Despite their tiredness Turlough and Juras agreed on an
immediate test. The aim would be to reduce acceleration to

relative zero – something which in itself would take several hours, and then attempt to move themselves forward marginally in time. The visual effect would be very limited indeed – but their instrumentation should give a clear indication of whether they had succeeded in doing that very rare thing – creating a working time-machine that did not explode in the operator's face.

By conducting their trial in deep space the couple knew that they were limiting their chances of survival. If something went wrong their options for escape from the ship were zero. On the other hand if they carried out the test on a planet their chances of survival could have been much higher. Yet the possibility of their test being picked up by Time Lords who constantly monitored the time waves, jealously guarding their temporal monopoly remained high. Such a discovery could result in a successful test followed by Time Lord action which would effectively stop any further use of their machine. They both preferred the greater risk and the greater freedom.

As the ship slowed, Turlough returned to his cabin to rest, only vaguely aware that Juras suddenly showed a burst of extra energy which kept her awake. He knew that without him she could not return to the storage room and interfere with the time unit, and he could see little advantage to her of sitting at the central navigation unit, fiddling with the controls.

Yet Turlough knew all about treachery. As he lay on his bed in his tiny cabin he thought of past times, and his own deviousness. He thought of Juras, and tried to imagine her in the same position, attempting to destroy as he had tried to destroy when faced with no other option save the mindless boredom of ten years exile on Earth. He thought of the totally evil and mad Rehctaht, dictator of a whole system until the Counter Revolution. Juras had worked for her, developing knowledge of that most bizarre and little understood of forces, gravity. What, he wondered, would have happened if Juras had completed the work before the fall of Rehctaht? Would she have handed it over to the mad woman? That he didn't know.

Uneasily he fell into a light sleep, his mind still partially aware of the questions unanswered about the girl who sat in the control room.

Two hours later Turlough was awakened by his auto-alarm and quickly walked back to the flight deck. There was no sign of Juras. He switched on the remote units and found her in her own cabin using the ship's memory link with Central Data on Home Planet. When he spoke she looked up suddenly. In answer to his immediate question she said she was just checking through some calculations she had made, using the much greater power of computers on the planet. It sounded a reasonable explanation but left Turlough feeling even more unsure about his companion. He scowled to himself and looked at the girl out of the corner of his eyes when she joined him on the deck. The feeling between them was more uneasy than ever.

Turlough was sweating slightly as he double-checked the instrumentation. From now on, having added what was, effectively, an alien element into the mechanism of the ship, it would be unwise to trust totally in the control systems that he had previously thought of as infallible.

The ship was at relative rest. The checks were positive. Turlough looked Juras face on and Juras reciprocated. Neither could find any reason to delay. Turlough pressed four touch controls far harder than was necessary. Nothing happened – at least nothing as far as they could see, which was by and large a positive sign. They began reading dial settings to each other. Their scanners were divided into two sections – one looking closely at the ship itself, seeking out any sign of stress, wear or unexpected movement, the other checking the planetary systems of the four nearest stars. If the ship was moving forward in time as they anticipated and hoped, then those planets should be seen to be buzzing round their respective suns at an insane speed.

The outcome, when they had finished analysing the read-outs, was good and bad. The ship was showing no sign of strain, but the planetary systems under observation were moving normally. The relief at still being alive was swamped by disappointment. They had checked, certified and rechecked. There could be no doubt that the time unit was engaged, and an active, functioning part of the ship. Which meant that as it was not working there was something fundamentally wrong with the way in which it was built.

If Turlough had been working on his own tht would have been enough. But now, with Juras having checked the operations against her own specialist knowledge they had looked at the mechanism from two distinct angles, and both had thought they had got it right. Unless . . .

Thoughts he did not want to entertain shimmered within Turlough's mind. He looked at Juras. What had she been up to whilst he was resting?

'Back to the drawing baord,' he said watching the girl carefully.

'Not necessarily,' she replied. 'Let's try and up the power slightly.'

'That may not be safe,' Turlough told her nervously. He'd lost enough weight worrying about the first test without rushing blindly into the abyss of higher power.

'There's probably a lot less risk now that we know that the whole thing isn't going to blow,' Juras argued. 'If it isn't working it will simply not work a lot more. The worse that can happen is a circuit overload, but that won't affect the ship's power units.'

Turlough remained silent, his brows knitted tight. He didn't like the idea, but could not say why without openly accusing the woman of having fixed the machine for purposes he could, as yet, only guess at. He could of course retreat into cowardice, but that was not an image he cared to develop, at least not in front of Juras.

'I said, there is less risk now . . .'

'I heard what you said,' replied Turlough. And then angry at himself for his own indecision, he almost shouted his agreement, and began running the checks ready for the second test.

The high power trial was as much of a disappointment as the initial run. The ship remained apparently at rest, yet there was no sign of temporal movement on the planetary systems under observation. There was however one minor change in the ship. Turlough spotted it first.

'The relativity correction unit cut in,' he said as they switched the power off. 'In fact, it is still running.' And then, as if the unit had heard him, it cut out. 'What would cause that?' he asked nervously, knowing only he (or possibly a Time Lord) could answer.

'It was as if the ship was working to keep us standing still,' said Juras.

'Except that it had no need to because we were not time-travelling. Besides why would it keep working even after the unit had been switched off?' replied Turlough. 'There was a good two minutes between reducing the time distortion to zero and the correction unit cutting out.'

Juras claimed to by mystified. It did not help Turlough's state of mind. 'What now?' asked the girl.

'We need to stop off somewhere close by to get basic supplies,' said Turlough. 'I only put minimal stocks on the ship when we left to avoid attracting too much attention. Regal is nearest – they have a supplies station in orbit around the ninth planet which makes the pick up nice and painless.'

Juras said nothing, as Turlough laid in the new course. If she was aware that Turlough was lying about the lack of provisions she did not show it.

As to Turlough himself, he was unsure of why he had told the lie. His feelings added up to little more than a sense of unease, an intuition that he needed time and an opportunity to observe Juras and see exactly what she got up to. He also wanted to have a chance to check out the connections of the time unit himself before they got much further away from their own world. The dive back into the galactic centre would ensure that if Juras were planning some sort of evil against him he might just throw her plans out of sequence.

During the flight Juras at last slept, and Turlough dedicated himself to the time unit, relaxed in the knowledge that for once he was not being overlooked. Yet try as he might he could find neither justification for his superstition towards Juras nor a fault in the theory on which the time unit was built. As to the machinery, that appeared to be in perfect working order. What had stopped it acting temporally was a mystery.

Four hours later the decelleration motor-unit cut into the cold fusion reactor in the heart of the ship. Muons, lasting the merest billionth of a second were created by the plant as the fundamental working blocks of the system, the cheapest energy in the universe – part of the collapse of the universe itself. Automatically the ship, attuned to its captain's wishes sent a faster than light beam across the void to inform Regal station IX-1 that the Hawk was on its way and requested orbit procedures. Automatically the ship sent a second message when no reply was received to the first. And automatically it informed the captain that all was not well when the third message also received no response.

Cursing his luck, Turlough sent the message manually. He too got no comeback. Pondering the possibility of this being part of a replusive Juras-Rehctaht plot he went to the viewing screen and ordered up maximum magnification. At this distance the ninth planet of the Regal system was clearly visible. They would have to skirt round the star about which the planet orbited, but that would delay them by no more than minutes. That the orbiting space station was not visible did not trouble Turlough since it could easily at that moment have been eclipsed by the planet. But when it refrained from reappearing after twenty minutes he began to show his concern.

Rapidly he reset the co-ordinates of the screen and picked up Regal itself, second planet of the system, and the only world among the nine capable of supporting life without artificial environments. With sudden inspiration Turlough typed in a set of commands which removed the visuals and put in a heat image. Apart from the reflected sunlight on the dayside of the world, Regal was not producing heat. But when Turlough had been there five years before it had supported one of the most developed civilisations in this sector of the galaxy. The whole planet should have been covered in power plants generating electricity for the massive mineral extraction industry and the local population. Regal was always banging on the door of the Imperial Clans for the latest developments in extraction technology. Yet it was dead.

Turlough left the screen on, and called Juras in her room. If she was involved in sabotage now seemed as good a time as any to have it out in the open. She responded to his call within a minute.

Rapidly Turlough put the girl in the picture. He looked at her squarely in the face. 'What have you been up to?' he demanded in conclusion.

She looked straight back at his gaze. 'Why do you always blame someone else Turlough?' she said. 'Haven't you just considered the possibility that I might be telling the truth? If there is anyone around here that you shouldn't trust it is yourself. Apart from being devious by nature you're too suspicious for your own good.'

But Turlough was not to be appeased. 'Just what were you doing last night when I was resting?'

'I have told you. Isn't my word good enough for you any more?'

Turlough looked away and began to feel uncomfortable.

'So what is it that makes you suspect me?' asked Juras. Her manner softened a little.

'Rehctaht,' said Turlough. 'You worked for her, and stayed working for her. Why?'

Juras sank deeper into her chair. 'When Rehctaht said she wanted me in her research labs it wasn't a request, it was an order. I could either obey, or follow you and your family into exile. When you were faced with that type of situation you chose to leave – which is fair enough, although I haven't heard you say since what a mind-expanding and uplifting experience it was for a Clansman to be stuck in a school learning science that was nine thousand years out of date. No one criticises you for being exiled – it made you a hero, but it didn't actually achieve anything. And it certainly didn't overthrow Rehctaht.

'I chose to stay, and it was an equally valid choice. When Rehctaht made her demand she was already quite mad and her command crumbling, but the facilities she could command were huge. I knew that she would never fully understand what I was doing and she would always be dependent upon me, which meant that as long as I made sure I worked in secret Rehctaht would always need me there. I would be the one who would control what knowledge she got. And since I knew that I would never let her get away with her main plan, I reckoned I was actually helping to safeguard the future of both the Clans and the Home Planet.'

'And just what was her main plan?' demanded Turlough. The story sounded plausible, but he wasn't ready to give up his suspicions that easily.

'To build a gravity unit. With that she thought she might then have sufficient knowledge to do what you have just done – build a time unit. She was quite wrong in that, gravity is little help here, but you know as well as anyone the way gravity technology has dominated our race memory for thousands of years. Rehctaht wanted to conquer her own past – our past. The new Rehctaht dynasty she dreamed of spawned from her artificially bred children would then last a million years, through her control of the time lanes.'

'Very well,' replied Turlough. 'You made sure she couldn't undertake the work by continuing to pursue your own favourite avenue of gravity beams. But what about after the counter revolution? Why didn't you hand your work and knowledge across to the Revolutionary Committee once you were sure Rehctaht was dead. That is Clan Law.'

Juras smiled. 'Turlough, I was going to ask you the same question! I haven't noticed a report to the High Clans on developments in time-travel. Now why don't you face facts? Both of us, in totally different ways have worked out a few of the basics of new developments in our own chosen spheres. And both of us, for our own reasons have decided to keep quiet.'

Turlough was not impressed. 'I kept quiet,' he said, 'because if word had got out of just how much I had learned from the Doctor it would have alerted the Gardsormr. What's more, if I am right and the Gardsormr are our enemies, then the chances are that someone within the Revolutionary Committees is a traitor, and I certainly don't want to hand the knowledge of time to a traitor. Whatever else you may think of me you can never deny my allegiance to the Clans.'

'So our answers are the same,' said Juras. 'The only difference is that you trust your answer, and not mine.'

Turlough looked unhappy. 'The truth more likely is that I know I don't trust my own answer,' he admitted. 'Deep inside me is the knowledge that I would like the power and the freedom of the Time Lords for myself, no matter how much I pretend I want it for the common good. I'll use my knowledge to help overthrow the Gardsormr threat, but even if that threat didn't exist I'd still try and learn about time-travel anyway.'

'So you can't trust me because you can't trust yourself, at least for the moment.'

'It doesn't say much for me, does it?' said Turlough.

The couple remained quiet for several minutes before Juras made a suggestion.

'We have a problem with the time unit and with Regal. Let's sort out Regal first, pick up the supplies, and then work on the time unit to try and get that going. If we both work together you can keep an eye on me and I can reciprocate on you. How's that?'

'Agreed,' said Turlough. 'Just one thing though. We don't need supplies. I just said we did to try to throw your plans off balance.'

'I know,' said Juras. 'Don't worry. I don't have any plans apart from being with you and working to solve the time mystery.'

Turlough relaxed slightly, as the couple turned their attention back to the screens. Turlough gave the order for the ship to move towards Regal itself. As they completed the turn Juras added another comment. 'How did you plan to keep your discoveries secret from the Time Lords?'

'Much in the same way as you with Rehctaht,' Turlough replied. 'By being discreet, and trying to obey their own rules about not tampering with time itself. But they'll find out about us in the end.'

'If we get the wretched machine to work,' said Juras, as they watched the growth of Regal on the screen.

Turlough's memories of Regal were neither positive nor negative. He had visited the place simply as part of his education as a young Clansman. He was escorted around factories and workfaces of mines, seeing for himself just how Trion technology could be put into operation on a scale suitable for transforming a whole planet.

The young Turlough's reaction to Regal was typical of most students from his world. The planet – indeed the whole system of nine worlds and over one hundred satellites – was one of the richest mineral centres in the region, supplying not only the needs of the Regalans but also half a dozen other systems within the area. Most of the workforce had some connection either with mining and processing, or with the leisure industry. The local populace worked hard in the mines and lived hard on the surface. He had been overwhelmed by the size of the operation, and proud that so much could come from the original research work undertaken by the Clans.

The central navigation system of Turlough's ship contained all the details necessary to bring the vessel into land at any one of one hundred and eighty five docking bays on the planet's surface. Normally, of course, he would never have dreamed of undertaking such an expensive operation, berthing his ship instead in orbit around one of the outlying spacestations and travelling by public system down to the surface. But now all that was impossible. There was no public transport for the simple reason that there were no spacestations. Come to that, it was starting to look as if there was no public either. Turlough was hardly amazed when the control system announced itself unable to locate a single one of the docking bays.

Juras, sitting beside Turlough, ordered a landing to where the largest docking point should have been whilst broadcasting the message that they were a peaceful freighter anxious to establish normal contact in order to secure a standard landing. No one heard them – or at lest if they did they kept quiet about it.

The landing, like everything else on the ship, was automatic, even when faced with the problem of not actually having anywhere that looked like a docking site to land on. What was, according to the ship's datasystem, the centre of a modern, fully equipped space port turned out to be arid wasteland. Tumbleweed blew along the ground stirred up by the backfire of the cold fusion jets. A slight breeze ruffled the bare branches on the occasional tree stumps that scattered the surface. There was no sign of habitation.

Turlough looked at Juras, that familiar frown once more on his face. 'Don't start,' said the girl, recognising the signs. 'We'll work it out. What are the options?'

'Wrong place,' said Turlough. 'That's the most obvious.'

'So we check the navigation units,' said Juras.

It took an hour. They found nothing. All the self-checks checked. So did the back-ups. In desperation they ran a check on the self-checks. That checked out perfectly. To all intents and purposes they were on Regal.

'The air is breathable,' said Juras, looking at the gauges in front of her. 'No radiation. We could go for a walk.'

'I'm not sure that would be wise,' said Turlough. 'We don't know what is out there.'

'Nothing, by the look of the scanner,' Juras told him. 'Don't Hawks carry Runners?'

Turlough nodded grimly. He hated the machines. They usually made him feel sick.

If Juras noticed Turlough's reluctance she didn't let it show. Instead she led the way back through the ship, past the hold with its installed but seemingly faulty time unit, past the cold fusion drive and finally down the step ladder into the lowest section. There, standing at ground level was a six wheel Runner, with its own muon generator on the back. The vehicle could comfortably fit four, or more normally two, plus a wide ranging collection of stores and supplies, could traverse all but the roughest terrain, and afforded excellent vision of the countryside through its all-glass roof, sides and floor. As the manufacturers pointed out, if something was going to attack you from underneath it was often handy to know just what you were fighting. In a Runner you could see it all.

The advantage of having a Runner on board a ship but at ground level was obvious. You could get inside the vehicle, open the access doors, and drive out into alien terrain without having to put a space suit on. Turlough was all in favour of undertaking this procedure, but Juras felt the need for some fresh air. After all the readings on the ship had been quite unequivocal. In the end Turlough persuaded her to travel in the safe cocoon of the Runner for a few kilometres just to be quite sure the area was as safe as the instrumentation said. Then, if all seemed quiet he would agree to open the windows. With that they settled down to a ride across the barren countryside.

After five kilometres Turlough had to agree that everything

did seem as peaceful as Juras kept protesting it was. The semi-desert stretched in all directions, there was no sign of life and the Runner's readings steadily gave the lowest possible levels of radiation combined with exactly correct levels of oxygen and nitrogen. Its own independent analysers confirmed, as had the ship's, that the gravity was that of Regal, and the level of noble gases in the atmosphere that one could expect on Regal. Juras touched the control. The dome across the top of the Runner retreated leaving the couple in what was effectively an open jeep.

At the exact moment the windows reached their lowest point the life readings on the panel in front of Turlough shot across to maximum and a frightening screech pierced the sky. Without waiting for further consultation Turlough leaned across in front of Juras and hit the close control. Agonisingly slowly the glass moved up as the screeches got louder.

It was the eagles Turlough saw first. He labelled them eagles in his mind, simply because that was the nearest he could come to working out what they were. However they differed substantially from the broad winged birds of prey he knew from the warmer climes of his own planet. The wing span of these creatures was larger – and the wings themselves multicoloured with luminous blues, greys and greens creating a mind-distorting effect enhanced even by the tail which continued the joyous revelling in the colour. Turlough found it hard not to look: the colours *forced* him to look. Dimly he became aware that Juras felt it too. The colours ate deeply into the brain – he had to watch. That must be why Juras was slowing down. How sad the glass was getting higher, cutting out some of the most beautiful colours. He should lower it again . . .

It was not until Turlough's hand was actually on the contact point that he realised what he was doing. 'Juras!' He practically screamed her name. 'Don't look. Keep your eyes away and get up speed.' The girl took no notice. With a sudden jerk of his arm Turlough hit her squarely on the face. Juras looked at Turlough in astonishment, and for a moment Turlough thought she was going to hit him back. But in time she too realised what hypnotic powers the birds possessed in their plumage, and rapidly changed gears to enable the Runner to pick up maximum speed.

The early evidence suggested that these creatures had the keen eyesight and powerful flight of the eagles from Trion. But now, with his eyes kept away from staring directly at the feathers, Turlough noticed the strange formation of the birds' six legs – or perhaps they could even be described as two arms, two legs and two grabbers. For several moments Turlough found himself wondering how the creatures ever managed to walk or sit, for where the conventional claws of a bird should have been there were instead crab-like pincers – six in all – each one over a metre long and each containing rows of teeth and serrated edges which made it quite clear that anyone – anything – caught inside those claws would never come out whole.

Turlough pulled his eyes away once more as he cowered in the depths of the Runner desperately hoping that the glass, even if it made it into the fully locked position, would hold off such a creature.

As the bird came in for its final dive Turlough spotted several more in the distance also flying headlong to the craft. Now other noises rented the air but the Clansman hardly noticed, his attention firmly on the dive of the first eagle. It hit the Runner side on, and got one claw in between the closing top of the glass seconds before the gap disappeared. With a sickening wrench it pulled itself away, injured but not sufficiently so as to inhibit a second dive. With the glass now fully closed Juras had the Runner under full power as she used the all-round vision to avoid getting too many direct hits from the flying creatures.

And then she stopped dead. Turlough pulled his eyes away from the dive of the group of eagles that had been following the leader. Ahead, more birds; a different species. These were flying directly at the Runner, at not more than a metre above the ground. A thick armour plating covered them, and they appeared to have no need to keep themselves flying, apart from the occasional flap of their wings. But it was the head – a solid white thing with red eyes peering above and a black downward pointing beak, that dominated the appearance of the creatures.

Even if the eagles seemed unable to break through the glass of the Runner these birds, heading straight at them at around two hundred kilometres per hour could well dive directly into the vehicle and smash it to bits, sure to survive themselves, thanks to their armour.

Turlough was sweating profusely as Juras turned the car and started moving at a ninety degree angle to the original path. As she had hoped, the armoured creatures dramatically overshot the mark and would take a considerable time to slow down, turn and get up speed once more. Juras turned at ninety degrees once more to resume her heading back to the ship. This time the way became blocked, not by a flying creature of any sort but by eight lumbering lizards. Turlough found it hard to believe. Where could such an assortment of beings have come from? Surely they could not be the natural inhabitants of the planet. The lizards were slow, and so proved no direct danger but it rapidly became clear that the Runner would have to skirt a long way round the group in order to avoid the huge tails of the three metre high beings. One stray swipe and the vehicle would be on its side and at the mercy of creatures who would surely be able to smash their way through with one twitch of a claw. As Juras made a wide sweep of the animals a group of eagles resumed the attack, and the life readings on the Runner's dash board illuminated with creatures approaching on all sides.

For the first time since the roof had closed Turlough spoke. His voice was shaking with fear but he had no mind to try and hide anything. 'It's unreal,' he said simply.

'I shouldn't bet on it,' said Juras. 'Those creatures look to me as if any one of them could get into the Runner.'

'But their behaviour is unreal,' insisted Turlough. 'There was not a single sign of any living being anywhere until you opened the roof.'

'Now is not a good time to tell me off for wanting fresh air,' Juras replied, swerving violently to avoid a new approach of the low flying beaked creatures.

'That's not what I meant,' shouted Turlough holding on grimly as the Runner completed a full circle and Juras tried yet again to get on a heading that would lead back to the ship.

'The instrumentation said they didn't exist. The roof came down, and suddenly they poured in from goodness knows where and attacked. But there was no sign of them before!'

'So you think they are figments of our imagination? Well you pop outside and try de-imagining them. I'll stay in here.'

'That is not the only explanation,' said Turlough. 'I've seen these creatures before – on the Slotsisland.'

And then, as if to confirm thoughts only half formed in his mind the instrumentation on the Runner showed a single life form straight ahead. It came out of nowhere, and seconds later could be seen as a speck on the horizon.

Juras spotted the being too, slowed slightly and prepared for a diversion, but Turlough moved to stop her.

'Head straight for it,' he commanded.

'Every other thing we've found here has been a hostile alien. Why not that?'

'Because I suddenly had the idea that something outside was controlling these creatures. And at the moment a single being appears on the screen ahead of us. The moment you opened the glass I thought that it might be dangerous and then we were under attack.'

'If these beings are part of your subconscious then your mind is in a worse state than I imagined,' said Juras.

'I didn't imagine them – the thoughts came to me,' said Turlough, and then suddenly lacking certainty he added, 'I could be wrong – it was just an idea. Take it slowly towards whatever is up there, and be ready to turn and drive at speed if need be.'

Juras accepted the instruction, largely because she could think of little else to do. At the present rate their muon drive would overheat long before they actually found a safe route back to the ship, and even when they did there would be no guarantee that the flying creatures they had seen would not choose to fly straight into it and make it unspaceworthy within seconds.

Ahead a humanoid: under two metres tall, wearing a white robe with a blue sash and red cloak. In his right hand he was holding a short white stick, whilst at his feet were flowers of some description – lilies and roses Turlough guessed, looking as if they had been just recently cut. Where they could possibly have come from on such a planet was impossible to imagine. On the man's head was a large brimmed hat shaped like a figure-of-eight. Piercing blue eyes, and flashing white teeth completed the colour schemes.

The humanoid male stood facing the oncoming Runner. Behind was the start of a forest of stunted leafless trees, the trunks bent through lack of water and nourishments. He remained motionless. Juras considered her options and ended up approaching at less then one kilometre an hour. Finally she drew to a complete stop a few metres in front of the being. Turlough and Juras looked hard. They took in the slightly pointed chin, a refined nose, and long slender fingers. All in all they appeared to be dealing with an unarmed, cultured young man probably only slightly older than Turlough. He opened his mouth to speak. Turlough rapidly turned on the receiver, but missed most of the statement. He spoke into his microphone and asked the humanoid to repeat.

'This is inhospitable country,' the man said. 'Please follow me,' and with that he walked calmly off, leaving Juras and Turlough little option but to drive slowly behind him. After five minutes they reached the brow of a hill. The man walked down, turned and disappeared into a cave. They drove in behind him and stopped. The man stood there, his skin illuminated by an unearthly glow from the very rock of the cave itself. He beckoned them out of the Runner, content to sit and wait patiently whilst they decided that they had little option, regarding them with a half smile playing on his lips.

'You are obviously not from this world,' said the stranger, once Turlough and Juras decided to emerge. 'What brings you here?'

Turlough looked at the man curiously. His demeanour revealed all the signs of his certainly not being a primitive, despite living in a wild and dangerous environment. He had an obvious acceptance, and possibly even knowledge of the concept of space travel. His clothes too were far too well kept and colourful for someone not fully in control of the situation.

'We thought we were on Regal,' said Turlough. 'But clearly we aren't.'

'Regal!' said the young man. His accent had started off as strange and hard to understand, but was rapidly adapting itself to something closer to the style used by Turlough and Juras. 'Then you are scholars. But you are on the wrong side of the world. The libraries and catacombs are all in the northern zones. The world of learning! The depths of knowledge. It has much to recommend it, much to be admired. I envy you your freedom.' As he spoke Turlough gained the distinct impression that the man was having fun at his visitors' expense.

'We're not scholars,' said Turlough looking nervously to Juras for support.

'Travellers,' said Juras. 'Hoping to stop and see the planet.'

'But no travellers come to Regal,' replied the man. 'Not in a thousand years. Only students of the old days.' The smile stayed on his lips. He was enjoying himself immensely.

'The old days?' said Turlough. And then with a moment's inspiration asked, 'What was it like in the old days?'

'Why, the planet flourished, but was eaten, demolished, destroyed and mostly forgotten.'

'*Eaten*?' Turlough found mythology hard to take.

'By the miners. They dug the planet to bits; the Trion Clansmen showing them how. They found gas fixed in crushed ice at the base of the planet's crust; a brilliant feat of engineering it was to remove the gas without boiling the ice. And then, when they had removed everything they could ever want everyone went. That was over a thousand years ago. Now there's just the scholars in the libraries, and a few simple hermits like me. We exist and live, watching, waiting.'

'But not so simple that you don't know about your planet's history.'

'You can't live here without knowing about history,' said the man. 'On this planet we have a lot of history, not much else.'

'Why do you stay?'

'What else should I do? I like it. Sometimes I travel to the north and spend some time with the researchers there, talking about the olden times. They give me food, and there is all the shelter one needs. There is something comforting about the past. It helps describe the present and develop the future.'

'There's nothing comforting about those creatures,' said Juras casting a glance back through the cave entrance.

'But they were as surprised to see you as you were to see them. This is their planet. We don't venture outside much – at least not this far south. It's safer up in the north, but here, with protection, the weather is more amenable. I don't like rain, do you?'

'Do you have records of your past here?' asked Turlough ignoring the climatic question. He'd had enough of weather reports whilst exiled in England.

The young man continued to smile. 'I'm not the simpleton you think,' he asid, and with that he leant against one part of the cave wall. Immediately on the other side part of the rockface came to life, revealing a picture of the planet as seen from neighbouring space. 'How far back would you like to go?' he asked. 'Reality is endless, the seam unbroken, time infinite.'

'Ten thousand years?' suggested Juras.

Touching what appeared to be solid stone the image was controlled bringing forth pictures of Regal as Turlough recalled it.

'How detailed can you get?' asked Turlough.

'How detailed would you like it? A grain of sand? A molecule of oxygen? A triad of quarks?'

'The year 8033 by your reckoning, the space port station of Leege, in the fourth month. I want to see the ships docked there.' The scene changed to outer space. The circular docking satellite appeared surrounded by visiting ships of all shapes and sizes. Connector tubes extended from ships to the hull of the satellite allowing passengers, crew and service teams to come and go as they wished. 'Go forward faster,' commanded Turlough. He watched intently as at almost comic speed ships came and went. Suddenly he shouted for a stop to the action before demanding a close up on one particular ship. He gazed intently at the picture for a moment before looking across to Juras. She looked back as Turlough gave a gentle nod of the head. The hermit caught sight of it too, but said nothing.

Turlough got to his feet, expressing his thanks to the man, saying how they needed to get back to their ship, and how they had learnt a lot. The young caveman pressed them to stay a little longer, to share in a meal perhaps, but Juras, taking up Turlough's theme, agreed they had already inconvenienced him enough, and they really had to be pushing on. The hermit made no move to stop them departing as they turned back to their vehicle. Both sat in the Runner, closed the lid carefully, double-checked it was actually fully secured and then gently eased it back to the outer world for a rapid return to their ship.

The young alien watched them go from the edge of his cave before returning to the control panel of his screen. Muttering to himself he adjusted several contact points and gained a picture of the connector tube that joined the craft that had so interested his young visitors. Gently he ran the picture forward until a young man – no more than a boy in fact – could be seen emerging from the tunnel. With a quick flip of the wrist the picture was made to freeze. There in mid-step could be seen Turlough. Somewhat younger than now, more flustered, more bedraggled, but definitely Turlough.

The hermit cleared the freeze and let the picture run on, following Turlough and a collection of other youths all bearing the unmistakeable air of junior Clansmen as they walked around the satellite dome looking for somewhere to eat. Having found what he was looking for the man turned the picture off, and sat back, a smile still playing on his face.

Idly he let his hands run over control positions invisible within the rock, and pictures of a variety of wild and undoubtedly fierce animals and birds appeared on the screen. Each one froze, before being transferred across the cave to take up a highly illuminated position on the walls. Once there each creature returned to life, only to find itself caged in.

Behind, the cave wall opened into sufficient space to allow each animal plenty of room to wander, fly, run or do whatever else it pleased. Only access to the cave, and beyond it the rest of the planet was excluded.

As his monitors showed Juras and Turlough drive at full speed in the Runner back to the ship the young man let out a slight, hardly perceptible chuckle.

04: 4D

Back at the ship, with no more interference either from wild animals or the young man from the cave, Turlough and Juras sat and considered their discovery. Neither was in any doubt now that they had indeed landed on Regal, and that the time unit had functioned perfectly.

'What we got wrong,' concluded Turlough, 'was the notion that we would be able to witness time passing whilst we were time-travelling. And now I think of it, I never saw the Doctor have the viewer of the TARDIS open whilst the vehicle was in sustained timeflight. Presumably that was why. Whatever you see is just an illusion.'

'So there are still further dimensional changes that we've never considered,' said Juras. Her face did not show the worry of her voice. Yet again Turlough gained the impression she was not pooling all her knowledge. For the moment, however, he decided to hold his peace.

'Whatever the changes are,' he said, 'they don't seem to cause us any immediate problems.'

'So what now?' asked Juras. 'Take off and fly to your famous out-of-the-way planet Earth?'

'One more thing to install,' said Turlough. But he said no more, unwilling to let Juras know what he had in mind.

'Don't start this again,' said the girl guessing the cause of his hesitation. 'I thought we'd got over not trusting each other.'

Turlough bit on his lip. Then he said, 'Let me try out what I have in mind. If it works you'll see it. If it doesn't it doesn't matter.'

'And if you don't get things to work,' replied Juras, 'I'll probably get blown into the skies of this desolate, windswept planet with you and the remains of the ship. Or worse, I won't get blown up, but the ship will, leaving us both stranded to talk for ever more with our local friendly caveman.'

'I promise you there is no structural change to be made to the ship as a flying vehicle,' said Turlough. 'It's merely a quantum problem. And you must admit, that if anything is experimentally my province then it's physics.' Juras nodded as Turlough continued, 'I know the basic principles, and have everything lined up. Only I didn't want to try it until I saw if the time unit worked. First law of physics: don't try two experiments at once.'

'Very well,' said Juras. 'How long do you need?'

'An hour,' replied Turlough. 'Ninety minutes at most.'

'I'll be in my cabin,' said Juras. 'Give me a shout when you are ready.'

Turlough watched the girl walk away towards the residential quarter of the ship before making his way to the time unit. He opened the central box, and climbed inside. As he had said to Juras, it was basically a simple problem of quantum physics. During the time spent on the TARDIS he'd turned the problem over and over in his mind. It was his field, after all, so he ought to be able to work out the solution. And certainly if he could devise a working time unit, he ought to be able to handle this small development in quantum mechanics.

There were however great gaps in Turlough's knowledge of time control, gaps which he had to fill from intuition. Now, thinking of what Juras had been up to in the intervening years, and watching that one modification she had made, he had seen, as if in a flash, a new way to route the circuits through a central controller. It made everything so much simpler. The result would be not a downmarket simplified TARDIS as he currently operated, so much as a completely new approach to time-travel itself. And it had one tremendous advantage: Juras wouldn't have the slightest notion as to what he had done. He might even surprise a few Time Lords.

Turlough stopped the self-congratulation, and pulled himself together. The extraordinary thing was, he had to admit, that if the spark for his revised plan came from Juras the background came from, of all places, Earth. Earth indeed, where they were still arguing if time-travel was a physical impossibility, and trying to show that nothing could travel faster than light. Turlough, with his near perfect memory, could even remember the journal in which he had read the piece – *Physical Review*, volume 9, page 2203. In effect it suggested that a rotating object could cause time displacement simply by rotating. All around such a massive object spacetime itself would be distorted. The lightcones would tip over and time-travel become not just possible but inevitable.

Turlough had known of the theory separately from this paper, but only now did he see the relationship between this quaint notion of a gigantic spinning object, and Juras' concern with gravity. A spinning object in space creates its own fake-gravity, as everyone who had ever walked on a space station knew. And particularly massive objects like stars bent the gravity waves of spacetime. Spacetime, gravity, spin. There was a unifying link.

'Now,' he said half aloud, half to himself. 'Positrons strike the unit as particles and waves, and are reflected back according to the angle of the surface. So first we spin in a way to use the energy.' He made a connection, and then another, deep inside the console in the centre of the floor. After a moment he crawled out, pressed a few contacts, observed the results, and, apparently satisfied, went back into the unit. He chatted to himself as he continued to work. More connections, more talk, another set of tests on the control panel, and back inside the machine once more. He touched a wrong connection, got a mild shock, gave a shout, and came out of the console. That, he knew should not have happened. He sat down.

Twenty minutes later he stood up and went back into the console, delicately prodding. On the fifth prod he found more electric current and let out a shout, but this time one of anger. Someone really had been meddling, and the number of suspects could be counted on one finger. From that point on Turlough worked at almost fever pitch, strangely happy now that he had made a discovery that seemed to remove all doubts about his companion.

He was just finishing when Juras, tired of waiting, came to

find him. 'Time to take off,' said Turlough at once.

'Work done?' asked the girl, trying to peer over Turlough's shoulder. Silently he closed the door behind him and led her back to the control room. Without pausing he patched in the new controls.

The ship travelled through space as no ship had ever done before. It moved far faster than light, slowly rotating about its own axis whilst travelling backwards through time, making its simultaneous way to Earth, England, and into the past which they had left before Regal.

Whilst Juras continued to work happily during the journey on her theoretical studies of gravity circuits Turlough puzzled over another of the TARDIS's mysteries – the chameleon circuit. That he had never seen it work properly caused him some heartache, it was a refinement he would have love to have had. But in the end, his complete failure to build one did not, he had to admit, really detract from his achievements.

What it did mean was that they still had to solve the question of landing. Where the TARDIS could simply materialise Turlough's ship physically had to land, and in landing there was nothing they could do to stop the spaceship looking like a spaceship. As Turlough said, even the primitives of Earth had worked out what an interstellar ship ought to look like even if they were several thousand years away from building one.

Meanwhile, the only way around the problem of trying to arrive unnoticed was to spy out the land in the temporal zone they wanted to be in, go backwards in time, land in a space that would remain unobserved and undisturbed for centuries to come, and then transmit themselves forward. It was a cumbersome operation, but preferable to creating a fuss by dropping out of the skies in what the local inhabitants would call 1982.

Dubious as the whole operation sounded it did not cause Turlough too much concern. That the revolutionary regime had brought him to Earth without being noticed in a region and time of such high population density was partly due to the speed with which Trion ships habitually charged into a planetary atmosphere. It also spoke volumes for the ability of

72

the natives not to examine what was going on around their own planet very clearly!

The place selected, Turlough brought the ship forward from the Devonian period (he had, he admitted, rather overshot – there had been no need to go back more than five hundred years), and stopped at the correct moment. If his calculations were correct the ship was now close to the location where he had hidden the electrolog illicitly smuggled onto Earth at the start of his exile.

The scanner showed them in a park. In the distance a few trees plus a large building, surrounded by outhouses. A small obelisk stood nearby. Beyond a group of teenage boys sat, chatting and occasionally looking at books and charts spread out on the grass.

'Recognise the place?' asked Juras as they emerged from the Hawk.

Turlough nodded solemnly. 'Oh yes, I recognise it,' he said in a quiet voice. The memories – his attempts to kill the Doctor (foiled on that occasion only because the Doctor slipped backwards as Turlough was about to bring a rock down on his head), and his involvement with the Black Guardian – were made too fresh by this return for him to be joyous at the success of his piloting.

As they left the ship Juras had a sudden worry about her clothes. Turlough regarded he one piece engineers' uniform. It did little for her femininity, but looked acceptable. 'They wore anything at this period,' he said with derision. 'If the clothes look unusual everyone thinks it must be a new fashion. As long as no one actually examines the material too closely we're OK.'

In burying his sacred package Turlough had, soon after his arrival, wandered deep in this wood, and away from the school buildings down the hill. He had had the perception to cover the little mound with earth; it would not keep a determined relic hunter away for long but had only been designed as an interim measure. If his calculations had been correct – and he was getting more confident about them all the time – he buried his package about three days before their current arrival. That would mean that by now he – the original version – would be away on a weekend trip to the seaside studying shells and attempting to imitate the other boys playing in the sand. He shivered at the memory of those dismaying, soul-decaying days. They could have landed earlier, but would then have run the risk of meeting Turlough the younger face to face—something that, as he knew from his time with the Doctor, could lead to all sorts of troubles.

The burial mound was inded as he had expected it. There were footprints nearby, retained in the soft earth following a recent fall of heavy rain, but otherwise nothing to worry about. Turlough and Juras worked hard for ten minutes digging at the earth to discover their treasure trove. The first thing he found was a pocket calculator so beloved of the schoolboys of the era. Turlough couldn't remember having had it, but put the matter out of his mind as he continued excavations.

Finally the package he sought appeared. With no care for the appearance of the ground around him Turlough picked himself up and walked back to the ship carrying the electrodiary, dusting himself down as he went. Juras meanwhile contented herself with looking around at the leafy undergrowth. 'You were lucky,' she said. 'Some were exiled to far worse places.'

In the light of the death of his father and mother in exile, Turlough found the remark in exceptionally bad taste, but let the matter pass.

Catching sight of a figure walking in the distance Juras quickened her step. 'We should move out instantly,' she said.

Turlough however had regained his love of bravado and was disinclined to move. 'If they see the ship it will give their Sunday newspapers something to worry about for a month or two,' he told her. 'And I don't suppose it will matter anyway. These folks have the most staggering ability to see genuine examples of alien civilisation as fakes and frauds, almost as if they didn't want anything outside their own little world to exist. Besides, they insist on believing that nothing can travel faster than light. Therefore, no one could visit from outer space, according to their view of the universe.'

The concept of insularity (something that no one on Trion had ever directly experienced prior to Rehctaht) fascinated Juras and she was ready to ask more about it, but she held her interest for the moment as they reboarded the ship.

Turlough connected his electrolog into the main circuits. Instantly the final entry appeared on the screen: *Abandoned on Earth; No escape possible.*

Turlough settled down to work. Juras left Turlough and returned to her own preoccupations. So intent were they both on their separate projects that neither bothered to regard the monitor focused on the outside world, even though it had been left on. Given that Turlough's bravado had dictated that they shoult stay on Earth rather than undertake research in orbit this really was something of an error. Indeed had they looked at that moment they would have seen a figure, familiar but out of place on this planet at this time. A singular young man, almost two metres tall, wearing a white robe, blue sash and red cloak and carrying a short white stick. All around him, where there had previously been only twigs and leaves were lilies and roses. A persona that knew perfectly well that the spacecraft sitting at the edge of a forest on top of a small hill looking over a minor public school, was indeed a Trion 976 Interstellar Hawk modified to allow time-travel in a way that had never been contemplated before.

Pushing his figure-of-eight hàt more firmly still onto his head the man gazed at the craft. The eyes stared more than they had the last time Turlough and Juras had looked on them, as he prowled forward. A long finger reached out and prodded the entry port, before withdrawing rapidly into the cloak. Then the hand emerged again and brought out what looked like a musical keyboard. The man touched a note. There was no sound, but ahead of him the ship shimmered, changed, twisted, reformed, deformed and returned to being the spacecruiser it really was. The muscular face of the man turned momentarily into a sweet smile and then back into a more neutral look.

Inside the ship the events were no less dramatic. 'Total power failure,' shouted Turlough. He didn't know who he shouted at. Juras was in her own room working on her theories and couldn't possibly hear him except through the intercom — and that, of course, had died along with everything else. Impatiently Turlough waited for the emergency back-up to come on. It didn't. He looked in the total blackness for any sign of light on any of the panels in front of him, but now all remained totally unseen. There was not a flicker of light anywhere. An urge within pushed him towards movement, but greter logic prevailed. The exit from the ship was electronically controlled – there was no over-ride; the ship builders had not anticipated both a primary and secondary failure. For that reason they had also failed to put in any mechanism to keep the oxygen pumps going once both systems were down. Turlough and Juras had about fifty minutes before they would start to appreciate that the air was turning thin. Another hour after that – an hour and a quarter at best – and they would be beyond caring.

If the young man outside had any notion of the effect his actions were having he revealed no sign of it. Carefully he lifted an elegantly long finger, and placed it on the single octave keyboard, three white notes from the bottom. Again there was no sound, but the ship stabilised for a moment. The man played more notes, a tune perhaps, but a tune unappreciated by any save himself. And then the alternating smiles were gone, the keyboard put away somehow beneath the cloak. Eyes slightly dimmed, he turned and walked elegantly away. Behind him the ship shimmered, melted, reformed and became rebuilt, exactly as it was before reassembled atom by atom after being taken apart, analysed and fully contemplated.

On board power returned. Turlough found he had been holding his breath. As the lights came on he let it out in a long gasp, and wiped his brow. Moments later Juras came through the door into the control cabin.

'I know,' said Turlough anticipating her report, 'total failure on primaries and backups. The whole ship went dead.' He looked at her carefully.

'Don't hold me responsible for that,' said Juras indignantly. 'Something – someone – external to the ship started playing games with us.'

'That makes no sense,' said Turlough, but despite himself he began running a full check of all the instrumentation on the control panel. Everything read normal.

Turlough watched carefully as Juras pressed in a number of

commands on the heat sensitive controls. The ship remained resolutely as it was. Juras tried again. Again no change. Whatever had happened was not in any way under their control.

'Further problems,' she announced at last, obviously mystified. 'Not only can I not get us to change into anything new I'm also unable to start up any circuits prior to getting us to move. The quark unit seems to have developed a mind entirely of its own.'

Turlough and Juras looked at each other thoughtfully for several seconds. Juras announced that she would go back to the drive room and go through the chromonal sections from scratch. Turlough meanwhile would work on refamiliarising himself with his entries on the Gardsormr, on the presumption that they would, eventually, be able to get the ship off the ground.

If Turlough had good spots in his complex personality they related to intellectual work. He accepted it, enjoyed it, would volunteer to undertake it, and mostly completed it faster than might be expected. This was not unnatural. Most Imperial Clansmen were the same. It was therefore not surprising that Turlough made rapid progress analysing his work of several years before.

He had intended to review the entries in the electrolog, updating them fully with new facts discovered during his time with the Doctor, before finally working on a complete new analysis of the entries. The fact that he was willing to undertake the review before getting down to the new analysis was testimony to his desire for intellectual accuracy. The fact that he rapidly spotted that the entries were not as they should be was testimony to his exceedingly accurate memory.

Turlough did not call Juras immediately. He checked and then double-checked the facts and searched his mind for any alternative explanation to the one that had leapt upon him. He found none. But he knew that in presenting his discovery to Juras he would need some sort of back up, or at least some idea of why it had happened. Such an event had to be connected with the unexplained changes that had taken place to the power supply of the ship. Yet how, and why? It began to seem as if there might be a knock-on effect in time-travel which almost distorted reality. Was that why the Time Lords were always so worried about other beings moving in time? And yet the Doctor had often interfered with events outside his own time stream. In fact he seemed to spend his whole life doing it, often at the behest of the High Council of the Time Lords on Gallifrey. Turlough was stuck for logical explanations.

Juras too was having trouble. Since landing she had run a substantial number of her standard gravity-related experiments and observations but the answers made no sense. The gravity of Earth itself was quite normal. And yet every time she attempted to verify some theoretical position with reference to the stars beyond, nothing worked. Worse, there was no explanation, theoretical or practical that she could find.

Turlough listened to her report before telling Juras his troubles. 'Someone or something has been tampering with my entries in the electrolog,' he announced. 'And before you tell me that is impossible, let me tell you that I know the log can only be activated by my voice, that it was all in order when I dug it out of the ground, and that therefore it doesn't make any sense. I inspected a handful of entries in the log as I dug it out; it was the only way I could be sure that the log had remained undamaged. Somehow something has happened between moving the log out of the ground and installing it here.'

'Just as something happened to the gravity waves that are reaching us from the space beyond this solar system.'

'The problem is that I can't see any sort of connection. In fact I can't see why there should even be such a connection. On the other hand coincidences such as this just do not happen.'

'Unless they are caused by time-travel.'

'That,' agreed Turlough, 'has been on my mind too.' And then he added, in a defiant mood that he had learned from the Doctor, 'We must proceed scientifically and find out what is going on.'

'How exactly?' Juras, just as capable of intellectual thought as Turlough, but sometimes more practical and less unyielding, brought the plans back to ground level.

And of course Turlough had to admit he didn't quite know

wht to do next, either scientifically or any other way. Juras had examined the time unit, just as he had previously, and there was no way their combined knowledge could discover anything which would lead either to the power failure, the log changes or the gravity anomalies they had experienced.

'We could go outside and check that the rest of the planet is as you remember it,' said Juras. 'Also we might find any localised disturbance that could itself be the cause.'

'Or,' said Turlough with typical trepidation of the unknown, 'we could hang on and see if any more disturbances occur. A fourth event could make the previous three clearer. Added to which, the Doctor always warned that it was dangerous to get too close to yourself in past time.'

Juras laughed, but said nothing further. Instead she returned to her cabin, and emerged, five minutes later, clean, fresh, and in suitable walking clothes ready for her second journey. 'Do I go alone?' she asked.

Turlough knew he had no choice. He followed, putting as brave a face on events as he could muster. After the experiences on Regal he wasn't prepared to take any extraneous planet on trust.

As they left the ship Juras asked, 'What would happen if you met yourself?'

'According to the Doctor, disaster. It happened once – not to me though, but to one of the teachers at the school I was sent to. Apparently he had known the Doctor previously. This militarist – Brigadier Lethbridge-Steward – met himself about four or five years apart, and caused quite a bang. Saved the Doctor's life, and gave the Brigadier an amazing headache that lasted for years – until he met himself again on the other side.' Turlough paused as he thought of the problems of meeting himself. He had no idea just how relevant that question was .going to become. Yet for the moment the issue remained academic, and he felt able to add, 'As far as I know, every time the Doctor met himself it was always a past self from a previous regeneration, and that change of body may well have made him less susceptible to the problems of time. But I don't intend going near where I was – am – in this time. At present I'm over a hundred kilometres away. We'll scout around the ship, take a few readings from outside and then return. If we find nothing at all we'll try another time-manoeuvre and see what happens then.'

As they left, Turlough tried a final excuse, suggesting they use the Runner, but as Juras pointed out there was no way better of attracting attention than using a clearly alien machine to drive around in. Turlough agreed to walk.

Turlough deliberately refrained from looking in the direction of the public school in which he had spent so much time before meeting the Doctor. Instead he directed Juras down the grass slope towards the road and the civilisation beyond.

After his initial objections he bore the walk with good grace and deliberately witheld suggestions that the stroll was doing them no good, until he felt that Juras too was feeling little was being gained. He pointed out the local sub-Post Office, explained the intricacies of road signs, talked her thorugh what he understood of the nature of a Small Business Enterprise Zone which had recently sprung up just beyond the school grounds, and finally answered a range of questions on the subjects of various local artifacts that filled the windows of half a dozen small shops lining the local high street.

On the way back Juras was silent, not because of the failure of her venture into the native world, but through a lack of clear ideas of what could be going on. Turlough respected her silence – he too was desperately puzzled and needed time to think – as he led the way along the path away from the village and school, and into the wood. Only when they faced the space ship did they stop. They stared. They backed off slightly. They looked around. They looked at each other.

In front of them was a smiling, young man with figure-of-eight hat, white robe, blue sash, and red cloak and lilies and roses at his feet. He was leaning against the ship.

'You,' said Turlough rather obviously.

The man smiled, as if pleased to be recognised.

'You are responsible for all our problems!' said Juras. 'Since you obviously followed us from Regal, and since equally obviously you can travel through time and space at least as effectively as we can, and finally since you are here, it is not too much to presume that you might get around to telling us who you are, and what you have been doing to our ship.' Turlough had never seen the girl so solid in her resolve.

The young man chuckled. A long finger emerged from his cloak; a long finger nail gently scratched the side of his nose.

'We are not totally powerless ourselves,' said Turlough with false anger. It had no effect, save that after a moment the tramontane stopped chuckling.

At last he spoke, 'Don't spoil yourself dear boy,' he said. 'You are more than you give yourself credit for. Full of faults, yes, but not so much as to hide totally some most valuable assets. Come,' he indicated with a wave of his hand as he turned and led the way inside the ship. It was an arrogant gesture. The ship was theirs, not his. Who was he, Juras wondered, to order them around like this? Turlough was beginning to get a sneaking suspicion.

'You are a Time Lord,' he exclaimed simply as he joined the others in the control room.

The outsider looked up from his inspection of the controls and forced an expression of mild surprise on his face. 'Well,' he said, pausing more for effect than uncertainty, 'yes. I suppose I am. But that really shouldn't affect you.'

'How can you say that? We've been struggling to make a time-machine tht works properly . . .'

'. . . And you've done it. Remarkably well, if I may say so. Brilliantly. Stunningly. Totally.' In the light of the ship's control room he looked even younger than he had previously – and had a mischievous air about him that was not fully to Turlough's liking.

'The least you could have done was help us out,' complained Juras.

'Help you?' The Time Lord seemed taken aback. 'Help you?' he repeated, to heighten the effect. 'Why should I possibly help you? As your friend, dear lady, has just ascertained through assiduous guesswork, I am a Lord of Time. We do not "help out" as you so sublimely put it.'

Juras looked at Turlough. There didn't seem to be much of an answer.

The visitor waved his arm imperiously around him. 'Besides

you don't need help,' he said looking straight at Turlough, and pointing a long finger at him. 'You,' (he emphasised the word, although it seemed to need little emphasis to make the point), 'have just created the first ARTEMIS. There's been discussion of it over the centuries, here and there, off and on, from time to time, but no one has ever actually gone back to basics and done it. Except you. You don't need my help, Clansman Turlough. I should be asking yours! Your work is excellent, superlatively superfine. Peerless, matchless and inestimable. Quite superb; impossible to over-rate.'

Yet again Turlough and Juras looked at each other, totally bemused by the interloper. Turlough tried a more practical approach. 'It's good to know that we have an . . .' He forgot the word.

'ARTEMIS'. The Time Lord helped him out.

'Just one problem. Wht is an ARTEMIS?'

Another wave of the hand, encompassing all around them. Everything this man did seemed to be a grand gesture. 'This, my friends, this, my dear Turlough and beautiful Juras, this time-travelling space ship.'

'But what exactly does ARTEMIS mean?' persisted Turlough. If he was going to be credited with a galaxy-shattering revolution he felt he ought to know exactly what he had done. Besides, modesty was not one of Turlough's better known traits.

'It means, that you have cracked the rotation-induced gravity problem in time.'

At the mention of the word 'gravity' Juras visibly jumped. It was as if she felt that Turlough had illicitly tampered with her property. Turlough however was too engrossed with the thought of himself having invented something that would go down in history for all time. Surely, he was already thinking, it would be better known as the Turlough Drive. Later to be shortened through familiarity to TD. He caught sight of Juras and returned to the matter in hand.

'Cracked it?' queried Turlough. 'I didn't even know we had a problem until we tried to measure our own movement in time against the rotation of planets. It was only then that I set out to solve the problem.' Such an admission he felt would emphasise the speed of his work – something that should be recalled in the official historical reports of this momentous development (whatever it finally turned out to be).

'That is exactly my point,' said the Time Lord. 'All Gallifreyan technology has for millenia been based on an awareness that revolution-induced gravity exists and affects all temporal manipulation. You did not know the details of the effect for sure so at first you ignored the problem. Then when the reality of the situation hit you in the face you, dear boy,' (he looked at Turlough and bowed slightly as he spoke) 'created an artificial adaptation unit. Artificial gravity from artificial rotation.'

'And that is ARTEMIS?' asked Juras. She was clearly getting rather miffed at being left out of the praise the Time Lord was heaping on Turlough. True, the time unit was his, but gravity was her province.

'Artificial Rotation Through Energetic Muons In Series. Enough to make you renowned through the galaxy, but for you, dear boy, Imperial Clansman extraordinary, just the start. What you also did was to use energetic muons as the power source for your time unit. And nobody tipped you off that that was a theoretical possibility.' And then, just for a moment, that all pervading self-confidence which had dominated every moment of the Time Lord's exposition of Turlough's brilliance, vanished, as he added nervously, 'Nobody did tip you off, did they?'

'Of course not,' said Turlough energetically defending his sudden fame. 'I never got anywhere near the power source in the Doctor's TARDIS, and it was obvious that the cold fusion powering the ship couldn't work to power a time unit, so I used the only other source of power I could think of – muons. Cold fusion creates them by the megaton. The ship creates muons, and the time unit uses them to travel in time. It is a drawback though,' he added as an afterthought. 'You can't travel in time without travelling first in space.'

But the Time Lord seemed not to hear such deliberately self-deprecating comments. Instead he continued his eulogy over Turlough. 'And next, to the run down of the universe itself!' He said it as if pronouncing the title of the most holy of works

83

in the galaxy. 'You must strive to work on the Entropy Mechanism – a feat only dreamed of in Gallifrey, a machine not even imagined elsewhere. I have had a few thoughts on the subject myself. Allow me to show you,' and with that he turned back to his little keyboard and began playing unheard melodies which turned into sketches and diagrams on the viewscreen.

Turlough peered at them in interest, although it was obvious that Juras was rapidly losing patience with both the other occupants of the craft. She coughed as a prelude to a caustic comment but was stopped by a sudden movement from the Time Lord. Spinning a full circle, arms akimbo, and forcing first Turlough and then Juras to duck he called out, 'We acknowledge ARTEMIS I. On to ARTEMIS II: Artificial Relativity Through Entropy Mechanisms In Sequence. ARTEMIS II. You have done it once, dear, dear boy. You can do it again. I feel it, I know it. That I should be the one priviledged to witness this feat.' And then with a sudden change of mood he looked straight at Turlough. 'You, my young friend, have a glorious brain. Turgid, devious, cowardly, unreliable, but brilliant.' Then turning to Juras he added, 'And you, beautiful lady, you also have a beautiful mind – diverted sometimes by your social engagements, but still just as brilliant. I have not forgotten in this moment of scientific triumph that you are here.' And then, to the world in general he commented, 'Each brilliant. Each worthy of a major place in history. A genius pair. Beyond comprehension. But put the two together, and . . .'

The sentence hung in the air unfinished. Turlough and Juras were spellbound, yet the unended notion of what the two of them together would create made Turlough feel uneasy. He turned to the Time Lord to demand further explanation but at that moment the Gallifreyan chose to sit down on the floor, curl up in a tight position and go to sleep.

05: MAGIC

Turlough carefully picked his way around the bizarre Time Lord and walked across to Juras. 'I'm open to suggestions as to what we do now,' he said.

'I'm glad to see you can still manage to speak to me after such elevation,' the girl replied sarcastically. 'Do you really think he could be a Time Lord?'

'Certainly possible,' said Turlough. 'All the ones I've come across have seemed singularly peculiar; this one is no more odd than the rest of them. In fact it is quite possible that this is yet another reincarnation of the Time Lord I travelled with – the Doctor.'

Turlough's suggestion brought a dramatic, unexpected result. The keyboard which the Time Lord had carried with him, and which was now placed by his side took on a life of its own. It played, seemingly without help from its owner. Disconcertingly the lights dimmed, but this time only for a second. On the main screens in front of the couple a message glowed in brilliant pink. 'The Doctor!?!?!' (it read). 'Don't be absurd.'

'Then what is your name?' said Juras, not sure if to look at the sleeping man, the screen or the keyboard. The reply came back on the screen. 'Some call me Pagad, some Magus. Mostly I am known as The Magician.'

'The problem is,' said Turlough, after the message disappeared and the lights showed no further sign of dimming, 'if he is a *real* Time Lord, he could well be in the business of stopping us travelling in time. That remains one of their main functions.'

'So all this about your being the greatest genius the Clans

have ever seen is just a ploy to stop you taking the unit back to Trion,' said Juras.

The thought cut Turlough to the quick. Stopping further discussion, he acted, engaging the time unit and the take-off phase simultaneously. Within seconds the ARTEMIS (if that was what it was, and it seemed to Turlough a fair acronym), was cruising away from Earth through the Solar System and as Turlough directed the ship out of the plain of the galaxy, into the future.

Juras was, to put it mildly, enraged, even though she recognised that she had been tactless in her last statement. When she calmed down she put her objections forward as logically as possible. Her main concern, it seemed, was with the removal of The Magician from the planet. 'Hijacking people,' she announced, 'whether they are Time Lords or not, has never been part of the plan as far as I knew. What is more, we are already overcrowded in here with just two of us, and now you've increased the population by fifty percent. And, you should have asked.'

Turlough's tension had been building up for some time and now found its moment of release. 'The overcrowding came entirely because you chose to stow away,' he told Juras. 'It has never been Trion law that stowaways have to be asked what should be done about other passengers invited on board by the captain. Besides,' he added mollifying his tone slightly, 'I know these Time Lords. They're devious . . .'

'*Devious*! Turlough you are the most devious person I have ever met. Even The Magician said so.'

'Not as devious as The Magician himself, I suspect,' replied Turlough going on the defensive. 'Possibly this one was sent here to stop us operating a time unit. And since operating a time unit is what we have both been trying to do I imagine you were not fully in agreement with giving in to him.'

'We have no proof he was going to abort the project,' Juras argued. 'If he had wanted to stop us it would have been on Regal. With all those animals around he could have taken us out at any time.' She snapped her fingers to emphasise the fact.

'What other explanation could there be?' shouted Turlough. He would neither admit he was as confused as Juras, nor that the reaction of sending them into space had been something of a panic measure. He had alternatively hated and then admired the Doctor during their time together, but even when remembering all the good things his erstwhile friend had done Turlough really did feel he had had enough of Time Lord interference, at least for the time being.

But Juras would not let the matter pass, and she was on the verge of shouting too. 'All right, great logician and genius. Now that we are travelling, do you know where, or come to that why? Or what caused the power failure and what is wrong with gravity in this part of the universe?'

Turlough chose to answer the first question. 'We are heading on a course back to Trion, with a marginal temporal dilation which should bring us back to the Home Planet two hours after we left.'

'That, if I may say so,' said a voice, 'is not a very sensible thing to do.' It was The Magician, struggling to his feet. He let out a long slow yawn, putting the keyboard in a pocket in his cloak whilst the others watched him. 'You know,' he said finally, 'you really should not shout quite so much. Even Time Lords need sleep—at least this one does.' And then, suddenly, he snapped back into his previous persona, long fingers again active, his head tilted slightly to one side, an air of all-knowingness filtering through from under his figure-of-eight cap. He produced a rose from his pocket and waved it in the air.

'And where, pray, would you have us go?' asked Turlough, his voice heavy with sarcasm. He regretted it at once—if this man was telling even half the truth he was making Turlough a hero.

'Nowhere,' said The Magician. 'You should stay in Earth orbit, in this time, check your chart of Gardsormr sightings, and then derive from that, as your magnificent brains can, details of when the creatures will next appear.'

'But the log is useless,' complained Turlough. 'It's been fixed.'

'Ah, such eloquence!' replied The Magician. ' "Fixed", as you so delightfully say, "fixed", yes. But "useless", no.'

'You changed Turlough's log?' asked Juras incredulously. It

seemed quite feasible that this strange Time Lord could have done so, but that he should then admit it was bizarre.

'Indeed, but merely because your records, good as they were, were incomplete. And inaccurate. Knowing the strain you were under whilst collecting them, Clansman Turlough, I can understand that, but still there were several sightings which had been erroneously entered. However,' he added with an expansive sigh, 'real geniuses do, I suppose, make errors in points of detail. It is the broad grasp of things that marks out the true brilliance. The way you instinctively utilised a natural phenomenon . . .'

'Will you stop calling Turlough a genius!' demanded Juras. 'I can well accept that it is completely in your power to change the electrolog, but I can't possibly imagine why you should choose to do that.'

'To help, of course. You have stretching before you a great mission, a tremendous adventure, a remarkable voyage, the headlong quest. Press on! Charge forth! Yet it would be rather sad if you started out on the wrong path just because your friend here had written a few co-ordinated data entries back to front.'

'I don't believe I ever did that,' said Turlough once more on the defensive.

'Believe what you like,' said The Magician imperiously. 'I know what's what. And besides I have seen the future. Time, the galaxy, the universe – they are my estate, my realm, my province, my heritage. I move through the temporal plains, observing, listening, recording, studying . . .'

'And?' Turlough and Juras spoke together.

'And?' mimicked The Magician. 'My children! You think I will tell you? Is that what you want? This is your great exposition, my friends. Your name to be written large in the history of your planet. Go forth and track down Gardsormr.' And then he added, with those dramatic changes of his voice that Turlough realised were his hallmark, 'And if you don't mind I'll come along for the ride.'

'It's not a pleasure trip,' objected Turlough.

'No, no,' said The Magician, moving his voice into another mode, with sweeping rises of pitch that took him up at least an octave. 'Not at all. No!' he reached a crescendo. 'The road will be long and tough. But,' his voice dropped dramatically, 'interesting. I would like to bear witness.' He swept his arm before him and ended pointing at the screen, before adding very slowly and very quietly, 'I should like to see. I wish to be there. I shall be there.'

'And help us out?' asked Juras.

'Can't do that,' said The Magician briskly. 'Against the rules.'

'Then why did you change the electrolog?' asked Turlough with a smile. 'That was helping.'

'And allowed,' answered The Magician. 'As I said, "I know the future," and the future says I helped you on that. I may be able to add the odd little bit here and there – but really you two, you do yourself an injustice. You are sitting in the admittedly cramped conditions of the galaxy's first ever ARTEMIS. You don't need me. Think of me as a guest.' He paused, looked at the two, and then added in as pleasing a voice as he could manage, 'What's for lunch?'

Turlough dialled up some tablets and nuts from the two centimetre square control box that acted as a kitchen, and took the result over to The Magician on a tray. He looked at it carefully, and then began pecking at the nutrition ignoring his companions. Turlough took the opportunity to lead Juras as far away as possible from The Magician – which in the cramped surroundings was not particularly far – before holding a brief conference.

'There's no way of making a judgement on him,' said the Clansman. 'He could be working for the Time Lords with the intention of throwing us off the right track, or he could be telling the truth. He could even be working for the Gardsormr, or come to that he could actually be a Gardsormr! We can't tell.'

'There must be a way,' said Juras simply. 'In the meanwhile, why don't we hold position, and run the analyses on the electrolog. That might give us something which can be put to the test.'

Turlough agreed and took his seat at the controls. Juras walked back to the Time Lord and sat next to him. Politely he offered her some nuts. She declined.

'I have a question,' the girl announced quietly.

The Magician licked his lips, then his fingers, and then scratched his nose. With a flowing movement he swept his head round to regard her directly. 'Mmmm?' he said. He made the sound last several seconds.

'What are the Gardsormr?'

The hands of The Magician disappeared under his long flowing cloak. 'Indeed,' he said. 'What are they? Who are they? Why are they? Where are they?' He seemed disinclined to say any more.

Juras decided to try another tack. 'Turlough doubts that you are who you say you are.'

'Of course, he does,' said The Magician. 'Inevitably he must. Otherwise it would all be too easy, too straightforward, too simplistic, too credulous, too implicitly hyper-orthodox for words. And do you know,' (he leant forward conspiratorially) 'I don't blame him a bit.' He leant back smiling contentedly to himself as if he had either just made a remarkable joke or had perhaps let Juras into a deep secret.

'But can you give us some proof, or evidence that you are who you say you are?' she persisted.

'None,' said The Magician. 'But that is because I am who I am. Were I something else I could. Did the Doctor ever prove to Turlough he was the Doctor?'

Frustrated beyond measure, Juras stood up and walked back to Turlough. He, however, had lost interest in The Magician's verbal games. The electrolog was giving results. 'If nothing else,' he said, 'these entries do make more sense than my originals. There is a definite pattern of Gardsormr movements for both Trion and Earth, and the other planet on which I observed them. Their visits ebb and flow—they go through a cycle in which they either increase until they are virtually encamped on the planet, or decrease until they only visit once every few months.' He paused for a second before giving Juras the final spot of information. 'Earth,' he said, 'is building up towards a peak. If this data is correct a Gardsormr ship is going to appear at any moment.'

Turlough pointed at the screen to show Juras exactly where

he anticipated the appearance of the Gardsormr ship. Within seconds it was there, a huge spinning top gleaming grey and white, sporting additional structures in all directions, not only practical for any sort of atmospheric travel, but also reasonable for the voids of interstellar space. It was a good design.

As they watched the ship dived towards the planet, passing the Moon and moving into orbit at a mid-point between the two objects, conveniently using the natural satellite as a backdrop to itself, a method guaranteed to cause confusion to anyone on Earth happening to be observing. After remaining stationary for under a minute the ship began to move again in its own orbit of the planet. Turlough gave the instructions to follow.

'Looks like a simple reconnoitre,' said Juras.

Turlough said nothing, concentrating on keeping the ship in sight, whilst holding a position as remote as possible. Four orbits later the Gardsormr ship took up its position between Earth and Moon.

'Preparing to leave,' conjectured Turlough. 'I think we ought to follow.' Juras could see no reason to disagree. The Magician said nothing. Juras sat down in the co-pilot's chair, leaving The Magician to make himself as comfortable as he could near the centre of the room.

Suddenly, as anticipated, the Gardsormr ship moved off. 'Lateral thrust 27-29-91, maximum force,' shouted Turlough. The ship obeyed. 'Full fusion, direct ahead.' The ship moved forward rapidly, giving an increase in apparent gravity to the occupants. Turlough and Juras felt the stress. To The Magician it seemed to make no difference. He was still happily eating his nuts.

Once the course co-ordinates were resolved Turlough relaxed. 'They're taking a standard arc out of the galactic plain. If they follow what would be our conventional procedure then they are going to end up at Trion or at least somewhere near it.'

'So there is a connection between Trion and Earth!' Juras exclaimed.

'And between Gallifrey and Earth,' replied Turlough.

They looked at The Magician. He smiled benevolently, but

his glance back gave nothing away. Turlough locked the course units on the ship. If the Gardsormr deviated from the course he would be warned by a shrill alarm. Both decided to get what rest they could in the tiny Interstellar Hawk. Turlough worried for a moment about what their uninvited passenger might get up to whilst they relaxed, but concluded that with the technology the man possessed he could probably do as he wished no matter what precautions he took. And they would have to sleep sometime.

The alarm shrieked in Turlough's ear. Within a fraction of a second he was upright before falling off his bunk and running through the rear portion of the control room, where The Magician still sat seemingly content with the way things were going. Turlough took his position at the controls.

The Gardsormr ship, he knew, must have deviated from the predicted path. Now he had to relocate it before he lost the image against a backdrop of stars. And yet the screen showed it hadn't deviated. The ship was still there.

The siren was still blasting. Turlough killed it before checking again. The Gardsormr ship was still in front of him, heading on its established curved path towards Trion. Perhaps there was something wrong with the instrumentation. Imitating an old habit of the Doctor's Turlough gave the control panel a solid thump with his fist. None of the readings changed. Then he felt and heard a bang. It had nothing to do with his hitting the control instruments.

'Something's grabbed the ship,' shouted Juras, now fully awake and by Turlough's side.

'Of course!' Too late Turlough saw the trap. 'The alarms went off because they launched a mini-sub to come back to us. And I missed it.'

'Can we pull out?' asked Juras.

'Not worth risking. From the sound of it we're caught in a grappling web. If we pull against it the skin of the ship will rupture. For once,' he added with half a grin, 'Turlough isn't going to recommend running away.' He turned to The Magician, still sitting in such comfort as he could muster in

92

the middle of the rear control area. 'Any suggestions from you?'

'Like I said, my dear, dear boy,' replied the Time Lord, 'not my place to interfere. You must sweat and slave, struggle and debate in order to overcome whatever malpractices should befall you. Plan and plot – that is your role in the affair. I merely observe.' He gave an imperious wave of the arm as if to indicate permission for Turlough to carry on the good fight.

'I am not putting on a turn just for your entertainment,' Turlough shouted as he turned back to the console. 'We could try and move in time,' he added to Juras in a calmer voice.

'Too late,' the girl replied, and as she spoke there was a second bang, and the unmistakeable hiss of the entry lock opening. Disengage now, and they would lose all their air.

As the lock opened Turlough and Juras strained their eyes to see their adversaries. They were frightened, true, but fear was mixed to a degree with the knowledge that at long last they would meet the Gardsormr. For Turlough, annoyed and affronted by the Time Lord's attitude of calm disassociation, it was now a time to act. As a single humanoid figure emerged at the entry port he touched a control on the desk. The figure flew backwards violently, emitting a low howl of pain as he did so. Juras looked to Turlough in surprise as he activated the air lock, and prepared for time movement. Then she saw what he had done. The doorway had become electrified. It was a simple device included on all these ships, and for good reason. Land on an unknown planet with a good atmosphere and you might well feel inclined to open the entry hatch just to let in some fresh air. What you wouldn't want to encourage however was the entry of any aliens who happened to be passing by at the time. Electrification of the floor, walls and ceiling tended to deal with most predators.

As the ship moved forward in time, Turlough started to shudder. He had been through a few episodes like this with the Doctor, but this was the first time he had become involved of his own volition. It would take some getting used to.

Turlough brought the ship back to normal time-speed a few years ahead of their confrontation, and tried to think out what to do next. No sooner had he finished checking the controls however than there came a second clang on the outer hull, followed yet again by the sound of the hatch being opened. Turlough at once re-activated the electronic pulses around the door. This time they did no good. Through the hatch came, not a solitary walking figure, but instead five glowing balls, each about thirty centimetres in diameter, floating at head height. One sphere remained glowing with a pinkish light by the entry hatch. One moved in front of Turlough, so close that he had to shield his eyes from the light. Two others took up similar positions in front of Juras and The Magician. The last moved to the control panel.

The alien object remained motionless for several seconds until, apparently satisfied, it moved away to be joined by the sphere that had been guarding the door. All five then began the task of shepherding their captives into the lock, and across the boarding passage into the docked mini-sub. The whole operation was carried out in silence and took under a minute.

If the ARTEMIS drive had made Turlough's ship crowded, the mini-sub, designed for only robot operation was far worse. The three captives were forced to sit on a metal floor, with heads bowed to keep from banging themselves on the ceiling. Turlough, whose faith in The Magician was rapidly cooling was pleased to see the Time Lord looking distinctly uncomfortable.

There was but one cabin, in which walls, roof and even parts of the floor were covered in controls. The spheres moved around from one position to another occasionally changing the intensity of their pinkish light as they fed in or received commands. The noise from the engine area of the ship was frightful, the light too dim for comfort. Within moments of disengaging the ship also became far too cold to accept.

Turlough tried to speak to the spheres. 'We can come to an arrangement,' he said, his teeth chattering. The spheres ignored him. 'We have a time-ship.' There was still no response. Speaking faster he added, 'This man is a Time Lord,' but it got nowhere. If the spheres could hear him they were obviously not interested in responding. Ejecting the humanoid three years (in real time) earlier was looking like having been a bad move.

'Not much left to bargain with now,' said Juras bitterly. She appeared to have little sympathy with Turlough, and looked set to blame him entirely for their present predicament. Not that that would bother Turlough too much. A few more minutes and they would all be suffering from hypothermia. She looked at The Magician. He seemed to be feeling the cold too, but showed no signs of coming to their aid. Turlough by now had his eyes closed, and frost was forming on his lips. Juras tried to move across to him to keep him awake, but found her legs had been curled up beneath her for too long. She looked round at The Magician again with the idea of speaking to him, but her lips felt dry. She licked them. Her tongue stuck. Frost was now covering much of Turlough's face. And then the world went black.

Juras awoke to warmth. She felt her legs. They were stretched out, no longer curled, stiff but warm. It was good. She risked opening her eyes, and wished she hadn't. The sunlight was too bright. She closed both eyelids tight, counted to twenty and then tried again. All around was jungle. Bushes, grasses, ferns, leaves, trees.

Jungles, of course, (so Juras rationalised with her still slightly befuddled brain) were not normally that nasty in themselves, but could become the habitat of a variety of unpleasant creatures. Added to which the fact that the Gardsormr, or at least their irritating spheres, had created yet another mystery to add to the paradoxes already surrounding them, did not lead her to expect an early solution to the problem of what she was actually doing lying in the middle of a jungle on a planet she did not, at least from this viewpoint, recognise.

Juras sat up and looked around. There was no sign of the others. She resisted the desire to shout out Turlough's name – if there was something nasty nearby there was no sense in advertising her presence too widely. Standing, she peered through the lush undergrowth. There was no sign of movement. No sign of life. The air was still. There was not even the sounds of the jungle that she associated with the wilder parts of the Home Planet.

Juras found she had been lying in what might have been an overgrown track. It invited her to walk along it. She obliged, choosing to walk towards the single sun high in the sky. After ten minutes the track petered out into nothing, leaving the option of either attempting to cut through the undergrowth without even a pocket knife to help her, or retracing her steps. She chose the latter, and was eventually rewarded for the right decision.

After half an hour there was a definite thinning in the undergrowth, and the first sign of a slight breeze. She welcomed it. It was hotter than she had at first realised and thirst was starting to get a major problem.

A man jumped out in front of her holding a reflex rifle. Juras didn't know if she was more surprised by the appearance of the man – he looked like a Trion with somewhat dated clothing – or his choice of weapon. The only time she had seen such a gun before was in the Central Museum at Charlottenlund.

The man moved towards her, rifle on shoulder ready to shoot, eyes narrowed, finger on trigger. In the universal move of surrender Juras raised her arms over her head. The man carefully walked around her until he could prod her in the back and urge her to continue walking. 'Move!' he shouted.

From that one word Juras knew the accent. 'All right all right,' she said, imitating the man's style of speech. 'Just tell me where you want me to go and I'll go. It's not as if I have anywhere else in mind.' She had hoped that these few words would get the man to realise he was escorting someone with the same accent as he himself had. Possibly a conversation would ensue, and with that an explanation. If he did realise he made no effort to stop, talk or explain.

The walk was a prod and push affair, Juras trying to take it slowly, with the captor, perhaps more knowledgeable about potential dangers en route, anxiously keeping speed up. Eventually they came to an encampment. A wall surrounded the buildings. A solid wooden door was pulled back slightly at the man's approach and he and his captive were allowed to enter.

Juras was paraded through simple streets enclosed on both

sides by a variety of low level buildings. In the distance a few taller more elaborate structures could be seen. The housing and general layout of the settlement gave no clue as to how one of the inhabitants came to have a museum piece of a rifle, and spoke with an accent immediately recognisable to anyone from Trion as equatorial eastern.

The inevitable cell into which Juras was eventually led was not as horrific as she might have anticipated. She had a bed, chair, table, plenty of light, running water and cup; it was better than many of Rehctaht's prisoners had got. On the other hand, having drunk her fill of the clear water Juras was left with nothing to do. No one came near her, no guards appeared at the door. The silence of the planet remained. At last she fell asleep.

She awoke in darkness. This time there were two guards. They escorted her through passageways, through the open air, and into a building, slightly, but not dramatically more imposing than the rest.

If Juras anticipated that she would be meeting the local emperor, high priest or other dignatory, dressed in glorious splendour, surrounded by lackeys, perhaps with a throne room cascading in jewels with the odd amulet thrown in for good measure, she was disappointed. The house appeared to be used for living, not glorifying. She was taken into one room and sat in a chair by a modestly decorated wooden table.

Opposite sat two women, both in middle age, and a slightly younger man. The guards retired, returning presumably to their jail. There was no sign of a single armament in the room.

'Your name, please.' It was one of the women who spoke. She wore a simple brown dress. Her hair, long and flowing, retained an extra element of youth that had gone from her face, victim no doubt of the exposure to the heat and humidity of the jungle environment. She spoke without malice or harshness, a form in front of her. She wrote with an electronic marker on a micropad – a technology totally out of keeping with the surroundings. As Juras looked at her she also realised that a micropad was itself inappropriate to the job of interrogation. She had seen enough such events on Trion during the last years serving Rehctaht. Imperial Investigators, as they were known then (interrogators as everyone more properly called them) used total recording techniques. Everything from changes in sweat rates on the palms of the suspects' hands to changes in the tone of voice was constantly recorded and analysed, with an immediate feed-back to the questioner on the screen in front of her. (Juras paused in mid-thought. Why, she wondered, were the good interrogators always women?)

'I am Juras Maateh, from Valerange, in Norring, on the planet Trion.' What had made her suddenly give her full address she wondered? The accent of her captor? The look of these inquisitors?

The three facing her took the answer calmly and recorded it on the pad. 'You are therefore a Clanswoman of the Imperial Clans of Total Science Knowledge?'

How strange on this wilderness of a planet, to hear the formal title, thought Juras. She did not deny the suggestion.

'Your occupation?'

'Engineer.' Her answer caused a stir – the three looked at each other with ill-concealed excitement.

'And how did you come to be on this planet? Are you on the run from Rehctaht?'

'Rehctaht is deposed and dead,' Juras informed the inquisitors. 'The Imperial Clans are welcomed back under decree from the Committee Of Public Safety now ruling Trion. The details of how I come to be here form a long and complex story.'

'We have plenty of time,' replied the solitary man at the table.

Juras gave a full and detailed account, starting from Turlough's exile, and ending with the following of the Gardsormr ship. It was received without comment although judging from the faces of her inquisitors Juras guessed that her arrival was to them, if not to her, a timely intervention. Even her frank admission that she had been working for Rehctaht brought no criticism or threats of instant death.

'Do you know why you are here or indeed where you are?' asked the older of the two women at the conclusion of the story.

Juras said no to both questions, but decided to offer some guesses. She told them she realised she could not be too far from the position they were in when the Gardsormr struck. She knew she could not have withstood the cold for long, and it would have been illogical for the creatures to capture them at any time other than when they were near the planet where they wanted to drop them. The blackness of the night sky enhanced her assumptions. Turlough's path had taken them on the fastest route between Earth and Trion, an arc out of the main plain of the spiral arm of the Galaxy. A night sky which was clear but revealed precious few stars suggested the edge of the galaxy – perhaps even slightly beyond that theoretical limit; a planet circling a long rogue star, far from any position that could lead to a chance rescue.

Her audience were appreciative of the deductive logic, and non-emotionalism of Juras' replies. They rose, and invited Juras to do the same. She complied.

Juras was led back into the street, past more houses to a central square. The sun was rising. Children played in the dust and dirt. On the steps of a house sat Turlough and The Magician, the Clansman scowling, the Time Lord grinning all over his face. When Juras looked round her escort had vanished. She ran across the square as Turlough looked up, saw her, and came to greet her. They hugged each other as they had not done since before the start of Turlough's exile.

The Magician looked on. 'Dear, dear girl,' he announced benignly. 'You are well? Not mistreated? Fit for action? Well for travel? Prepared for adventure? Ready for battle?'

Juras guessed he knew exactly what had happened, and ignored the comments. She looked instead at Turlough. 'What have you found?' she asked as soon as they disengaged.

'Not much,' Turlough told her despondently. 'He won't tell me anything,' he added, gesturing with annoyance at The Magician, who continued to smile back. 'I was picked up in the jungle, brought in, questioned and led out here.'

'Did they question you too?' Juras asked The Magician.

'Of course, of course, young Juras. The questing heart of the Trion spirit never faulters, never stumbles. Such inquisitiveness is wondrous to behold. If only more of the galactic races would follow your lead. Why, the progress! The advancement! Consider how far forward we could all develop. Imagine all worlds, questing together in unified harmony.' The Magician's delight in using ten words where one would do had not deserted him.

'Trion spirit?' Both Turlough and Juras caught the implication.

'A slip of the tongue,' said the Time Lord. 'I'm allowed those – although unless I'm mistaken – and that is rare – you are about to be told. Look forth and take careful note, for even a genius such as Turlough can sometimes learn a little from other, lesser, brings. Contemplate briefly, truth will be revealed. Hark!'

The group of three that had questioned Juras were heading towards their captives. Turlough stood to meet them, pulling at his cuffs nervously. 'Welcome to New Trion,' said the elder woman as they drew close. 'I'm sorry you had to undergo the indignity of our questioning, but we have to consider every new individual who joins us. You will be very worthwhile recruits. A Clansman, Clanswoman and Time Lord. Excellent!'

'To what exactly have we been recruited?' asked Turlough pompously.

'Nothing,' replied the woman. 'You can come and go as you please, but we hope you'll stay and help us in our struggle.' Everyone sat down in the dusty street by the side of a wooden building. There was, it seemed, no general meeting hall or special room for the government, at least not in this region. Perhaps, thought Turlough, it was not such a bad way for non-Clanspeople to carry on their business. Why have a government when a small informal group will do? It was an interesting political speculation, but, at least as far as a New Trion was concerned, irrelevant.

'We have all, in the past few years, come to New Trion as you have done, transported suddenly in alien ships of differing designs,' the three were told. 'We each have our own names for those that control the craft – you call their masters the Gardsormr – perhaps that is the right name, we cannot tell. But, like you, we none of us know why we were brought here.

100

Yet slowly over the long months we have built up the beginnings of civilisation, with this basic community, trying hard to avoid the problems and errors that we encountered on Trion. You are the first to come here with news of a counter-revolution, perhaps the Committee Of Public Safety will result in a style of life like ours . . .

'Sadly, however, we are not a utopia. Two things bite into our lives and keep us resentful and mystified. One is already obvious to you – we are unable to leave this planet. We have no technology beyond that we invent, save some that we have found – although more of that later. Our population, though growing fast, is too tiny for any real industrialisation. Our main need is to survive. Yet even this simply objective is disturbed by a second problem. To the west, through the jungle and beyond the mountains, there is another settlement of Trions. They should be here, working with us, but they demand their separate existence. We are from Noved originally, they are from Dnalevelc – and you know the natural difficulties that arise between us on the Home Planet. Here these difficulties become insurmountable. There are no relationships between the two groups, and we fear the worst; there may be war. We have to guard against them, and that defensive posture drains our meagre resources still further.

'But now with your help perhaps we have a chance. With an astrophysicist and an engineer surely we can now build pure and complete defences that will finally put an end to the problems we face. They will continue to live their lives, and we ours, in peace. After that we may even look forwards to the building of space ships that will take us out of this planet and back to our own world.

'Now we shall take you and show you where you can work.'

Turlough looked at Juras. As she could see he certainly didn't relish the idea of building a space ship with his bare hands, although if he could effect matters so that he was perhaps the project director, instructing others in the way of escape . . . He looked at The Magician. Surely he would not allow a genius to be demeaned by such basic engineering work!

101

06: MOBILE?

The little party left the town on donkey back, in the opposite direction from the way Juras, and before her Turlough and The Magician had entered, making their way across two bridges spanning a wide tidal river before coming back on themselves to view the settlement from the far side of the water. By the time they finally stopped, night was falling once more. A night of blackness, relieved by no moon and precious few stars. In the final glows of the twilight the settlement had taken on a reddish hue, contrasting with the greens of the water. A small flock of swallows flew just above the water level, wings beating silently. Behind the town grey-white mountains shot up to the sky—to left and right the jungle dominated—much of it lost now in the increasing gloom.

At one edge of the town a tower was revealed marginally above the other buildings, its top now almost totally lost in the darkness. Turlough suddenly realised—there was no artificial light in the settlement. Surely they were not expecting interstellar travel before electricity?

He turned from the scene and looked at Juras. She was standing in front of their guide, a man approaching middle age but still looking as if he could actively wield the long sword carried by his side. With the rays of the setting sun behind her Turlough saw her as more beautiful than he could ever remember. She was wearing a long dark dress she must have obtained locally, with a mauve sash running from one shoulder to the waist on the opposite side. Her long hair, only partially brought under control during their rest at the settlement twisted and curled, as if joyous of its new found freedom. Her cheeks had been reddened by her experience of intense cold followed by the exposure to the sun. Her blue eyes stared straight past him as if examining something in detail. In all she looked more like an empress than someone just abandoned on the most out-of-the-way planet in the galaxy.

Turlough reflected once more how she had ever become interested in him – why she had actually bothered to follow him, track him down, stay with him. Sudden pangs of jealousy welled up in him. If he was not careful, she would go with one of these hardy men, geared to survival on this utterly uncivilised planet stuck in the middle of nowhere.

Turlough was relieved from his reverie by a movement on the water behind Juras. At first he thought his eye had been caught only by a lone sailor laboriously punting his way across the wide river. But then as he adjusted his eyes to the distance he picked out lights in the sky, themselves reflected in the still water, flashing irregularly from just above the treetops on the opposite bank.

'That is what we have brought you to see,' said the guide catching Turlough's gaze. Juras turned and looked too and as she did Turlough seized the opportunity to hold her hand. She looked at him surprised, but did not resist. The guide ignored the development. 'Our research area is kept deliberately separate from our homes. There are questions of security.'

The man on the punt was getting closer, evidently intent on rowing them all across the water towards the flashing lights. On the journey Turlough looked away from Juras for long enough to consider the face of The Magician. He had the aspect of a man loving every second of the adventure. Perhaps he really did know what was going to happen, in which case Turlough and Juras were providing for him the ultimate entertainment – real life drama in which the viewer could experience everything first hand whilst knowing in his or her heart – or, in the case of a Time Lord, hearts – that all would be safe at the end. It was, Turlough thought, like watching one of those dreadful adventures so beloved of people on Earth. Everyone knew that the hero would survive and the evil one would at least get caught, if not die. Yet despite this pre-knowledge the people of Earth still found it enjoyable to share in the game of watching. If that really were The Magician's position then Turlough could relax – they would escape and survive. It was the first comforting thought he had had since being captured.

Whatever Turlough expected after crossing the calm water of the estuary it was not what he found. The island to which they were delivered was rocky with a steep hill rising up in what was by now almost total gloom. At once he thought of the iron age hill forts he had been lectured about, and seen once or twice, whilst he was at school on Earth. (He must stop thinking about that dreadful experience, he realised. Clearly it had had more effect on him than he liked to imagine.)

The boat landed on a shingle beach and the little party trudged a well worn path through luxuriant undergrowth. Suddenly in front of them was a huge wall of rock, in the centre of which was a series of steps leading up the wall into a tunnel. Cut into the rock were narrow viewing points, but no faces could be seen. The rock rose about thirty metres, but behind, dominating all else, were three greater towers, looking almost as if they were cut from the mountain behind them. Each was rounded, with occasional outcrops here and there, ending at the very top with a slender tower. The entire set of structures looked vaguely familiar to Turlough, but he could not exactly place them.

They entered the tunnel. It was short and led to steps down again, onto the pink ground below. Juras moved ahead of Turlough but still contrived to keep her hand in his. He could feel her trembling slightly and perceived a need to act in a more protective way, guarding her perhaps, although as yet he was not sure what from. Added to which he knew that she could probably feel his hand sweating too much under the strain of the situation.

A few seconds' stroll led to a square building again some thirty metres high, in front of the three towers seen before. At close range they appeared more massive, more imposing than ever. Blue vines covered the walls.

Inside the square building a corridor led to a large room, probably used as a meeting place. At one end was a range of benches and experimental gear. Elsewhere, a small number of chairs were scattered around. Juras, Turlough and The

Magician sat with their escort. A young man joined them. He introduced himself as Sseradd Encha.

'It has fallen to me to try and develop our defence strategy,' he announced immediately the introductions were completed. 'You've seen a little of the environment – it is not promising. But after living on New Trion for some months those who came before me discovered the planet's most valuable asset – these remnants of a past civilisation. Who they were, what they did, we do not know. But they were technologically developed. They did not leave behind any space vehicles, sadly, but we have found a lot else, here on this island. This is where we would like you to help us.'

'What is the security aspect?' asked Juras.

Sseradd looked around as if checking the credentials of everyone in the large room. 'You have probably been made aware of the problem we face with at least one other settlement on this planet – a settlement that has itself attempted on several occasions to attack us with flying bombs, explosions and sabotage. Much of our work here has to take on a defensive aspect because of that, but we still have hopes that spin-offs will allow us to develop the escape vehicle we all eventually seek.'

Something in the explanation caused concern with Turlough. 'Do you want us to work on your defensive capability or your spaceship?' he asked bluntly.

Sseradd smiled and spread his hands wide. 'In a perfect world,' he answered, 'it would be a matter of escape only. But the survival of our community must come uppermost in our minds. It would be no good, I'm sure you would agree, if we worked for years developing our escape only to have it stolen or bombed out of existence at the very moment of launch.'

'You want me, a member of the Imperial Clans of Total Science Knowledge, to help with your war effort!' announced Turlough. The Clans undertook research and development, and at times in their history had listened with care and attention to the requests of the Trions for developments in particular areas. But they had never, ever, worked on warfare. Occasionally their developments had found military uses, but that was the responsibility of the Trions themselves, not the

105

Clans. If asked to develop a bomb the Clans always politely said no.

'Defence,' countered Sseradd, still smiling well aware of Clannish morality.

Turlough turned to The Magician who sat watching the exchange, fingers intertwined. 'A moral problem dear boy,' he announced in response to the look. 'What will you do? How will you choose? A legacy of your historical development – does that code still have meaning on a distant isolated planet? Does personal survival overrule ancient law? Is defence ever justified against an unknown aggressor? How to distinguish between Gardsormr and warring Trions? Such questions, such investigations! Consider your responses.'

Turlough turned away in disgust knowing there was little hope of help from that direction. Juras on the other hand appeared disinclined to say anything. Not wanting a fight on foreign ground in splendid isolation Turlough let the matter rest, at least for the moment, although he realised instantly that his social position back on Trion as the genius that The Magician had proclaimed could be in grave doubt if he started helping out the castaways.

The party was shown to its quarters, simple rooms with bed and table. Communal washing facilities were a short distance away. Turlough joined Juras in her room. Together they walked across to The Magician's chamber but found it empty. Disconsolately Turlough sat on the bed. 'It's ironic,' he announced. 'I left Trion because I refused to help in the military build-up of Rehctaht. Now I find myself trapped on New Trion and faced with the same problem, except we haven't got any way out.'

'Will you refuse to co-operate?' asked Juras. By working with Rehctaht she had already crossed the forbidden line.

'Will you?' Turlough looked at her face on.

'I'll bide my time. There's more here . . .'

'Than meets the eye,' Turlough concluded. 'I felt that, but at present I can't quite put my finger on it.'

'Then make life easy,' urged Juras. 'To discover what's what you need access to people, places, events. You certainbly won't get that through lecturing these people on ancient Clan Law.'

'You really do think it was cowardice that made me go into exile from Trion, don't you?' said Turlough bitterly. Suddenly he was at his most accusative. Yet even as he said it he wished he hadn't. Looking at Juras he desperately wanted to be on the best of terms with her, but found it impossible to retreat having laid down the challenge. That old warmth he'd had with her before he was exiled was gone, perhaps forever, although even now he found it impossible to believe that she had betrayed such a fundamental Clan belief.

Juras smiled disconcertingly. 'You went into exile. I worked for Rehctaht. In the end Rehctaht was overthrown. You invented the ARTEMIS. Maybe my time on gravity work will come. Who is to say which of us will eventually have the greater effect? Possibly it needs both approaches to bring about change.' The twinkle in her eyes deepened. 'Or maybe looked at from a different direction it needed the stupidity of both of us to land us in this mess.'

Turlough was relieved, the pressure gone, at least for the moment. He laughed with Juras, and put his arm round her. The Magician came in. 'Get some rest,' he ordered, eternally smiling. 'You won't believe what the next week holds. This is just the start, dear friends. A world of experience is about to open up. I tell you, you really will not believe what you are about to do!'

In the morning, Juras and Turlough were briefed and shown their work. It was clear and simple: to make a nuclear fission bomb. There was not even a pretension of non-military activity. Despite protests that he was more familiar with fusion than fission, and was anyway an astrophysicist not a power engineer, Turlough was introduced to his new colleagues and shown the work they were involved in. Juras was directed elsewhere.

Turlough understood the problem rapidly and knew, with a certainty bred of his Clansman's training, an immediate solution. He also knew that if it were put into practice it would mean the likely death of himself and quite a few of those on the planet from plutonium poisoning. He made an excuse and left his workroom to find Juras. They met in the large Assembly

107

Room where they had first been briefed; she had been on her way to find him.

'You know what they are up to?' said Turlough.

'And I think I know a solution,' replied Juras.

Despite himself Turlough was ready to fly into a rage, especially if the solution was the same one that he had come up with. But Juras put her hand against his mouth. 'Let me put it down in black and white for you,' she said. They walked across the wide room. Technicians continued working around the benches at one end as the couple pored over pencil and paper. Saying as little as possible for fear of being overheard, Juras began sketching plans and writing equations. Turlough watched as before his eyes a variation on the nuclear bomb theme appeared. Juras's version was much the same as his only she did not seem worried about the safety angle.

Turlough took up the pencil and completed the drawings, emphasising the problem he saw. He looked at the result and thought hard. Yet no matter how he viewed the problem there was no way he could see of stopping the reaction from running away with itself to such a degree as to cause an unacceptable level of danger. Finally he said, in as neutral a voice as possible, 'I think there is a stability problem.'

And then, no sooner had he stated the problem than Turlough saw the answer. Juras's original had included one element Turlough had ignored – the use of energetic muons. Now he saw a use for them. A nuclear reactor added to an ARTEMIS drive would create the power they wanted, but it, too, would run away. Feed back the reaction into the artificial relativity chamber and it would be like putting a break on itself. Still unsafe, certainly, but it could hold for a while.

Above all, it looked like a fair plan for a space shuttle which whilst being built, would look like a nuclear bomb! With luck it would hold itself together long enough to get off the ground and far enough through time and space to reach some sort of civilisation. After that they could jettison the lethal mechanisms before they did some serious damage. Turlough told Juras. They set to work.

The work was hard but, in a strange way, enjoyable. Turlough and Juras both had the confidence of individuals who felt that they had made important discoveries in their own fields, and the chance to work from scratch gave them the opportunity to develop further modifications they had previously not thought of. Given the work already being undertaken on nuclear missiles elsewhere on the base, it was not too hard to avoid directly handling the dangerous materials, although the likelihood of the whole operation blowing up in their faces was never far away.

It also became clear that Turlough would need to inspect more fully the original developments of the civilisation that had lived on this planet. He made his request for a pass, it was processed by a bureaucracy that appeared to grow larger every time he encountered it, and two days later he was given the papers that enabled him to see the central nuclear installation. What he found was that the original civilisation that had built it had, thankfully, been fully aware of the dangers they were playing with. Their safety features, now inherited by the Trions, were the best Turlough had ever seen.

Having viewed the plant he took the opportunity to look around the ruins. Along many walls there were carvings and markings. There was something vaguely familiar about them. What Turlough did not come across, however, were any signs of the opposition, whose existence presaged the need for nuclear strike. It was, he thought, this same fear that had given rise to the domination of Rehctaht in the first place. His belief in not getting involved in the development of instruments of war was reinforced.

Noticeable by his absence during these days of intellectual toil was The Magician. His bed was rarely slept in, and he made few appearances at the communal meal tables in the Assembly Room. In fact it was not until Turlough requested, and was granted, a half-day off work to give himself a chance to clear his mind and review matters to date, that a meeting with the Time Lord finally occurred.

Determined to give himself at least a couple of hours away from the claustrophobic atmosphere of the research station, Turlough had taken himself onto the river in a small rowing boat. But no sooner had he reached the tidal flow in the centre of the water than he found his little craft being pushed, against his will, downstream. Having failed to row against the pressure of water flowing to whatever sea or ocean lay beyond, Turlough rapidly adopted the policy of directing the boat into the quieter waters nearer the bank of the river. As he did he spotted the Gallifreyan sitting on an outcrop, with no indication whatsoever as to how he had got there. His smile was the same as ever – indeed he looked the same as ever, poised on a rock, in front of the winding path that led down from the islet's upper reaches to the water. He waved happily to Turlough but made no sign of wanting to get down. Turlough rowed hard and finally moored next to the outcrop. He clambered up and sat next to the enigmatic figure, panting hard from his unexpected exertions. Only when he had got his breath back did he ask, with more than a hint of sarcasm, if The Magician had a view on the work to date.

'My dear Turlough,' came the reply. 'Everything is for you to decide. What is the unknown dynamo for the reality that surrounds us? Be resolute and find undoubted strength. Do you still doubt your abilities, still question your destiny, after all I have told you? Be calm, clear and strong!' He paused and then added, 'What was your major criticism of the scientists of Earth?'

To Turlough, having just been caught out by a tidal flow as he rowed a primitive boat across a river that went he knew not where, his opinion of Earth scientists was not at the centre of his mind. Yet it was a point that had occupied his thoughts considerably during his exile. Turning the matter over in his mind he said simply, 'Their stupidity.'

'But,' replied the Time Lord, 'surely that can be explained by their primitiveness. As you yourself have said many times, it really is a remarkably backward place.'

'But being primitive does not excuse being so totally wrong,' countered Turlough, settling himself down more comfortably on the rock and contemplating the waves below. 'Those characters calling themselves physicists seriously believe that it is impossible to travel faster than light. Can you believe that?'

'I find it quite easy to believe,' replied The Magician. 'But what do you put such nonsense down to?'

'Their timidity, I suppose,' Turlough told him. 'Every time

they come up with some development that might just take them out of the Dark Ages, they instantly start worrying about whether it is right or not. And not just the scientists. Politicians, philosophers, novelists, they all love to jump on the bandwagon of retreat. It was their terminal disease; invent something and then run like mad away from it. In fact I wouldn't be the slightest bit surprised if within fifty years of me being there they actually start rejecting science all together and head back for the Bronze Age.'

The Magician let out a long languid laugh. 'An accurate assessment,' he pronounced, 'based on the data available to you. And a fair insight into human nature too. But as you will discover, dear boy, there is more to Earth than meets the eye. There is a link between Earth and your friend the Doctor, but it is not to be revealed to you yet. However that is another matter. For now, remember what you have just said of Earth science and ensure you do not fall into that trap. Your ethics prevent you from making war machines; their ethics prevent them doing everything but creating the means of death. Yet there are ways out. Find them, digest them, use them. Pursue them!' He stopped speaking and gazed nonchalantly across the lake.

Turlough continued to sit next to the Time Lord, and like him gazed across the water seeking inspiration. It was a relief to be away from the monotonous stone walls that had made up his world for the past two weeks. The waters had a calming effect on his mind. At last he asked, 'You know my thoughts on you?'

The Magician merely smiled. 'Do tell,' he said.

'That knowing the future you are not worried about escape from this planet. So I need do nothing save sit here and watch the waves with you. Escape is assured.'

'Logical,' said The Magician. 'Aren't you happy with your own development programme?'

'Happy enough,' agreed Turlough, 'unless the enemy, whoever, or whatever they are, appear first. But again your presence and confidence is reassuring. Is there an enemy?'

'Oh yes,' said The Magician. 'There are always enemies. And even friends can turn against you. How long, dear boy, could you possibly last if the rulers of this little settlement thought that you were deliberately refusing to work?'

'So you have manoeuvred the situation such that I'm obliged to work for them whilst you do nothing!' shouted Turlough, suddenly losing his temper. 'You're not going to give me any help at all are you?' Then, as instantly as his anger had blown up, it subsided. In a strange way he could see the cleverness in The Magician's ploy. He was almost getting to like the Time Lord.

'Close your eyes,' said The Magician suddenly. Unable to think of any reason to disagree, Turlough did as requested. 'What do you see?'

'Nothing,' said Turlough still anxious to prove The Magician wrong about something, 'except the pink of my eyelids.'

'Turn your head towards the island,' urged The Magician. Turlough did as commanded. 'Keep your eyes firmly closed,' continued The Magician. 'Tell me what you see.'

'Pink eyes,' said Turlough sarcastically. But then stopped himself. 'The island,' he announced. He looked harder, or did he look? His eyes remained completely closed. The island was rising out of the lake. Sea was pouring off its lower parts as it continued its impossible upward motion. The three towers of a past unknown civilisation were by now almost lost in the clouds. And still it rose. Now the bottom of the rock had totally cleared sea level. It hovered unmoving, untilting, with billions of tonnes of water pouring off all sides. It was impossible and yet it had happened. The scene retained its reality, the rock hanging. Impossible, but there.

'Open up,' said The Magician.

Turlough did as instructed. With a shock he saw the world returned to normal. There was nothing untoward about the rock. The water lapped the shore, the rock floating in the sky was now returned to the island sitting in the sea. The Magician was grinning.

Despite repeated questioning The Magician would give away nothing further. He had given a vision. That was enough. By his own rules, whatever they were, he claimed he could go no further.

Turlough climbed back to his punt, and rowed up river and then across to the island shore. To anyone watching from a distance his behaviour could only have been described as fundamentally peculiar. Once safely across the currents Turlough stopped rowing and looked back at the rock. The Magician was still sitting. He gave a hearty wave. Turlough turned to look at the island. He sat, for several moments, oars pulled in, head in hands. And next, as suddenly as he had stopped Turlough picked up the oars and began rowing towards the three towers with all his might.

No sooner had he docked than he pulled the boat onto the edge of the ramp and ran at full speed towards the inner sanctum. He found Juras at a bench in the Assembly Room working on the safety factors that had been a prime concern since they began the work on the modified ARTEMIS.

Juras looked up in surprise. 'I thought you . . .' she began as Turlough tried to regain his breath. He held his hand against his heart, leaning against the workbench for support.

'The safety margin,' he gasped between breaths. 'We need to dig deeper.'

'Explain' commanded Juras. It ws a reasonable demand. Digging had never been part of their plan at all. Concrete walls and water filled moats, yes. But digging?

'I have just seen the Mobile Castle,' Turlough announced as he grabbed paper and began drawing. He outlined a cross section of the island with its three distinctive towers. He marked the area of the fission laboratories, devised out of what he had for some time suspected was a primitive power station. Below that he drew the imaginary bottom of the island linked into the planet's crust. At this point he inserted a number of crossed lines, representing fractures in the rock. 'They may not be exactly there,' he announced stabbing the pencil at the diagram, 'but they must be somewhere around.' Turlough then added lines of force from the power room. Juras looked at him blankly, but she had too much respect for Turlough's mind (and his lack of enthusiasm for physical exercise) to know that this would be a wild goose chase. Turlough added a box to the drawings and marked it ARTEMIS II. He then drew further links down from the power station towers to the fission room, and re-emphasised the subsequent force lines to the fractures in the rock. Finally he wrote two equations underneath and collapsed into a chair, still gasping for breath.

'What about the population?' asked Juras. Turlough looked puzzled. 'The people on the mainland,' she explained. 'They should be with us.'

Turlough remained silent. He had no desire to help anyone on this crazy planet except himself, Juras and The Magician. The fact that the inhabitants all came from Trion struck him as neither here nor there. They were not Clanspeople, and the law was clear. The Trions look after themselves. Indeed, Turlough reasoned, if they hadn't been so concerned about their stupid, (and as far as he could see) non-existent war, they could have used this nuclear installation as the basis for their escape long ago. As he sought some way of expressing his opinion, Juras added, 'Safety will be a factor.' She was wrong of course – safety was far less of a factor with this plan than with the previous version which involved building their own small scale ARTEMIS I. 'During the tests we should get everyone to the island, just in case.'

Turlough nodded but said nothing more. It was a feasible ploy, and the political leaders of the settlement might just fall for it. On the other hand, with luck he could find that the scientific élite on the island would veto the idea and that would put paid to that. In the meanwhile Turlough had more pressing things on his mind – not least the connection between the Mobile Castle, most sacred of monuments on Trion, a Time Lord who knew the future but wouldn't let on what it was, and an out-of-the-way planet populated with Trion exiles bent on killing each other. Come to that, where did the wretched Gardsormr fit in?

07: TRANSPORT!

The revised plan involving ARTEMIS II had a lot going for it besides the additional safety of Juras and Turlough. Not least it reduced the time taken to organise the operation by something in the order of 90% – for which Turlough, for one, was grateful. Yet having solved the problem theoretically in his moment of insight as he rowed across the river, he was becoming bored with the practicalities and waited impatiently for time to pass as the new system was built.

Juras meanwhile sold the local leaders the idea of the need for safety during the first major test of the revised nuclear system, and late one evening a week later the grand population of some one thousand people poured across the placid river onto the island. In their makeshift control room at one end of the grand Assembly Room Turlough and Juras sat quietly until the word was given that everyone was inside. They then switched on their force barrier, now conveniently stretching from water's edge on one side, over the towers, and to the edge on the far side, and waited. After thirty seconds it was clear all was working well. Not one particle of air was moving in or out of the island.

To the locals this was a fall-out protection measure, to Juras and Turlough something rather more daring. Keeping an eye on The Magician to ensure he was still smiling (he was), Turlough initiated the switch-on. Silence – but only for seconds. There then came the most awful scream of tearing rock and shaking foundations.

Panic ensued. There was a clamour for the machine to be turned off. Juras was pushed over as a group of politicians ran forward to the controls. Turlough was knocked against a wall but had foreseen the chaos. The control mechanism was now locked in place, through a numeric code. No one could remove it now save himself. Not even Juras.

And then suddenly they were all on the floor, as the screaming, tearing sound came to a halt and the entire building lurched upward. Anything not tied down flew across the room – including people. Juras had known the moment would cause injuries, but there had been little she could do. A warning, any warning, would have aroused suspicion.

As people at last began to pick themselves up a dominant figure pushed his way into the central research area. 'Explain!' shouted Sseradd. 'This isn't a nuclear test – or if it is, something has gone dreadfully wrong.'

Turlough looked for Juras. Instinctively he felt she could do better than he at admitting what had been perpetrated. But Juras was out cold, her head having hit the side of the work bench during the great jolt. At that moment however, and much to his relief, Turlough heard a familiar voice wafting across the room. 'Friends, friends.' The Magician; at last he was doing something useful. 'The Clansfolk have supplied you with much much more than a bomb. They have indeed provided more than you deserve with your continuous talk of war and fighting. They have given you exactly what the Imperial Clans ought to give you. Escape. *Guaranteed* escape.'

'Escape from what?' demanded Sseradd. He looked and sounded unconvinced.

'From your petty war, your imprisonment, yourselves.' The voice of The Magician rose and fell dramatically and he waved long fingers describing a grand arc across the room. 'No, they didn't build you a bomb, although they could have done. You have instead a space vehicle. You are travelling in it. The island, friends, is a space machine. Years ago it was done on your own planet – The Mobile Castle. Have you all been so blind as to not recognise the three sacred towers? And it is a testimony to the Clans' great desire to help every single one of you that has led to the gathering of the entire population here. Go outside, friends, and look at the sky. Slowly you will see it change. Go to the edge of the cliffs, look for the lake. It is gone. We are travelling between the stars. En route for Trion.'

Sseradd wouldn't give up so easily however. 'A complete and utter trick,' he yelled. 'How could this be the Mobile Castle, when we all know it exists already on Trion! We have been duped. Seize these three.' The inevitable guards stepped forward ready for action.

A knife was held at each throat. The Magician spoke, incongruously relaxed in such a threatened position.

'Fraternal Trions; is this the way to treat your benefactors? Test the hypothesis! You call yourself a logical scientific race, or have the leaders of New Trion become so loving of their positions of power, so happy to be big birds in a tiny sky, that they dread the throught of a return to the real large world – a return home? Is that what they cower from, being once more little Trions in the galaxy at large?' The Magician had given this last word every gramme of energy he had. It had no effect on Sseradd nor his immediate followers in the guard, but others, less powerful, and (as The Magician supposed) with less to gain by keeping the beleaguered community together, made their move.

'How long before we get back?' shouted one.

'Two days,' said Turlough.

'And by then the antagonists from beyond the mountains – the enemies now in our midst – will have overrun us totally,' sneered Sseradd.

'What will you do, Sseradd?' called another, 'just slit the throats of all of them and then work out how to turn the machine off?' It was a good point and gained a lot of muttered agreement in the vast hall.

'We shall force them to explain exactly what they have done,' replied Sseradd, desperate to hold on to his authority.

'But I offer you proof of what I have done,' declared Turlough.

'Proof!' said the politician, his voice heavy with contempt. 'Tricks and games.'

'We'll see the proof,' came the shout from around the room. After years of reduced circumstances there were many who would grasp at anything – even a trick – if it offered just the slightest chance of a way out.

'Use the observation tower,' suggested Turlough. 'The

117

telescope will show you New Trion falling away below, a great gap torn on its side where the island has been pulled out of the mantel itself. And if you don't believe that go out and look with your own eyes at the new star.'

They needed no second bidding. Rapidly the hall emptied. The guards holding Turlough, uncertain for a moment, left the chamber dragging their captive with them. Reluctantly Turlough allowed himself to be pulled along.

By the time he got outside many had climbed into the tower to use the single telescope discovered by the enforced colonists. Others simply stood and stared at the new star – still large enough to be made out as a sun, bright, blue-green, but already shrinking. In the confusion Turlough ducked from his captors and made his way back to the Assembly Room. He found The Magician tending Juras. She had several nasty lacerations, but appeared to be recovering quickly. Turlough turned away from her, back to the main control consul. Now was the time for laying in the course, which he did with such precision as he could, given the lack of star charts. There were simply not enough stars around for him to recognise. He followed his best bet, heading in the presumed general direction of the Home Star at the edge of the central cluster, trusting his memory to be good enough to make the last leg of the journey.

As he finished the input people began to return to the Assembly Room. Although the force field could hold in the atmosphere and some of its heat, there was no doubt that they were going to suffer a cold journey. Already the majority wanted to stay in the Assembly Room and ensure that all doors were shut.

Turlough relaxed momentarily, but it was too early. Sseradd was not going to give up power so easily. He used the increasing cold and outside gloom as a weapon. 'We'll freeze to death,' he announced to the Assembly Room. 'Is that what you want?' He was backed by half a dozen of his staunchest supporters, all men and women who had experienced power on the planet, and now rallied together for a final assault. 'Recall the journey here in the ships! You know what happened. What do you remember most about that journey?' The question was rhetorical, but none the less successful for that. There was muttering. He had hit a chord. 'Cold. Freezing cold,' continued Sseradd. 'And what do you see now? What do you feel, but that same cold!'

'Space *is* cold, you idiot,' shouted a voice. It was Beyla – a woman of about thirty. She too had experienced power, but had constantly urged an end to thoughts of war. She was a minority, but one that was listened to. 'We are going home, fools. Does that mean nothing to you? Or are you afraid of what home will mean now there has been a revolution? Afraid you'll be on the wrong side? Afraid that a journey home will mean instant arrest?'

Approval of her speech echoed around the hall. Sseradd for all the advantage of being on the platform had lost the initiative. Turlough moved to speak, but Juras held him back. 'Let them slog it out,' she said.

'I tell you it is a trap,' Sseradd was shouting. 'How do you know where you are going, or what is happening? What do you see outside? Black sky. Nothing but black sky. Who is navigating? The one man who hijacked our entire community! And you trust total power to two people?'

The feeling of the crowd swayed. Turlough and Juras were outsiders. Newcomers. And Clanspeople as well. Why should they be trusted?

'Sure,' said Beyla. 'Back to that jungle-infested planet, ready to start a nuclear war that will effectively mean the end of us all.'

'There will be no war,' proclaimed Sseradd.

'Then what are you building nuclear bombs for? Turlough and Juras had to hijack this island to stop you from blowing us up.'

'Nuclear weapons are our ultimate defence.' Sseradd was adamant. It was a well-rehearsed argument.

'For how long? Until the western communities beyond the mountains build neutron bombs. And then we build cobalt and satellite bombs, and so it goes on. There never is a way out of this madness. I say we go home.'

'You are running into a trap.'

'I can show you the future.' The room quietened at once. Turlough had got his moment right. He walked forward at what seemed to himself a snail's pace, but which was calculated to give further impact to his speech. 'This island will travel in time as well as space,' he announced. 'We can go forward and see what the future holds for the rest of the planet.'

'Another trick,' said Sseradd elbowing Turlough out of the way. 'He is looking for a further excuse to play with the equipment.'

'I don't play,' said Turlough seizing on the word. 'If I wanted to trick I could have done it anytime. I offer you information. I don't know what the future of the planet holds, I merely inform you that the equipment we have installed here enables us to travel forward and look. If you do not wish to, that is fair enough. You can decide.'

It was an effective speech, and Sseradd, for all his faults was well enough versed in the politics of the crowd to know when it was better to fall in with the will of the mass, rather than force issues too far. He let it pass.

Sensing his victory Turlough left the platform, and turned to the control panels. Juras was by his side. 'What was that about?' she demanded tersely. 'What do you expect to gain by letting them look at pictures of clouds?'

'Nothing,' Turlough replied, 'except time. We go forward fifty years and look – and all the time we travel further from the planet – and remember with this system the more we travel the faster we travel. By the time everyone has got tired of temporal manipulations at a distance we'll be getting towards the galactic centre, and they'll be able to see we really are going to Trion. If nothing else they will start to see a lot of stars in the sky which will make them believe we are going home even if it turns out that I can't navigate this hunk of rock properly.'

Turlough turned and resuming his platform position addressed the crowd. 'Two hours,' he said, 'and we shall have moved fifty years forward. Then you shall all be able to see if New Trion is still there, or destroyed by war.' What he didn't add was that it would also give him time to talk to The Magician about how it was possible that this was the Mobile Caslte in this time zone, when he had experienced the very same place, as a historic monument only a few weeks before.

Turlough attempted to take the island out of time drive at the fifty year mark. However, moving short time spans was, he found, much harder than larger ones. As soon as he engaged the Mark II time unit, it seemed under a mind of its own to shoot forward or back. It could take longer to travel fifty years than five thousand years. As it was he overshot and revealed the galaxy one hundred and ninety years hence, rather than the fifty he had promised, but he decided that it really was not a very important slip, and omitted to reveal his error to the assembled populace.

Turlough stayed in the warmth of the Assembly Rooms leaving the brave, the foolhardy and those with their own form of thermal heating to tackle the weather and venture into the third tower. Five minutes later he was wondering if it had all been such a good idea as the first who had been across returned full of chatter and mutterings.

Turlough recognised Imlama Kurke, one of the leaders of the astronomy group of the settlement. Whatever it was that was being observed was probably true if it related to observations she had made. Turlough had previously marvelled at her ability, and had a mental note that she would be the first person he would take into his confidence if he found navigating harder than he imagined. She ran straight to Turlough. 'The Star is there,' she said, 'but New Trion is radiating in all wavebands.'

Turlough was shocked. He had not in any way anticipated destruction. After all, if this warring faction left the planet who would launch a nuclear war? His devious mind twisted and turned. If the future showed nuclear fallout he thought maybe there had been a war – in which case he could yet be forced to return the island to the planet from which it was wrenched. But then this island would then fail to form the Mobile Castle on Trion. Alternatively, even if he did go to Trion with the island he would have to take the rock far back in time in order to create the Castle, and even then, he'd have to try and land the thing, and he certainly had little idea of how to do that.

Turlough was vaguely aware of shouting by his side. It was Imlama. 'Go back,' she was demanding. 'Take us back and

121

find out when it happened. We need to watch the events that led up to it.'

Suddenly Turlough realised he had been given the biggest break possible. Shunting forwards and backwards would give him more time to move the island towards the galactic hub, and more certainty of final escape from New Trion.

He used standard mathematical procedure, halving the time difference, then halving it again, going forward or back in time according to whether the radiation was still there or not. They rigged up a permanent radio link between the observation tower and the Assembly Room to stop people having to run across the freezing landscape. Finally, in real time the observers witnessed and relayed their observations of the effective destruction of their planet. It started, Turlough was relieved to hear, not in the area of the island and the settlement, but far out to the north. 'Why there?' everyone wanted to know. Why indeed – except that immediately after the first flare there were signs of strikes beyond the mountains where the dreaded enemies of the settlement were known to be located.

'Are you sure no one lived on the northern continent?' asked Juras.

'Never heard of them if they did,' said another. 'Northerners!' He said the word with an element of disgust. It was traditional Trion bigotry. Everyone from the eastern hemisphere thought the westerners insane enough to start a war anywhere, and considered the northerners who lived outside the Clan settlement areas dirty, uncivilised, and wild. Accents and custom dominated opinion and overrode any unity that the common language of the planet might one time have brought.

Turlough let the matter pass. It was clear that the destruction of New Trion from the point of view of civilisation was caused by something or someone indigenous to the planet. There was definitely no sign of an outside invader, nor any untoward activity from the Home Sun. It had to be a nuclear war between tiny communities each of probably no more than a thousand people, unable to share a planet that could easily accommodate and feed ten billion.

He sat at the controls, the atmosphere around him deeply depressive – even those opposed to the flight back home were disinclined to act against Turlough. Their argument to fight the mad westerners seemed unattractive to even the most militaristic.

A shout down the phone link from the tower brought everyone back to attention. It was Imlama. 'A ship has arrived,' she announced. 'It's circling the planet.'

Turlough grabbed the receiver. 'Describe it,' he called.

'It's a sphere,' said the astronomer, 'with a sharp edge at the equator, and coming to a point at top and bottom. There are shields all around – oval, each about one tenth of the size of the ship itself. And it's got amazing manoeuvrability. This thing can shift and dart.'

'Gardsormr!' exclaimed Turloug and Juras together. 'But what are they doing at the planet after the spread of the fallout?'

'Come to that,' said Imlama listening down the line, 'why did we ever get deposited on New Trion in the first place?'

'I'd supposed,' said Turlough, 'to breed. But that hardly seems a likely assumption now. Maybe to blow ourselves up.'

The atmosphere in the chamber was hardly uplifted by the news of the Gardsormr arrival, nor the revelation that the ship departed as rapidly as it had arrived. When it subsequently became apparent that the ship was heading directly towards the island no one moved to stop Turlough immediately swinging the rock into time drive and gently edging it back towards their own real time. By the time they emerged back into observable space New Trion was becoming too faint to view easily, but Imlama rapidly found more exciting things to study as she swung round and viewed the galactic core in detail. Her excited announcements down the line that it was possible to see Trion Sector killed off any further protests from Sseradd. They were almost home.

123

08: NEW TRION ON TRION

The arrival of a small asteroid heading straight at the Home Planet broadcasting a message which stated that it was inhabited by people who had gone missing up to four years before, caused, not surprisingly, total consternation on Trion. The fact that the rock also contained Turlough, whose reputation continued to develop in direct proportion to the time he was away from the Home Planet, merely served to increase interest and speculation.

That the rock also contained a variety of individuals who had left before the collapse of the Rehctaht regime and who, it must be admitted, had not believed a word of Turlough's story concerning the end of the revolution, was a further twist in this most unlikely episode in the history of the Home System. But all was overshadowed by the widely circulated rumour that Turlough had cracked the time problem, and succeeded not only in building a steerable asteroid but also a time unit. For many this was too much. It was, they claimed, at best a fairy story, at worst another tasteless publicity stunt by the owners of Njordr Nerthus who had found themselves yet another useless chunk of rock in the midst of nothingness.

Speculation ran wild. Turlough and Juras — now herself a top-of-the-hour news item — found it impossible to appear in public. They were hounded, questioned, touched, prodded, shouted at and endlessly harrassed. Privacy, which had just about been possible before their departure, became a thing of the past. Only their apartments were safe. If anything they had had more freedom on New Trion.

Upon his return Turlough said nothing about the Gardsormr, and requested that Juras do the same. Yet there

124

was no stopping the voices of the hundreds who had been rescued from New Trion, and many were only too glad to relate to the media how Turlough had revealed personally to them the true nature of these terrible creatures from outside the Home System. People whom Turlough could not even remember from the flight of the island (some of whom he began to consider as nothing short of imposters), claimed deep, long, and meaningful personal friendships. Listening to their stories Turlough found he had to pinch himself to recall that he had only been on New Trion three weeks, and the flying island two days. His supposed friends made it sound like years.

But it was the Gardsormr stories that remained the major problem. Given that these beings were now the firm allies of the New Regime, the suggestion that one of the great living heroes of the Home Planet should actually be propagating the view that these unseen creatures were responsible for the incarceration of a thousand sons and daughters of the Homeland on an alien planet for no apparent reason, was too much for many patriots, already jealous of Turlough's rapid rise to prominence.

Sseradd found a particularly neat way out of his problems. Posing as an eternal enemy of Rehctaht he claimed that Turlough's behaviour, tantamount to the hijacking of an entire planet, combined with his outrageous allegations, revealed a certain instability of mind (undoubtedly the result of pressure of work). The man, he said, should be treated with care, and his word with a certain degree of caution. By underplaying, Sseradd was making sure of revenge.

After four days of public turmoil Turlough and Juras were given notice of a summons to appear before the next meeting of the Committee of Public Safety. It was not a call to be trifled with. Holed up in Turlough's house deep in the rain forests, the two heroes, now in danger of finding their unexpected popularity turning totally against them took time to review the situation.

'Foresight,' said Turlough, deep in self pity, 'would have been helpful. Once I'd latched onto the idea of powering a rock back home all other thoughts strayed from my mind. If I'd never mentioned the Gardsormr to those characters on the planet they'd never have known who was imprisoning them.'

'We still have no evidence that it is the Gardsormr,' countered Juras, coming to more practical matters, 'and it is that that the Committee will get us on. All we know is that the ships which have tracked around Earth and Trion are the same, and that the ship we were following was of a similar design. It is not beyond the wit of any race capable of space travel to introduce some lookalike vessel in order to put the blame for their actions on some other set of creatures. The Gardsormr are only guilty in your mind because of your original premise that they helped Rehctaht.'

'Didn't they?' demanded Turlough.

'Not as far as I know – but that's neither here nor there. I only worked for the woman, I didn't see her state secrets.'

'But you can see the logic of the argument,' persisted Turlough. 'It must be the Gardsormr.'

'You don't have to convince me,' said Juras. 'It's the Committee we have to worry about.'

'And the Committee will be full of people who have built their political reputation around a treaty with the Gardsormr. To recognise that there is even the start of a possibility that they are wrong would be to commit political suicide.'

'So what is to be done?'

Turlough sat and thought. He had a deep respect for Juras's ability to analyse problems, and for her grasp of political reality, but he knew that at the end of the day his often instinctive grasp of situations had an uncanny knack of being correct. His own deviousness revealed to him the way in which others thought – often with more clarity than they themselves would ever recognise.

His face downcast, Turlough stared blankly through the windows of his house, into the forest beyond the clearing. On the wall next to the window the VT light flashed continuously showing someone was requesting permission to land at his private reception point in the basement. It had been like that ever since he had returned. The light remained unanswered.

'There is also,' he said at last, 'the unresolved issue of the Mobile Castle. At present there are two such things. One floating above our heads and the other where it has always

126

been, sitting next to the Museum of Natural History.'

'You have the same sort of problem there as you have with the Gardsormr,' said Juras. 'You have no proof that there is any link between what we flew in and the Mobile Castle. They just happen to look the same. Who knows, maybe the original Castle was built by the same race that left the ruins on New Trion. That would explain the design similarities. The rest is coincidence.'

'I don't believe in coincidence,' said Turlough. 'If I did I wouldn't keep searching for a link between the Doctor and Earth. I'd just accept that Earth was the planet I happened to be outlawed to, and it also just happened to be the place that the Doctor liked to visit. But I don't believe that for a second, and as a member of the Clans of Total Science Knowledge neither should you.'

Turlough returned to silence. His eyes strayed across the room and again watched the VT light flashing repeatedly on and off. Suddenly, without warning, he leapt out of his chair, and touched the control unit on the portable touch panel which had been left lying in the middle of the floor two days before when Juras had arrived. The control opened a sound-only link to whoever was asking permission to enter.

'My dear, dear friends,' said a highly familiar voice, 'I know you need privacy and some time alone together, but I would have thought I could gain a moment of your precious seconds together . . .'

'Magician!' said Turlough. 'I had forgotten about you. Come, join us, and tell me what to do.'

The line went dead as the Time Lord left his vidphone at the VT terminal. A minute later Turlough cleared the lift to bring him directly into the living room.

The Magician had not changed at all. The same clothes, the same look, the same long fingers, twisting, turning. On his head the figure-of-eight hat. In his buttonhole, lilies and roses. Seizing on Turlough's invitation he sat down on the sofa and stretched long legs before him, as he put his hand behind his neck. For a moment Turlough thought he was going to launch into a speech, but he remained quiet, enjoying the view.

At last Juras broke the silence. 'Where have you been?' she demanded.

'Sightseeing,' came the reply. 'Your planet is remarkable. Almost as remarkable as Earth, which is saying something.'

Turlough sat up straight, full of attention. 'Is there a link?' he asked.

'Between Earth and Trion?' replied The Magician. Turlough nodded. 'My dear boy, that is for you to discover. What would your life be like if I gave you all the answers! Abolish research, lay down and die. A sad life, an appalling fate. Destiny meaningless, eternity a hollow frustration.'

'Less frustrating if you gave us a clue,' said Turlough. 'Any good throughts on what we do in front of the Committee of Public Safety?'

The Time Lord continued to relax, arms and legs now stretched to their greatest possible length. But then, just when they thought that he had decided to totally ignore the question he said, 'To go or not, you mean?'

'How can we not go?' said Turlough derisively. 'The Committee rules the planet.'

'Very well,' replied The Magician. 'And what will they say to you?'

' "Retract all statements about the Gardsormr, stop being a meddler, talk to no one and build us a fleet to time ships",' replied Turlough imitating the voice of Naale Niairb, a leading member of the COPS.

'And what will you do dear boy?'

'Argue,' said Turlough. 'I *always* argue.'

'Very well,' replied the Time Lord. He appeared to be enjoying his new style of cross-questioning. 'Is there an alternative?'

'I could do what they ask,' Turlough told him.

'And what would the consequences be?'

'Of agreeing to retract all my statements on the Gardsormr, none. I'm not out to sway public opinion, merely to satisfy myself, and if I'm right, to then reveal the truth about the Gardsormr to the planet as a proven truth not a supposition.'

'And the time-ships?'

Turlough paused and thought, turning to Juras to see her

128

opinion. During his time with the Doctor, Turlough had accepted without much question the belief that all attempts by other races to develop time-travel should be stopped for the very safety of time itself. But was that so? To a Clansman no knowledge was sacred. And supertalented or not, Turlough had been able to copy sufficient of the TARDIS's system boards to enable him to devise the ARTEMIS approach. Building a time unit was not simple, but neither was it impossible. But was it morally reprehensible?

'It all depends,' said Turlough, 'on just how delicate history is. If it is so fragile that each journey into time could irreparably change the universe as we know it then time-travel becomes highly dubious. But if it has just as much effect as a trip across the ocean then it doesn't seem to matter.'

'And what attitude will the Committee of Public Safety take?'

'Knowing them,' said Turlough, 'they'll keep it for themselves on the grounds that it is too dangerous for the common crowd to handle.'

'And you, my dear?' The Time Lord looked at Juras.

'I agree, the Committee will keep it for themselves. In not letting it spread they are probably right, at least until we can devise a harmless experiment that will reveal just how dangerous time-travel can be.'

'But that is not our concern as members of the Clans,' said Turlough with deep feeling. 'My problem is to decide if in facing the Committee, I am likely to find my own freedom restricted. Would they dare tell a Clansman what to do?' And then, answering his own question he added, 'After Rehctaht I suppose anything is possible.'

'You can say what they want to hear, or tell them the truth,' said Juras.

'Or respond to events!' said The Magician enigmatically. 'My children, as I have told you before, great things are afoot. Bêhold!'

His timing, as ever, was perfect. No sooner had he said the last word, than the communications set cme to life, overriding the zero controls that Turlough had set. Overrides were only used for announcements from the Central Presidium, or for officially sanctioned news flashes. In the days of Rehtcaht, Presidium pronouncements came out almost daily. Now there were few, with real power having moved to the Committee of Public Safety.

'An urgent message for citizens Juras Maateh and Vislor Turlough – respond at once,' it proclaimed. The COPS had used the override having found Turlough not responding to any incoming calls. It seemed ludicrous not to answer. Turlough touched the heat sensitive plate that allowed the comset to come to life. The COPS could see him – he could see them.

'That asteroid you rode on,' announced the Committee Chairman without preliminaries. 'The orbit is decaying. We're sending up auto destroyers to break it up before it hits the atmosphere. Your observations immediately, please.'

Turlough looked astonished, and took several seconds to find his voice. Then in a rush he replied, 'Chairman – you must not destroy it – the nuclear plant that we used is not well enough protected. You'll unleash unstable radiation directly into the atmosphere.'

'Suggestions?' demanded the Chairman tersely. 'You have seconds.'

'Let me back up there – I'll correct the malfunction.'

'There isn't time,' the Chairman told him.

'Let me try,' said Turlough.

'Report to Eastern Aerodrome at Tronna immediately.'

The transmission was cut, and Turlough rose. 'It couldn't decay,' said Juras simply. 'I saw you set the orbit. There's enough power in that system to keep it safely up there for ten thousand years.'

'I know that,' shouted Turlough over his shoulder running for the VT lift. As he entered the cabin he turned ready to call a goodbye to Juras and The Magician, only to find himself pushed forward by both of them. They descended to the VT station together.

'The invitation was for me!' said Turlough as the lift came to rest and the three bundled into the truck. Turlough pushed the command buttons for the airfield. As he did, a thought struck him. He looked at The Magician. 'Are you intending to come

130

with me up to the island?' he asked.

The Magician wrapped his robe around himself more comfortably, relaxed despite the rush from the room, and smiled. 'If you will allow,' he said with exaggerated grace. 'The time will come when even you, young Turlough, will find that you will need just a little help from me. A rare event I know, and one that edges close to compromising my Lordly role, but still it is and must be.'

They arrived. Turlough had not had a chance to try to dissuade Juras, and for two reasons he didn't bother. Firstly, he knew he would almost certainly need her engineering knowledge and skills if the Gardsormr really had attempted to move the island out of orbit. And secondly, if The Magician were to be travelling with them, they ought to be safe.

The ship was very small, and looked like nothing so much as a conical canvas tent. Turlough had never boarded a ship so fast in his life. They were hardly seated before the neutrino-jets ignited. Even the safety time zone which had effectively saved Juras on their first flight out together was bypassed.

It was not until the ship was coming in to land on the island that it sank into Turlough's mind just what sort of vehicle they were on. If there were neutrino-jets firing, and if from the outside it looked like a tiny canvas covered tent, then it was a Neutrinova, the final offering of Clan technology before the Rehctaht revolution. Given that the Committee had one available it was a reasonable ship to provide – small to the point of tiny, faster than anything before. The problem was it was only built for one, not three.

Both Turlough and Juras looked in frozen horror as the tiny craft accelerated to the impossible sub-light speed of 40%, before breaking, turning, tilting and landing. The anti-thrust units worked perfectly – they felt nothing.

The first discovery they made was that the local force wall that had kept in the atmosphere on the island had been ripped away – although how or why was not clear. The three donned space suits, left the tiny ship and ran as fast as the suits would allow them in the vacuum towards the Assembly Rooms. Turlough made straight for the main control panel. With only a cursory check at the safety controls he engaged the main drive to take the rock away from Trion. It was a horrifically dangerous move. If the Gardsormr, or anything else come to that, had actually jammed the controls, such an action could have merely speeded up the island's descent. On the other hand a booby trap could have ensured that no one got out of the Assembly Rooms alive. Alternatively a link between the nuclear thrust and the central atomic pile could easily have made sure that there was simply no Assembly Room for them to get out of.

And yet their luck held. The drive engaged, the island's crumbling orbit gradually rectified and the immediate danger was removed. Turlough felt he had aged ten years. They had actually been on the rock one and a half minutes.

Juras went to the transmitter to report results. Turlough laid his hand on hers. 'Wait,' he commanded. Juras looked at him curiously. 'Before we tell them, let's decide what happens next.' He turned to The Magician. 'That discussion we were having before the Chairman of the COPS came through. That must have been relevant. *Everything* you do is relevant!'

'Perhaps,' said The Magician. 'But relevance is a matter of time and space. What matters to you can hardly be considered to be of importance to a traffic warden in a village you never even heard of on Earth. You may sit on a train, or in a car on that planet, and watch events pass that concern you not and affect you not. Yet for those involved directly they can be the most agonising moments of life. The mother who has just lost a child; the lover just deserted. You may see them by the road side but know nothing of their grief.'

Turlough looked at The Magician in some surprise. Even by his standards that was something of an irrelevant speech. 'What I do know,' said the Clansman, 'is that I still have no idea if there is any real reason to restrict time-travel to an élite few, or if it can be opened to everyone. If it has to be a few, for fear of corrupting time itself, the last few I would trust with that knowledge would be the COPS. If we go back, that dilemma still has to be faced.'

Juras sat down and looked at Turlough, her hands crossed. His politics were becoming more and more confused by the day, she felt. 'So is the power to decide only safe in the hands of the great Turlough?'

'No! We must continue to live by the tradition of the Clans. And yet, in a strange sense, you are right.'

'You haven't started believing in magic have you? Or was it all that praise about your scientific brilliance?'

'The Magician's presence guarantees we are on the right track,' replied Turlough. And then turning to look straight at the Time Lord he announced, 'It will take us no more than five minutes to dismantle the ARTEMIS drive from the island and install it in the Neutrinova.' The Magician still smiled. 'See?' Turlough continued now looking back at Juras. 'He smiles, we must be right. We dismantle the drive, board the Neutrinova and then push the island towards the Home Star. The nuclear fallout will drip gently into a far vaster pile and cause no problem at all. The Gardsormr will have lost the chance to use the island again as a weapon and we have a new ARTEMIS.'

Turlough sat down and looked at The Magician. The Time Lord was strangely silent after the hectic activities of recent events. All was calm.

And then Juras attacked. Her weapon was simple and effective – a longarm sword left by one of the Central Guards during the final evacuation. Lethal at the best of times, with Turlough and The Magician wearing space suits it was clear that one tiny prick could bring instant asphyxiation. For them this was not the best of times.

Turlough backed away, collided with one of the desks which still contained experimental equipment from before the flight of the island, edged along it, keeping his eye on Juras, hoping continually for a chance to head for the door without turning his back on the girl. At present she was wielding the sword in front of her ready to swipe at the airlines at the first opportunity. However she also had the option of throwing the weapon over a short distance. It might, or might not, connect with the target. Turlough didn't fancy taking the risk.

Not wishing to take his eyes off Juras, Turlough had lost sight of The Magician. He held back a desire to shout. Either the Time Lord was going to help him or he was not. Shouting was unlikely to change his outlook on life. Maybe the Gallifreyan had been smiling all this time because he would be safe and well; his ticket to see nothing more than the early death of Turlough!

Turlough pulled himself back to the reality of the situation before him. It was hard to see the full detail of Juras's expression under her space helmet, but there was no mistaking the intent with which she advanced. Backing off, Turlough repeatedly tried to speak to her, calling her name, asking her what was wrong. All he got back was the sound of breathing.

Turlough edged round a bench. It put him in the main corridor leading towards the exit. Irresistably Juras came after him. He passed another pile of debris and kept retreating. And then he slipped. Someone had left a box of myolyne crystals in the middle of the walkway – another sign of the rapid and joyous evacuation. Falling backwards Turlough caught a glimpse of Juras lunging at him. He moved sideways as far as the constrictions of his suit would allow as the weapon came down and just missed his face. The sword stuck in the wooden floor, giving time for Turlough to haul himself to his feet.

As he rose Juras freed the blade and ran towards him. This time however the myolyne worked in his favour. The box had split and small crystals were lying in all directions on the floor. Juras, having eyes only for Turlough had not seen them. As she advanced her foot slipped and she fell. Yet falling back she made no effort to protect herself and hit the rear of her head. Turlough felt sure that such a blow would at least induce concussion, if not long term unconsciousness, but Juras was not so easily stopped. She rose, picked up her sword and continued towards Turlough. The Clansman, however, had had enough. He turned and ran for the door, all too aware of the running steps of Juras behind him.

'Left!' It was the sudden sound of The Magician. Turlough obeyed and jumped to one side, just in front of the door. Juras moved to follow, but found herself trapped. From above a net had descended totally engulfing her. The more she struggled, the more she became entangled. In such conditions the sword became useless. Turlough stood, shaking, staring in horrified terror as Juras's frantic slashing motions became less energetic.

At last she stopped, and stood, staring straight ahead, emotionless, almost anonymous, and certainly not the Juras Maateh Turlough had known for most of his life.

Seconds later the girl collapsed and lay on the floor. Still Turlough did not move. It was as if his brain refused to accept what had happened. Only when The Magician descended from the lintel above the doorway and started to remove the net from his victim did Turlough return to reality.

'Is she safe now?' he asked.

'Not until we get her into the ship and hook her into the medical unit,' the Time Lord answered. And then looking up and finding Turlough still taking no part in the action shouted, 'I thought you had some feelings for the girl. Help me lift her. I'm The Magician, not the Doctor.'

Reluctantly Turlough lent a hand, but as he did he looked more at The Magician than at Juras. Something in his words did not ring true.

Once inside the ship they connected small disks to her heart, head, arms and legs and initiated the medisearch and correction program that all Trion craft carried. The health control machine would work through the results it found, referring back, if necessary to the master centre on Trion itself for a second opinion, before administering any corrective electro-chemical procedure, and issuing instructions concerning psychological and sociological life style amendments that might be thought wise.

Meanwhile, under The Magician's instructions, Turlough returned with the Time Lord to the Assembly Rooms, to undertake the job they had previously agreed upon – the dismantling of the time unit, and redirectioning of the island towards the Home Star. Yet no sooner had they taken up positions in front of the controls than there was a sudden jolt. Turlough looked at The Magician to see if he could be the cause. The Gallifrean gave no sign. The jolt occurred again – and again – and then settled down into the familiar bumpiness of atmospheric turbulence. Only when he had been at the task for some minutes did Turlough glance at the master controls. Truth dawned. The orbit of the island was still decaying. The main drive had only appeared to engage. In fact nothing had happened. 'We're on the way down,' he shouted in despair.

'Then stop staring at the screen and take us up,' replied The Magician.

'I can't,' Turlough called back, helpless in his panic. 'I've already got half the control panels out. If I try and run it now it will simply short out.'

'Then I suggest,' said The Magician dryly, 'that you stop shouting at me and work as fast as you can.'

'We should evacuate now,' Turlough called back, still not moving.

'Then this island will crash into Trion and result in a level of nuclear fallout that will result in your death anyway. Face death, Turlough, and try and save yourself through the one course of action open. Get the time link out, close the circuits and try again to take this island up. I'll send a message to the surface to suggest that they might delay shooting us down, just in case that is what they are contemplating doing.'

'How do you know they're thinking of that?'

'I don't – now will you just get back to work?'

At last Turlough did as commanded. The turbulence was now so bad that it was getting hard for him to work at the contacts he had inserted when the island had first dislocated itself from the rest of New Trion. However there was one compensation. The odd shape of the rock was meaning that they were gaining a few seconds more than Turlough had originally imagined, as the rock repeatedly bounced into and off the upper layers of the planet's atmosphere.

Finally the time unit was out, Turlough snapped shut the circuit breakers and touched the heat sensitive controls. And then nothing. There was no thrust of power, no movement, no cessation of the turbulence as the island shot into space.

The Magician saw what had happened. 'Get into the ship,' he shouted. Turlough did not need telling twice. He ran. As the door of the Neutrinova closed about them, Turlough took the ship up, and kept going at maximum acceleration. Even though it made no difference, he kept his hand pressing hard against the controls. By the time the island tumbled through the atmosphere and exploded in the biggest nuclear

136

outpouring the planet had ever seen they were far enough away to avoid even feeling the shock wave.

Juras contained a strange look in her eyes. Turlough kept his distance as The Magician checked the print-out and finally pronounced her fit and well. The ship's medicontrol prescribed an initial period of rest, but then with a build-up of activity to ensure she got back to her previous level of fitness. There seemed little chance of that in the tiny spacecraft, but then medical computers had a habit of not being very practical when it came to the life style advice.

'Who hit me on the head?' Juras wanted to know as The Magician moved away.

'You did,' said Turlough sardonically, 'whilst you were trying to lop off my head with a sword.'

Juras refused to believe it. 'What really happened?' she demanded turning to The Magician.

'It is as Turlough tells you,' he said with a sad smile, brushing some dust from his figure-of-eight hat and fixing a new rose in his button hole. 'You attacked him and showed every intention of relieving him of the ability to breathe. A savage, vicious move rarely seen in the past life of Clanswoman Juras Maateh.'

Still Juras refuted the evidence. The Magician sought to allay her concerns. 'However, no harm done,' he said. 'We'll just run a test on the EEG brain patterns and see what got into you.' And with that he began to place more small pads on Juras's forehead.

Turlough on the other hand was not prepared to let the subject go as easily as that. ' "No harm done"?' he repeated incredulously. 'Trion is awash with radiation. Most of the population is already dead and the rest soon will be, and you say "no harm done". You have just wiped out the entire Imperial Clans. Nine thousand years of science and technology. The longest continuous scientific community in the Galaxy, gone. And you say "no harm done"!' The Magician opened his mouth as if to speak but Turlough, now in full flow, would not accede to interruption. 'It has gone wrong, hasn't it?' he demanded. 'This is not the future you saw and expected, the future that left you smiling and coming along with us for the joy ride. Admit it, Time Lord. You had no idea what was going to happen to us on the island.'

The Magician carried on with his medical work. 'Yes,' he said gravely.

'Yes what?' shouted Turlough although they were barely a metre apart.

'Yes, I had no idea what was going to happen. Yes, the destruction of Trion was certainly unfortunate.'

'Unfortunate!' Turlough found he couldn't believe his ears.

'Repeating my words does not actually solve problems,' The Magician told him gravely.

'So what do you suggest we do? I must say that for a Time Lord who doesn't like to get involved, you've certainly got the knack of gyrating to the centre of galactic affairs.'

'Would you have preferred that I hadn't got involved inside the Assembly Room? I could certainly have let Juras chop you to pieces. Trion would have been destroyed, just as now. The only difference is that so would you.'

'I wouldn't have chopped anyone to pieces,' said Juras still unable to acknowledge the full effect of her actions.

'You nearly did,' Turlough told her.

'Well, I don't remember,' she said defensively. 'And I don't believe it.'

'Whether you believe it or not is neither here nor there,' said Turlough angrily. 'Take a look at Trion through the spectrometer. You'll find a surge of lines that are somewhat incompatible with life.'

Juras moved to look for herself, but The Magician held her back as he completed running the results of his tests on Juras's head. The screen gave a result. 'Look,' he commanded. Turlough, who had been gazing through the short distance observation screens at Trion turned. He found The Magician and Juras staring at a collection of wavy lines. The Time Lord was pointing to one outburst in particular. 'That spike,' he said, 'is artificially induced. A crude device but clever. Someone's got at you.'

'Who?' asked Juras. It was an obvious question, but still a necessary one.

'That I really can't say,' replied The Magician. Turlough looked at the man, wondering if his accusations about the Gallifreyan not knowing the future were as true as he had just alleged.

'Can the spike be removed?' asked Juras.

'Not without knowing exactly how it was put in,' replied The Magician, still staring at the screen. He had developed a mannerism of rubbing his chin. It was becoming a habit.

'When was it put in?'

'Recently,' he replied, 'it is a relic from some scurrilous activities in your none too distant past.'

'Rehctaht,' said Turlough.

Juras seemed dubious. 'You would think of her,' she said.

'Don't you? You yourself admit she was mad.'

'Mad for power, but not in this way. She trusted me – that's how I got to the position where I could work on the gravity unit.'

'Whoever it was,' said The Magician, 'your brain contains things that shouldn't be there. And whatever it is remains dormant until triggered – as happened in the Assembly Room. It is a sophisticated and very nasty device.'

'And as a result of that,' replied Turlough, 'Trion is now a scorching relic of civilisation.'

Silence came to the little craft. Turlough switched the drive units down – they had in fact been going nowhere fast, shooting straight up out of the galaxy. The viewfinder stayed where it had last been fixed, focused on Trion. Occasionally Turlough glanced moodily at the screen. Sometimes he looked at Juras, who had now fallen into a deep sleep, presumably recovering from the activation of the spike in her brain. The Magician sat away from the viewfinder, eyes gleaming brightly, his cloak wrapped round him. He looked in deep thought.

Turlough felt a painful ache run through his entire body. The muscles on his legs hurt, not from the physical exertion of the work on the island but the fear and tension of the whole operation, an operation which had ended in a failure he had not even contemplated when the call came through from the Central Committee. Perhaps he had become overconfident

139

from his long association with the Doctor. Several times he had seen death staring him straight in the face, and each time he had escaped. It had given him a belief in the fact that he could not lose. Now once again with a Time Lord at his side he had not lost his life, that was true, but his planet had gone. The suffering that must be going on down there now was unthinkable. Anti-radiation injections would be insufficient to help an entire planet. For those that survived, there would be little left on Trion – no safe food would grow any more. And of course there would be the millions who were killed at the moment the island hit the ground. Plus the resultant firestorms sucking people into their raging infernos . . .

He closed his eyes, trying to force out the pictures. Taking on a will of its own his brain switched suddenly to a memory of his visit to the Slots. He thought of their ancient civilisation, officially part of Trion, but in reality removed from it. How had the Slots reacted? Had they known? Did they even know now it had happened? If they had escaped the immediate blast they may still be unaware of the creeping disease of radiation sickness that would soon engulf them all.

The thought had occurred to Turlough that perhaps he could contact some outlying civilisations and ask for help or aid – but the COPS would have already done that. If anyone was interested in aiding the planet, which under the rule of Rehctaht had openly spurned involvement with the systems beyond, then arrangements would have already been made. Trion was paying the price for allowing, if only for a brief spell, rampant revolutionary nationalism to dominate its communal life.

Turlough's rambling thoughts returned to some sort of order. The Gardsormr. He had blamed Rehctaht for what had happened to Juras. But it could also have been the aliens. Or both. Either way, the Gardsormr would soon be appearing. Turlough remembered the future situation on New Trion. Sudden radiation, followed some years on by the arrival of the aliens. Conscious that The Magician was watching him, Turlough touched the controls that began to edge the Neutrino-drive back towards his planet. At the same time he used the power to thrust the newly installed time unit forward slowly, keeping his eye on the scanner all the while. Not more than five years on he saw what he expected. Gardsormr ships, looking from this distance like innocent spinning tops, twenty in all. Slowly he accelerated the time unit, until he reached a point where the ships left once more. He advanced on the planet, and looked below though the hazy atmosphere. There was no sign of life.

Turlough centred on the zone where had had his house. The area seemed to have taken much of the worst of the blast of the explosion caused by the disintegration of the island. The forest in which he had spent so much time and upon which he had looked so lovingly was gone. In its place was something quite new – although at this altitude he could not quite work out what. At first he took them for landed Gardsormr ships, but as he descended it soon became clear that this could not be the case. They were fixed – some sort of dome structure replicated over and over again. They had to be a Gardsormr settlement; he could think of no other purpose. With an immensely heavy heart Turlough pulled the ship away from the desecrated landscapes of his home planet.

Finding Juras still asleep, Turlough undertook one further piece of exploration – he returned to New Trion. The journey of several days in real time now took only hours with this type of ship. As he had expected, he found the same situation there – mutilated landscape and Gardsormr domes. With a weariness greater than he could ever recall feeling before he set a new course, and closed his eyes to a Galaxy that he felt he no longer really wished to know.

09: JURAS?

Juras looked at the viewing screen. It was that dull grey streaked with flashing light that was the familiar artifact of ultra fast space travel. She struggled to her feet and walked the tiny distance across the craft to where Turlough sat staring blankly at the controls. Before speaking she looked round at The Magician. He seemed to be in a deep sleep or even a coma, sitting cross-legged on the floor, barely breathing and certainly not moving.

Turlough looked up and saw her. He managed a weak smile. 'All right now?' he asked. She sat down next to him. 'I had a terrible nightmare,' she said softly.

'It wasn't a nightmare,' Turlough told her sadly.

There was a silence as the message sank in. A small blue light flashed on the screen. Turlough touched some controls, and the ship slowed for the final approach.

'Earth?' asked Juras.

'The final place to look,' Turlough replied. 'I'd like to see what happens there.'

'Still chasing your link between Earth and Trion?'

'Still not sure,' confided Turlough, 'but even if not, there remains something special about this planet, to explain why the Doctor kept coming back. Even if it doesn't involve Trion directly it certainly involves the Gardsormr.'

'Maybe he just liked the place,' said Juras reasonably. 'I know some people who always went to Ohwrotco for their vacation. I can't see anything in the place, but it doesn't make it special. They just . . .' Juras cut her chatter when she saw the effect it was having on Turlough. It seemed he was almost close to tears. And then she remembered the dream. Only he had said it wasn't a dream. Trion, her friends, that silly vacation resort, were all no more . . .

Turlough pulled himself back together. On the screen the familiar greens and blues of Earth were revealed in full splendour. 'This is about the time that I was here,' he explained. 'At that period there was a very strong chance of nuclear war between two great coalitions – one in the east and one in the west. Both sides accused the other of being war-like, and neither would believe any talk of peace from the other. What was worse, the people in each camp did feel their leadership was right, and saw everyone on the other side as the real live enemy. The situation is very similar to that which we found on New Trion.

'And do they blow themselves up?' asked Juras.

'That's what I want to see. Let's take a look fifty years on.'

But fifty years was too long. By that time, on the surface was to be found no sign of civilisation, no cities, no towns, just scars and ruins on what had once been a beautiful planet. The effects of radiation dominated. Grimly Turlough retraced the time gap until he came across the actual moment of the outbursts that caused the nuclear explosions. And there, soon after the clouds cleared, as he knew there would be, were the Gardsormr spheres, surrounding the planet. Turlough pulled the Neutrino ship through time to escape recognition by the Gardsormr, and then brought it to a halt.

As the ship circled the desolated Earth both Turlough and Juras sat staring moodily into the screens. They were now only too painfully aware they had no home, no planet, no friends, nowhere to go. Turlough flirted briefly with the idea of going back in time to Trion and establishing himself there, but he knew he could never live in such a situation, knowing always what lay at the end of the road.

'You could always go to the Gardsormr's planet.' It was the voice of The Magician, standing behind them, suddenly wide awake.

'Two of us against an empire?' said Turlough. 'I know I'm widely regarded as a coward but even for a Time Lord that seems a pretty reckless concept. We'd end up on another prison planet, only this time we might not be lucky enough to get out before the bomb drops.'

'So what will you do?'

'Avoid your Socratic questioning for a start,' said Turlough. The smile on The Magician's face annoyed him deeply. The Time Lord said nothing, and Turlough stared moodily at the screen. He stayed there for a good ten minutes before the orange warning lights all over the ship caused him to react instinctively to swing away from a fleet of Gardsormr spheres that had risen from the planet and were heading straight for him. He shook them off easily, but the event had a galvanising effect on the young Clansman. He touched the controls and the ship sped around the planet in a new orbit. Juras asked for an explanation.

Turlough looked grim. 'I am going down. Once and for all I'm going to find out what these aliens are up to, why they destroyed our planet – and this one come to that – and I'm going to stop them.'

'But you just said . . .'

'I know what I said, and I know what I'm going to do.' And then calming slightly he added, 'If I don't do something about the Gardsormr there is no point in living, is there?'

'I'll come too.'

'Not safe,' commanded the new Turlough. 'That spike in your brain is still there and could be set off at any moment.'

Juras thought about the problem. Then she said, 'If you leave me on the Neutrinova that could just result in my getting this ship up into the sky and leaving you on the planet. If I come along at least you'll be able to see me.'

'Sounds reasonable to me,' said The Magician, 'adventures for all, a marvellous idea, an excellent plan, tremendous spirit, the vital principle in all Trions, that animating force that gives you all the breath of life. Quite superb.' He was still content, still smiling, still showing no sign of recognising that Turlough had placed a large part of the responsibility of the destruction of Trion upon his shoulders.

Turlough took the ship down. The ground was hard, burnt and discoloured as if by great heat, although the compass and maps suggested it had once been a temperate area with regular

144

rainfall. It was southern England.

They landed not far from a collection of Gardsormr domes. There was no sign of life. Radiation levels however, were far lower than they should have been this close to the time of destruction, and the air was breathable. They took radiation pills but dispensed with the heavy and cumbersome anti-fallout uniforms.

Each dome measured around two hundred metres across, reaching maybe ten metres in height at the centre. There were fifty or more of the constructions that Turlough could see, and probably more behind stretching along the flat plain at regular intervals. In the opposite direction could be seen the ruins of a city. Closer, a few outcrops of greenery shot out of the earth – incongruous in their abundance.

The hard ground revealed no sign of tracks. An eerie silence pervaded. Cautiously Turlough, Juras and The Magician left the Neutrinova and walked slowly towards the nearest of the domes and circled it at what they hoped was a safe distance. At the far side a doorway was revealed with a heat control set into the panelling. There were no signs nor instructions, no warnings, no obvious physical alarms. There was also no way of knowing what was inside without entering. Turlough touched the control.

The door retreated silently. The three pushed forward and rapidly eased back into the open air – the smell from the interior was quite appalling. However Turlough was determined not to let his newfound courage desert him. Cupping a hand over his mouth and nose he pushed forward into the dome. The light was diffuse – only a grey whiteness was let through the dome's covering despite the brightness outside. A central avenue led down through the dome entrance to the far end. The floor was dusty and marked out with two tracks. On either side of the central passage were metallic tubs a metre high, stretching back to the wall of the dome and running the entire length of the building. The tubs had no tops on them – and the smell came from inside.

Turlough walked across and peered in, and then reeled back. He was violently sick on the floor. Juras helped him to his feet, but Turlough was in no mood for gentle assistance.

Stumbling, and with hand still over his mouth he lurched back the way they had come and out through the dome door. Juras, taking a desperate look at the container walls, but unwilling to risk her stomach's strength on whatever was inside followed behind.

Turlough was gasping, and clearly in need of water. There was a stream nearby and, despite Juras's misgivings, he moved towards it and washed his mouth thoroughly in the clear liquid, before gently sipping at it.

Recovering slightly he looked around. 'Where's The Magician?' he asked.

Juras didn't know. 'Back in the dome I suppose,' she said. 'What did you find in there?'

'Slugs.'

Juras found it hard to believe and repeated the word. Turlough was in no mood to debate the weakness of his stomach. 'Slugs is the only word I have for them. Large slugs. Two metres long, twice as thick as your body, and with mouths like I've never seen.' The thought of the creatures was enough to affect him again. He took another sip of water.

'Slugs are slugs,' said Juras.

'Fine,' said Turlough, 'Go and see.'

Juras did not need telling twice. She got up and walked rapidly back to the dome. The door was still open, although The Magician was nowhere to be seen. She walked up to the first tank and peered inside. Despite the warning of Turlough's description she was taken aback. The creatures were indeed slug-like. Black, slimy, and as huge as Turlough had indicated. Yet it was the mouth and eyes that dominated the creatures. Within seconds of her looking over the top of the tank there were at least twenty of the creatures gazing at her, and most were making their slimy way along the bottom of the tank to get closer. As the vast fat bodies slithered so they opened and shut mouths that contained teeth – sharp teeth – more than Juras could count. After three seconds she had had enough and ran back to the door. She hadn't been sick, but it had been a near thing.

Outside Turlough was recovering. As Juras rejoined him so The Magician appeared from behind another dome. 'All the 'same,' he said quite oblivious of the effects the creatures had had on the two Trions.

'What is?' asked Juras, sitting next to Turlough.

'Each dome – the same as the others. I thought there might have been some variation.'

'Never mind the domes,' said Turlough, 'what are those creatures?'

'Slugs,' said The Magician with a knowing smile.

'Not like anything I've ever seen,' said Juras.

Colour was beginning to come back to Turlough's cheeks, as he got his mind in action once more. 'Odd though,' he said, 'there's no sign of animal farming.'

'Should there be?' asked Juras.

'Normally,' Turlough told her. 'If you have a bunch of animals in pens or cages you give them something to feed on. Here there is nothing. There's no food, no water in those tanks. Just the floor. What do the creatures eat?'

'That,' said The Magician, 'is an excellent question. Your mind is now working again. And with your established discipline proving unhelpful in this situation you are turning your brain to better things. The way is open – we may progress. Trion will be proud of its son. I congratulate you.' He saluted.

'Trion is dead,' said Turlough softly. And seeing his comment had no effect on The Magician he added sarcastically, 'How about an excellent answer to the question of how those creatures survive?'

'That is for you to work out, my boy. Now you've hit the question it shouldn't be too difficult. Not with your brain. No problem at all. An excellent start. The conclusion is close, your mind is on course.'

'One thing is for sure,' said Turlough, 'they can't be the Gardsormr.'

Juras wanted to know why. 'Because the Gardsormr build space ships,' Turlough replied logically. 'How does a giant slug plot an interstellar flight path and programme a computer?'

'Maybe that's them in a baby form. Perhaps they mutate into something else.'

147

The group fell silent, contemplating the revolting sight seen inside the dome. Turlough forced his mind away from the gastropods and back to the events that had led him to this spot. So far, his adventure into the future of Earth had merely resulted in him being sick. He had discovered something that must have a relationship with the Gardsormr, but he had no idea what. He suggested a return to the ship. No one objected.

As they walked the short distance across the dry plain the sound of an interstellar craft landing was unmistakeable. It was coming in near to the Neutrinova itself. Juras, Turlough and The Magician found themselves stranded in the openness. Already the downdraught of the craft was blowing up a gale and within seconds it threatened to knock them over. With no chance of making it back to the domes they threw themselves onto the scorched earth and covered their heads as best they could.

Like most efficient drive systems, the power unit of this spaceship shut down the moment it was no longer needed. Instantly there was silence and the wind dropped to zero. Cautiously Turlough raised his head. To his relief the ship he saw was not a Gardsormr vessel, but rather one of a type that seemed to figure in his memory but which he could not quite place. Something emerged from the craft – something not quite human, not quite Triic. Turlough stood, and recognised the Slot whom he had met during his brief visit to the Slotsruin. He walked over to greet the alien. 'A second meeting,' said the creature simply.

It was a singularly banal opening, but Turlough made no comment. 'Your presence is unexpected,' added the Slot.

'No more than yours,' replied Turlough. 'You are out of time and space, being here. Why weren't you destroyed when the island crashed onto Trion?'

'A reason for the existence of our Slotsruin; at the correct moment it switched on and gave us protection.' He paused and looked beyond Turlough at the domes. 'What does your presence here now signify?'

'A search for the creatures that destroyed Trion.'

'And have you found them?'

'Only their pets.'

There was a silence between the two beings who had previously shared a planet, but now apparently shared a common enemy.

'And you?' enquired Turlough at last.

'I have an interest in common with you,' said the Slot. 'And perhaps you are more able to deal with it than I. My race has long since lost the concept of warfare and fighting. I will depart.'

'Wait,' called Turlough as the creature began to walk away. 'I have no idea what to do here.'

The Slot turned back to Turlough. 'Follow the guidance of the Time Lord,' he said, before continuing his walk to the ship.

'But how did you get here – in this time zone?' demanded Turlough, falling into step alongside him.

'How did you?' countered the Slot. And then pausing for a moment, he said 'You have developed a time mechanism. It has always been possible that the Clans would accomplish that feat. You now possess real power. Use it with care.'

'Do I get no more than poignant advice?' said Turlough with growing frustration.

The Slot looked past Turlough to The Magician with what might have been acknowledgement on his face. 'You exist at the centre of a major crisis, Clansman. Act with caution, much depends on you.'

'And you? Do you have a part to play in this crisis, as you call it?'

'I have the past and future of my race at heart. It is something you would not fully understand. The Clans and the Slots have always shared something – both being non-Trion, yet of Trion. Thus do not be too surprised at my involvement. Nor be too surprised by our own possession of technology different from the Clans. Of all Trion races ours is the oldest.'

'But there is nothing left on Trion save your island. What places us all together here, on Earth?'

'I protect the past and future of my race,' repeated the Slot, and with that walked back to the ship.

Turlough was experienced enough in the ways of the Galaxy to turn and run when he saw the Slot close the airlock of his

149

craft. He knew that if the alien was about to take off he could do so within seconds. He ran towards his own ship, urging the others to do the same. But they need have had no fear. The Slot's craft stayed on the ground.

'I never heard of the Slot going into space,' said Juras when they gathered inside the Neutrinova.

'Nor existing through time,' said Turlough. 'It's over fifty years in real time since I went to the Slotsruin, and yet that Slot looks just the same as he did then. Either they don't age, or he has a time unit too.'

'So just another problem. What now?' asked Juras.

In honesty Turlough admitted to himself that he didn't know. But he recalled how often during his travels the Doctor had been asked by companions, unable to see any solution to current problems, 'What now, Doctor?' Always there had been an answer. Immediate, decisive, even if on occasion it might involve the toss of a coin. Juras, if not looking on him with respect, was, since her brainstorm on the island, treating him as the leader of the expedition, and his decision to take a look at the Gardsormr domes had done him no harm in her eyes, even if he had ended up suffering a sudden and dramatic decline in health.

The young Clansman searched his mind. What would the Doctor have done in these circumstances? He forced himself to say something. 'I think we should have a word with the Gardsormr,' he said. He listened to himself in bewilderment. It sounded like the Doctor speaking. The only problem was he didn't quite know how he was actually going to fulfil the suggestion.

Juras on the other hand was very impressed by the new Turlough. Knowing that the decision meant a space ride she was already strapping herself in. The Magician did the same. Faced with such an immediate acceptance of his statement Turlough had no alternative but to believe it himself. He took the ship up.

Given that the Gardsormr were supposed allies of Trion, Turlough guessed that he would be able to make ship to ship communication. He tried the standard frequency. 'Gardsormr ships, this is Trion.'

150

There was silence, and then, 'Trion, identify yourself.'

Turlough thought rapidly. 'Identification is hardly necessary,' he said. 'You are the destroyers of Trion and Earth. We shall destroy your ships.'

Turlough expected bravado, anxiety, counter-charges, or something similar, but not what he got. 'Very well,' said the voice of Gardsormr.

Turlough looked at Juras and The Magician in amazement. ' "*Very well*" ?' he repeated. 'How can a being say "very well" to total destruction?'

'Perhaps they don't mind,' said Juras.

Turlough surveyed the screens in front of him. He looked for attack, but there was no sign. However as an extra precaution he time-slipped slightly, effectively making the Neutrinova invisible to the non-time mobile Gardsormr.

'Why are you waiting?' asked Juras.

Why indeed? Turlough had pushed himself into a corner but could find no way out. 'Because merely killing a fleet of Gardsormr ships won't solve any of the real problems we face. It won't tell us *why*. It won't explain the link between the Doctor and Earth, nor Earth and Trion, and it won't above all else bring back everything we've lost.' He turned to the console again, gently easing the ARTEMIS drive back to the temporal location at which he had spoken to the Gardsormr. As they emerged he spun the ship sideways in case of any Gardsormr fire. It was unnecessary – there was none.

'Gardsormr,' said Turlough again, 'farewell. And say farewell to your slug creatures on the planet below. They will go too, as will the domes on your prison planets, and on poor Trion itself.

'Trion,' the response was immediate. 'Your quarrel is with the Gardsormr. Leave the domes.'

Turlough spun round in his chair and looked at Juras. 'A response!' he exclaimed. 'They care about the domes. We're on the right track.'

'So do you knock them out of the planet?'

'I'd like to,' admitted Turlough, 'but I don't quite see how. There's no weapon system on the ship and I certainly don't fancy close quarter combat with the creatures in the domes.

We'll have to bluff our way through.'

Turlough returned to the transmitter. 'Gardsormr,' he said, 'are you aware of the nature of this ship?'

'You have time-travel,' came the reply.

'We shall use that facility to remove you and your domes from the face of history.'

'Why do you hate us so?' asked the unseen alien.

Turlough found the question hard to believe. 'You destroy my planet and my people, and you ask why I want to destroy you.'

'We did not destroy your planet.'

'The evidence suggests otherwise.'

'Your planet was destroyed by the collapse of the orbit of the space island.'

'Semantics!' shouted Turlough. 'Juras and I piloted that island to Trion as the only way of getting off the prison you put us in.'

'We save, not destroy,' countered the voice.

'Saving means refraining from killing all life on at least three planets.'

'We did refrain. You have chosen the wrong enemy.'

'I find that hard to believe.'

'You have seen our domes,' said the voice. 'What decisions have you come to about what is inside?'

'We presume that the creatures there are the early forms of yourselves. They prove we are lifeforms each repulsive to the other – you to us and us to you.'

'Wrong!' said the voice strongly. 'Without them civilisation on Earth and Trion cannot survive. In turn the creatures cannot survive without the right nutrients. Those nutrients are what you would call nuclear radiation. They have no desire to destroy – merely a willingness to live.'

'But their living,' said Juras, joining the conversation for the first time, 'involves millions of others dying.'

'You are full of misunderstandings. Where is the famous science of the Clans of Trion? Or perhaps you are not really from that planet. If you are you would do well to consider the evidence for all that you allege. Beware of calling us beings who feed on the misfortunes of others. It is not so.'

'Misfortunes seems to put it too lightly,' said Juras.

'What happened on Earth?' asked Turlough.

'Nuclear war – politicians rushing ahead too far too fast. It is always a dangerous scenario.'

'But you encouraged them – you paved the way,' said Turlough.

'No,' the Gardsormr voice was emphatic. 'I did nothing. On each planet Gardsormr observed and waited. Our greatest crime was to attempt to save life not to destroy it on all three planets.'

'So there is a link between Earth and Trion!'

'In that they both have dominant races that distrust their fellows to the extent that it can, sometimes, lead to nuclear war, yes. There may be more but that is not for me to discover.'

Juras had a sudden thought. 'Why don't you organise your own fallout on a deserted planet. There is no need to use Trions or Humans.'

'We are getting nowhere. You continue to believe, despite having no evidence, that we are guilty, when the opposite is true. We cannot convince you, Clansman.'

There was a long silence. Turlough turned to The Magician for help or inspiration but found none. Finally he said into his microphone, 'I've listened to your pleadings, and I do not relish the role of being judge and jury. I need time to consider.' And with that he slipped the ship once more into another time.

After some minutes Juras said, 'It all leaves many questions still totally unanswered. Not least who sent the island spinning out of orbit in the first place.'

'And what the Slots are up to,' said Turlough. 'Like the Gardsormr said, we still need more evidence.'

'So we must go and find it although it may be a gigantic Gardsormr trap,' said Juras.

Turlough agreed but he had no idea how to find even one clue. The one thing that came to mind had his brain shivering before the words even came out of his mouth. It had a similar effect on Juras. 'We'd better have a look around the domes after nightfall – just to see if anything untoward does crop up.'

Despite the horror of the idea it did offer some possibility.

Providing of course (and on this they were all in agreement) there was no question of actually going inside a dome once the single sun had gone down. Having agreed, they landed.

Juras, Turlough and The Magician moved forward cautiously, each holding a tiny torch. Having no idea what they were actually looking for it made a plan of campaign subject to instant variation. They walked carefully between the domes, pausing from time to time to listen. They heard nothing. Either the slugs made no sound at night, or else were pausing to listen to the Trions, who were in turn pausing to listen to . . .

In the warmth of the summer's night they sat by the stream. On one side the domes, black against a starlit sky, not nearly as beautiful as on Trion itself, but a real improvement on New Trion's bleakness; in the other direction the flat plain. In the distance the dark outline of ruined buildings; nearer the occasional outcrop of vegetation. Turlough remembered how Earth had been during his previous visits. Such thoughts didn't help. He found he had closed his eyes, opened them, and then closed them again rubbing away false impressions. They re-opened. What he was seeing couldn't be right. In the distance was a light. But this planet was dead, apart from the Gardsormr. He watched. It was at ground level. And heading their way.

Turlough nudged Juras who looked away from the bright half moon. It took her eyes a minute to adjust but then she saw it too. When asked what it was, The Magician would, as expected, offer no opinion, save to tell them that the Gardsormr had been right in suggesting they were jumping to conclusions. They had seen a desolate part of a planet, where they had expected a profusion of life, and assumed that it was all dead. None of them had done a proper survey from the ship. Life, even here, was possible.

Rapidly they headed back for the Neutrinova, climbing aboard as soon as they arrived. The screens gave a greater picture of what was coming towards them – a land buggy pulling behind it a cart. The buggy, apparently powered by petrol or diesel, drove close to the ship, but failed to slow until it reached a dome. Only at that point did the driver emerge – a

Slot! It opened the door of the dome and drove the truck straight in. So that was why the central lane was so vast, thought Turlough. Rapidly he turned all the sound amplification units straining at the dome in question. From within the sound of an explosion could be discerned, followed by a scream of bloodcurdling proportions. Next the sound of machinery, and then silence until the buggy started up again emerging from the far end of the dome and driving back the way it had come.

Turlough had a sudden thought. All external events on this, as with every other Trion ship were automatically recorded. He keyed in the visual of the approach and departure of the buggy, pressed several hand controls and then gave a satisfied grunt.

'I'm getting better at this detective work,' he said. 'The disk recording shows that buggy to have been more laden down on the way back than on the way here.'

'So the sound was the sound of a slug being killed, and taken away,' said Juras. 'The questions are where to, by whom, and what for.'

'There are always more questions,' said Turlough. For the first time since leaving Trion he gave half a smile.

10: PHARIX

They set off soon after first light walking at a controlled pace
across the plain towards the ruined city, following the
direction of the truck observed the night before. They
remained, as ever, weaponless, aware still of the spike in
Juras's brain, and the total unknown nature of whatever it was
that they were walking into.

Turlough was scared. He wouldn't admit it, of course, but
he was. It was only the horror of a life of endless wandering
with no Home Planet to return to, no friends, not even
enemies, that caused him to walk with an apparent resolve and
solidness of purpose towards the city, past the occasional
plushness of greenery that simply should not have existed.
Buckled roads and field divisions appeared, before the ruins of
the first houses. At these outer fringes there was neither sign of
life nor of any existence beyond the disaster that swept
civilisation away. They kept walking.

Further in, other roads joined, and the ruins became more
intense. Houses gave way to larger buildings, perhaps one time
shopping centres, amusement arcades, factories – it was hard to
tell. And then, at what must have been the city centre itself,
there were signs of repair. Several buildings had been chopped
down to a single storey and a make-shift roof put on.

Turlough found his mind once more returning to thoughts
of what the Doctor might have done at such a point. Walk
straight into the building probably, without the slightest
consideration for what might happen. He followed the idea,
but kept a close eye on The Magician, just in case that eternal
smile should suddenly leave his face.

Turlough pushed the wooden door and stood well back.

Nothing happened. Juras meanwhile edged to the side of the building and peered round. She called out. He ran to her quickly.

Along the track that ran by the side of the building was a path of smooth slime. It led to an outhouse. Turlough walked towards it, carefully stepping away from the revolting flow. The outbuilding had windows half a metre above eye level, covered in dirt, but allowing a chance to look inside. Juras brought up some bricks lying nearby and Turlough climbed up. Once at the right level he put his face to the window and brought his hands around his eyes to keep down the back glare from the sun. Without a word he jumped down and sat at the base of the building, his knees pulled up to his face.

Getting no response from her questioning of Turlough Juras climbed the bricks herself. She looked briefly and came down. 'Slugs?' asked The Magician. Juras nodded, before moving away from Turlough, and disappearing around the side of the building. Reluctantly the Time Lord decided that once again he was going to have to look for himself. Carefully he eased himself up onto the bricks and peered in through the grime.

Taking up much of the length of the room was, as he had correctly anticipated, one of the giant gastropods they had seen the day before in the dome. It was slit open from head to tail, and yet incredibly still showed signs of life with the head raising itself regularly to look back sadly at the gash that had been rendered through its entire body, only for the head to then fall back to the floor. As it fell back the head repeatedly knocked itself against uneven stonework and gradually opened up deeper and deeper cuts from which a thick black mud emerged. Even for a Time Lord who had seen everything it was a revolting sight.

And yet despite the vision, in the room were two crippled humanoids. Each was covered in a thick, coarse sackcloth from head to toe.

Little could be seen except for their faces; skins covered in boils and growths, shapes strangely distorted, with necks too short and heads too big and held on one side. It looked like the inevitable result of too much radiation.

The Time Lord turned from his perch ready to descend, but

as he did so the few bricks gathered by Juras slipped. He tumbled to the ground, banging his head against the windowsill as he did so. This, although apparently occasioning no long term damage to The Magician, did cause him to let out a loud yell, which was certain to raise the alarm within the outhouse, even if the crash of the bricks had not already done so.

The sound of the crash brought Turlough and Juras to the Time Lord's side. At the same time they heard the door at the rear of the building open. Helping The Magician to his feet Turlough rapidly indicated what seemed to him to be the safest route out – around the back of the larger building, along the far side and onto the main street. Not pausing to glance at the mutilated creatures, who he was sure would be following, he ran at top speed, checking only briefly that Juras was close behind.

They were almost at the far end of the building when a door opened missing Turlough's face by millimetres and causing him to jump rapidly to one side. From the opening came another hooded figure, this one with coverings so far forward that it was impossible to make out the face at all. The creature carried a long pole which it prodded at Turlough. The Clansman stood stock still in surprise as Juras came to a dead halt next to him, rapidly joined by The Magician. Immediately behind came the hooded figures from the outbuilding.

Given all that he had been through recently Turlough didn't feel that the odds were stacked against him at this point. Three radiation cripples armed with no more than a single wooden pole against two fit Clansfolk and a Time Lord: the outcome was inevitable. Turlough made a rapid move to one side, and found himself in receipt of an explosion on one side of his head. He slipped to the ground, and revealed a look of sheer surprise on his face, unable to imgine how the event had happened. The creature from the main building still stood with his wooden pole raised. Now the other two were also armed.

'When I say,' said Turlough softly to Juras, as he raised himself up once more, 'turn and run back the way we came.'

He wasn't sure if The Magician heard it, but he reckoned that even if not the Time Lord ought to be able to answer for himself. Turlough gave the shout. He turned, felt pain spread from his right shoulder through his whole body, and collapsed on the ground. Juras fell beside him.

The three crippled creatures stood around the two Trions and began prodding them with the poles. The message was clear. They were to enter the building.

Turlough prayed as they moved through the door that there were no gastropods inside. The pain, he felt, he could take, but not the sight and stench of slugs being ripped apart by barbarian cripples.

A dark corridor led into a small room. There were boards at the windows, rubble on the floor. Two of the three Earth creatures crouched facing Turlough, Juras and The Magician. The third guarded the door.

'Who are you?' one asked. The voice was high and unstable. Turlough was unable to work out if it was male or female. Fortunately for his sensibilities the being made no attempt to remove its hood.

'I am Turlough,' came the obvious reply. His mind raced to try to consider what the Doctor would have done. Clearly he would have gained the initiative. A question, an offer of help, these were the hallmarks of the Time Lord in such situations. Turlough opened his mouth to speak, but was stopped dead by a further question.

'Who is the Doctor?'

Turlough's mind spun even faster. And then another question in that high unstable squeak. 'What is a Time Lord?'

This, thought Turlough, is getting out of hand. It was as if the creatures merely wanted to ask questions. They had no interest in the answers. He had to gain control and lead Juras and The Magician out of this place, and away from the repugnant half-dead animal outside.

'Why do you fear the Land Snails?'

Land Snails? thought Turlough. An odd name, and yet appropriate. The creatures didn't see them as repulsive – nor come to that as the destroyers of everything around. Perhaps, his mind raced on, they don't know about the Gardsormr.

'Who are the Gardsormr?'

Now that was a difficult one. How to describe creatures no one has ever seen but who destroyed your own planet? And then he stopped his brain racing and stared at the creatures. He thought, 'G equals M to the power minus one by L cubed by T to the power minus four.'

'What is G?' said the creature.

'An algebraic way of representing gravity,' said Turlough, and then to Juras, 'They can read minds. Every question they ask relates to something I thought.'

'What is M?' the creature persisted.

'Another part of the equation,' said Turlough. He thought of the whole set of equations that formed the basis of the ARTEMIS drive.

'You are not human?' These creatures were nothing if not persistent.

'That is how they trapped us outside,' said Juras. 'Every time we tried to make a getaway they knew where we were going.'

'And now,' added Turlough, 'they are trying to work out who we are and what we are.'

'We might as well tell them,' said Juras, 'otherwise they'll just gradually get it out of our brains.' And then to the creatures she said, 'He was thinking of gravitational forces. G equals M to the power minus one by L cubed by T to the power minus two. It is the dimensionless number problem. Turlough said "minus four" but he was wrong. It is "minus two".'

'Does it matter?' asked Turlough with a pained smile. 'I'm not sure these creatures are going to be particularly worried.' Then he too turned to the creatures and addressed them.

'We come from a planet called Trion. Our world has been destroyed by nuclear explosions just as this one. We are here to try and work out who is responsible, and if there is a link between the two planets.'

'Why should there be a link?'

'There is no solid evidence – only circumstance. The race we call Gardsormr, and which in the mythology of Earth is called Midgardsormr have shown a great deal of interest in both

160

planets. We think they are responsible. It might be that these slugs – Land Snails – are their children.'

'We know the Midgardsormr,' said the creature.

'But we cannot read minds like you,' said Juras. 'Tell us about it.'

The two creatures in the centre of the room turned slightly to each other as if conferring. The second one took up the story. Its voice was deeper and more stable. It was almost certainly male.

'The legend of Earth says Midgardsormr is the serpent of the world. At the time of the great crisis, it rose from the sea and flooded the world. Midgardsormr fought the final Lord of Earth at sea, but the great boats of the Lord capsized and the Lord was defeated. Then Surtr destroyed mankind with fire, burning up the corpses as he travelled.' The voice of the crippled deformed creature was emotionless.

'How did you escape?' asked Juras.

'A few sentinels do penance and serve Midgardsormr lest Surtr return.'

'And the Land Snails?'

'Surtr left the land and travelled to the sky, and those left were unable to feed themselves well. Then the Midgardsormr put down foundations to grow the Land Snails. We are the servants, and we process food for the Midgardsormr. In return the Midgardsormr give us food for ourselves as he rests above the clouds gathering strength for the next great battle.'

'WHen you process the food do you see the Midgardsormr?'

'No one sees Midgardsormr.'

'What do you do?'

'We take the Land Snail to the north village and leave it. The New Ones deal with it and leave us food.'

Turlough and Juras lapsed into silence. Turlough took a look at the Time Lord, but he gave out his standard attitude of self-satisfaction. It offered no clue. It was time to leave, he thought.

'You must stay here,' said the servant of Midgardsormr, reading Turlough's mind once more. 'The Midgardsormr will decide what must happen.' And with that they left the room.

'What now?' asked Juras.

'Whatever it is,' Turlough told her, 'it must be a surprise to all of us. Those creatures read minds remember.'

'Not necessarily all the time.' It was The Magician. He had got into the habit of speaking so rarely that his sudden statement caused some surprise. He continued, 'Before I inadvertently fell off the bricks two of those creatures were working away inside the outbuilding, and showed no sign of knowing we were there. Either their mind reading works only over very short distances, or they have to be alerted to the need to mind-read before they do. We may be safer than you imagine.'

'I don't particularly want to be safe in here,' protested Juras, looking about. Certainly the room was singularly bleak. On the other hand it did not look totally secure. The boards at the windows particularly looked of a type that would pull away with one heave. Juras walked over, determined to give it a try. Yet as she put her hand up to the boards there appeared a resistance that pushed her away. She tried several times, but failed to get within the last few centimetres, no matter how hard she pushed. Turlough, seeing the problem came over and gave it a try himself, but suffered the same fate. Juras tried the door, which looked equally rickety and insecure. Yet that caused her the same problem. Juras and Turlough returned to the centre of the room where The Magician remained seated.

'This technology is odd in such people,' observed Juras.

'You mean if they can do this, what are they doing cutting up giant slugs for alien benefactors?' said Turlough.

'And come to that why exist in such primitive surroundings and believe in fairy story myths? Have they always been telepaths on this planet?'

'No,' said Turlough, 'it must be a side effect of the radiation, or some sort of recent mutation.' Then he added, 'I've seen this technology before. At the Slotsruin – and the Slot we met after we landed on Earth said that the Slotsruin had come to life to protect them from the radiation when the island landed.'

'So how did Slots' technology get into the hands of these primitives?'

'You have two choices in deciding what to do,' said The Magician.

'More games?' asked Turlough sarcastically.

'Perhaps,' The Magician told him. 'But they may help you out of a jam.'

'Tell us the alternatives,' commanded Juras.

'You can sit, debate and wait for something to happen – which could mean either a short or long period of time, or you can try and initiate action.'

'Quite brilliantly argued,' said Turlough, his voice heavy with sarcasm. 'What would you do?'

'Not for me to say, dear boy,' The Magician told him, reverting to his most annoying stance in relation to contemporary events.

Juras, however was more willing to pursue The Magician's ideas. 'What sort of action?' she asked.

'Escape of course,' said Turlough before the Time Lord had time to answer. He got up and paced the room looking for possible exits. But as was immediately apparent, apart from the door and boarded window, there was no way out. The walls were brick, the floor concrete, and the ceiling, although probably only plasterboard was well out of reach. Lacking any other action Turlough began walking round the walls hitting them every few paces in the hope of possibly activating a trap door, or maybe finding a section that was not brick after all. He completed his tour having had no luck but having gained a very bruised fist, and sat down disconsolately. 'We have to take some action,' he said. 'There's no telling if these Earthmen are going to feed us, or come to that wht they are going to feed us on. I, for one, do not intend to sit around waiting for a meal of sliced slug.'

'What is the weakest part of the room?' asked The Magician.

'The entrance and the window,' said Turlough automatically. It was a standard question, which always had the same standard answer.

'And how do you open them?'

Turlough refrained from more sarcasm, and thought. So far they had tried either himself or Juras pushing. It was time for greater experimentation. 'Push on the shutters again,' Turlough commanded. Juras did as she was told. 'You too, Magician,' he said, and the Time Lord himself took up a place.

Turlough then added his two hands. For a moment it looked as if none of this would have any effect. All six hands were restrained by the invisible barrier, but slowly it became clear that the barrier was heating up. After thirty seconds it was getting uncomfortably hot. Fifteen seconds more and Juras removed her hands, rubbing them to remove the heat that had built up on her palms. Rapidly Turlough and The Magician followed her example.

By now the wooden shutters appeared to be glowing. Turlough retreated across the room and picked up some small bricks. Gesturing for his companions to get out of the way he flung the rubble with all his might at the window. There was a sizzling sound as the stones, rather than bouncing back from the force wall were absorbed by it. Turlough repeated the exercise. The same result occurred. 'Help me throw more,' said Turlough. 'The force field is absorbing energy, and that is causing it to heat up. There must be a critical level to hit soon.'

Rapidly the room was emptied of the accumulated rubbish on the floor as it was hurled at the gap. As more went in so the colour changed, glowing first red, then blue and finally white. But the bricks, stone and cement chippings on the floor were exhausted and still the force field refused to blow. Although it continued to allow the rubble through there was no indication that it would not return to its original form when allowed to cool, and cool it certainly would unless more material could be thrown at it in the very near future.

Turlough could think of nothing else to do. In desperation he turned to The Magician. 'Ask me a question!' he commanded. 'I must know what to do next.'

'What choices do you have?' asked The Magician obligingly.

'We can wait till it cools down and see if anything happens, or try and leap through it now whilst it's still white hot.'

'Fine,' said The Magician, without explaining himself further. Turlough felt that on this occasion he had hardly got value for money. Without asking for opinions he could guess that there would be general agreement against trying to leap through. They awaited the result of the cooling process.

To Turlough's total surprise the result was positive. Even before totally cool it was clear that the wooden boards over the window had themselves suffered in the heat, and it soon became possible to assert that the force wall was likewise damaged. There was still an unpleasant repulsion, but it was now possible to touch the board. Turlough walked across the desolate room, took a run at the window, launched himself at it, and hit it shoulder on. He woke up seconds later on the pathway outside, every muscle in his body aching. Juras and The Magician stepped through after him, confirming that this final action on Turlough's part had removed the force field totally.

'They took leaps like tht all the time on television when I was here before,' said Turlough, picking himself up. 'I had no idea it would hurt so much.' He rubbed his shoulder again. In the near future, he knew, there was going to be a very large bruise down one side of his body, from where he had hit the window, and another bruise on his back from where he had hit the path.

There was immediate agreement that they should now conclude the journey around the building they had been trying to make before imprisonment. Hungry and tired, but nevertheless with greater caution than they had shown on the way in they began the long trek back to the Neutrinova.

Dusk was falling by the time they reached the edge of the city, and their ship was almost lost in the gloom. As they passed the last ruined house Turlough heard a noise behind. Hurriedly he ushered the others down a slight slope and into the cover of the crumbling walls. Within seconds a small truck pulling an empty trailer drove by, and disappeared into the half light of the plain. It was the same vehicle, or at least a similar one to the one they had seen the night before. Despite the dimness they were able to make out the driver. It looked like a Slot . . .

Turlough was about to comment on this fact when he felt a sharp twinge in the centre of his back. The pain increased fivefold. 'Don't move,' commanded a voice, presumably in direct relationship with the pain in Turlough's back. 'Just tell me what you think you're doing.' The voice was deep and husky; nothing like that of the telepaths that had imprisoned them.

'Staying out of the way of the trailer that went by,' replied Turlough honestly.

'And why would you do that? You look to me like the sort of people who would be ready to spend time with those aliens.'

'Because we have just spent the best part of today imprisoned by a group of creatures that may well be related to them,' Turlough told the man.

The pain in his back relaxed a little. Turlough tried to move, but found that the pressure returned to maximum. 'Who are you, where are you from?' They were questions asked a million times a day of travellers between the stars. Turlough performed the introductions.

'You own that little ship on the plain?' asked the man. Turlough agreed. The pain in his back vanished completely. Cautiously he turned. He was facing a man, thankfully normal in appearance, about thirty, suntanned and dressed in clothes that befitted a rugged outdoor life. 'David Swallow,' the man introduced himself. The pain in Turlough's back was revealed to have been caused by the barrels of a rifle. Behind the man in the ever deepening gloom Turlough could make out another figure, a woman. 'Erica,' he added, following Turlough's gaze. The woman came forward. She too carried a rifle (it had been in Turlough's back) and also wore the practical clothes befitting a hard life. Yet the couple looked well-fed and healthy, in total contrast to the creatures they had found in the town.

Erica led the way beyond the crumbling walls and into a back room of a nearly intact house. She lit a gas lamp. The place was well stocked with cans of food. A small gas stove stood in one corner. 'Tell me your story,' commanded David Swallow, as they all took seats. He put his rifle down near enough for him to grab if need be. It was almost as if the man had carefully calculated where the chairs should be in relation to the door, himself and the rifle. Even the old movie trick of tipping the table up against the man wouldn't work. It was screwed to the floor.

Turlough gave a full account. Whilst talking he reflected that much must have happened on the planet since he had met the Doctor here. Apart from the obvious effects of nuclear fallout, there was now an apparent acceptance of space travel, aliens, and goodness knows what else. Things had changed fast. Too fast.

When he had finished his story Turlough asked if David Swallow would reciprocate. He seemed almost delighted to do so. 'History is patchy now,' he said, 'so I don't guarantee total accuracy, but I can tell you the stories handed down.

'There was a war, you'll have realised that much, although the legends have it that it was as much a mistake as anything. One side or the other thought the opposition was launching missiles, and sent out their defence systems to knock the things down. In fact there weren't any missiles, just an enormous meteor, the likes of which hadn't been seen before. So the missiles hit the meteor, and the whole lot crashed into the Atlantic. There were tidal waves and wholesale destruction whilst the super powers knocked hell out of each other. In the end there was just a burnt-out wasteland. A surprising number survived, although many were totally deformed and quickly died. A few did all right though and started putting some sort of society back together in the parts of the countryside that didn't actually glow at you through the night, although I think everyone knew that even the survivors must have picked up so much radiation that their children, if they had any, would hardly be normal.

'Then out of the blue the spaceships land. Spherical things, flattened at the top, and they start rounding up all the humans they can find who are fit enough; get them to build domes – you must have seen them near your ship. There are thousands of those things located right across the country – perhaps in countries too for all I know.'

'Did you ever see the creatures from the ships?' asked Turlough.

'No – they used little round things to push us around and give instructions. Turned nasty on you if you didn't do what they said. Anyway, the work wasn't too hard – they had all the right equipment, and they provided food. So we built the domes – I was just a kid at the time but still got drafted in. Then when the building was done they just let us go. That was a bit of a shock for some people, because we'd all got used to the slave way of life, plus the daily supply of food.

'So a lot of people hung around the domes waiting for something to happen, but it didn't. At least not much. The spheres moved things in and out, but kept the doors locked and we could never see what they were up to. And there was no more food so people were forced to come back into the cities to find supplies. There were still enough tins, and the population was small so we made out OK. The next thing we realised the radiation level was down–right down to zero everywhere.'

'How long did that take?' asked Juras.

'About a year I'd guess although without proper instrumentation it was hard to judge. But we had a fellow with us at the time who used to work in the nuclear industry and he made a few tests. According to him the level dropped far too far, far too fast. It was almost as if the radiation was being sucked out of the atmosphere and the ground. And out of the people too. The deformities went, the ground began to grow food. Over the other side of the city there's a little community springing up, good and strong. We call it Eden.'

'Why aren't you there with them?'

'We are the watch. Watching the trucks pull in and out. After the radiation had gone right down the spheres came back. We thought they might be interested in more labour, so we prepared ourselves to say no–by then everyone was more concerned in just working in the fields and getting things back together again. But they didn't take anyone, they were more interested in bringing in their own workers, the Pharix. Horrible deformed creatures they are too.'

'We met them,' said Juras with a shiver, 'cutting up the Land Snails from the domes.'

'They work for the spheres and get food in return. But who they are or what they are we don't know. The trucks come in every night bringing in a new carcass. We just watch to make sure that is all that happens. Eden is guarded, and there's a watch on all roads. There is no way in without our knowing.'

'We got by,' said Turlough with unnecessary bravado.

'And didn't know we were following you. You got caught by

168

the slaughter house and spent an hour trying to get out. Do you think we would trust you this much if we hadn't seen you gawping at the Land Snail in the shed, and seen the mess you made of getting out of the grasp of those creatures?'

'What happens to the bits of the Land Snail after it has been killed?'

'The Pharix keep some of it and the truck drivers take away the rest for burial.'

'Burial – where?'

'Everywhere, anywhere. In the city, in the desert, in Eden. We get a delivery by truck each day.'

'You take dead Land Snails in Eden?' said Turlough disbelievingly. 'Apart from the stench the whole operation is revolting – macabre. Why do it?'

'The stench is bearable,' David Swallow told him, 'and it is the rotting flesh of the Land Snails that makes the ground good for harvesting. It makes things grow – fast.'

'So that is why there are pockets of grassland among the desert,' said Juras.

'If you've seen them, you've seen a graveyard of the Land Snails.'

There was silence in the room. Outside it was now dark, a half moon illuminating the clear sky. Turlough felt tired. A shiver went through his body.

'We need to get back,' he said. 'And then we need to find who or what is behind this whole operation.' Erica and David Swallow made no objection to their group leaving, and watched from their derelict house as the little group slowly made the long walk back across the plain. Only this time they had far less enthusiasm for walking through the glades.

Turlough slept fitfully on the floor of the tiny craft, images of the horrors he had witnessed in the outbuilding seeping irresistibly into his mind. In the morning he rose before the others and left the Neutrinova staring out across the plain back towards the ruined city. On the far side, he knew, was Eden, a community suddenly sprouting new life from a ground that by all theories of science should be totally barren.

Turlough turned the problem over and over in his mind, yet it would still make no sense. The story of the meteor colliding with the Earth and starting a nuclear war sounded so similar to the events that he had helped initiate on Trion that there had to be a connection. Which simply added to the belief that Turlough held that the Gardsormr were behind the whole operation. Yet there was little else he could glean from the story David Swallow had told him. If the slugs were the young of the Gardsormr who was arranging for them to be killed off? And why bother just to feed the deformed telepaths they had met in the city centre? Or perhaps the idea was to refurbish the Earth itself. But if so who could be behind it? Not the people of Eden, for if what David Swallow had said was true, they had been participants in the affair without knowing why, who, or how. Now they were beneficiaries, keeping watch in an attempt to ensure that what they had been given was not removed.

Was it really the Land Snails that caused the end of the fallout, as the story implied? If so that was just another element that made no sense. And what of the Slots? He had met one already, and was certain that the driver of the truck carrying the carcass the previous evening had himself been Slot. What possible connection could they have with the whole operation? Turlough walked back into the small craft determined to confront The Magician with his problems, but before he could speak the Time Lord approached him. 'Information,' he said, 'that is what is needed. Use of the brain – intuition combined with learning. A tactical approach carefully thought out. The maths of possibility.' He seemed pleased with his statement.

'I was about to tell you that,' said Turlough.

'Information,' continued The Magician, 'is bought, never found.'

'I don't seem to be using the right currency,' said Turlough grimly.

Together they stood at the entrance to the little craft and looked across the plain. A moment later Juras joined them. 'There's a ship coming down,' she said. Turlough and The Magician turned to look at the screen. The ship was large – and spherical with that distinguishing flattening on the top. The Gardsormr were coming into land.

'They're coming down right on top of us!' shouted Turlough.

Immediately he sat at the control desk, and prepared to take off. But it was too late – there were ships landing all around him.

The Magician laid a firm hand on Turlough's shoulder. 'This is your information, landing at your doorstep. If the spheres are the key to the problem then seek out your information, do not run away. Find the truth – and use all options that present themselves. Devour knowledge, be a mental omnivore, that is the way to reality.'

Turlough was beginning to get the idea that much of what The Magician said was making little sense, but he let the matter pass. Nervously he turned away from the controls and prepared to meet the occupants of the spheres.

Eight ships landed in all, forming a perfect circle around the Neutrinova. Despite the insistence of The Magician that this was the great opportunity to meet the enemy at last, Turlough and Juras opted to keep the ship firmly closed to the outside, and watch developments on the screens. At first it looked as if the occupants of the ship were doing the same, although as an increasingly excited Magician pointed out, to land in such a formation must mean that the ships' occupants were ready to do business. Then doors opened simultaneously in each of the spheres and out came the sinisterly familiar Gardsormr machines, floating a metre off the ground. Turlough and Juras were already very clear that there was no way in which they were going to do business with the spheres, after their experience on the way to New Trion. This time it was Gardsormr proper or nothing.

The spheres surrounded the Neutrinova and remained hovering. Turlough kept the ARTEMIS controls on line ready for a rapid ascent and dash back in time should the spheres attempt any sort of attack. Silence pervaded. Eventually they grew to taking watch in turns, Turlough and Juras calm and impassive, The Magician, now in a totally new role, excited and anxious for developments. As evening drew on Turlough turned to the Time Lord. 'Perhaps you would care to take a walk outside and introduce yourself to the spheres?' he asked.

It was not meant seriously but the Gallifreyan's entrancement with an occasion which had so far revealed nothing was becoming unbearable.

'Not my place, old boy,' said The Magician inevitably. 'It is your destiny. Out there is your future. This will be a monumentous occasion, remembered through the annals of time itself. Were I to go it would mean nothing. Nothing at all. Take heart and go forth. Prepare for immortality. Memory in perpetuity.'

'Why don't you just tell us what the future holds and then we can get on with it?' said Juras.

'Because that is not how it works and besides you would remove from history one of its greatest moments,' said The Magician. He would allow the matter to be debated no further.

Juras continued to watch the screens. Across the plain the nightly truck for the dome was making its regular journey. The spheres took no notice. Events followed their normal course. The return truck, weighed down with the half-dead Land Snail made its way back to the city in the dying light. Unseen in the distance David Swallow and Erica sat in their ruined house and watched it go by.

Without warning the control panel sprang to life. 'Trions,' it said. The voice was hard and metallic, just as before. 'What do you seek on this planet?'

'Answers to a million questions,' said Turlough.

There was a burst of static on the voice channel. It was so unusual to find interference of that type on communications at such a close distance Juras and Turlough both instinctively looked at the controls. All indications were normal. They took their eyes off the screens for just one second. It took another few seconds to refocus and yet more time to readjust their eyes to the dark outside after the brightness of the green control lights. And at the end they were left looking at the unmistakeable telltale lights of combined grabbing and scanning beams. There was now no chance of physical escape, and temporal escape was impossible without sufficient motion to power the ARTEMIS drive. Once more the Gardsormr had trapped them.

The voice came back on. 'Clansmen,' it said, 'you are

172

caught. Leave your ship and walk across.'

Turlough and Juras looked at each other, or rather Juras looked at Turlough and Turlough looked at the blank haze that had come over Juras's eyes. He had seen that look once before on the island – and that was not one of his favourite memories. She was walking towards Turlough, hands outstretched, although at least this time she wasn't carrying a sword.

Turlough backed off and glanced quickly at The Magician. He was grinning and showed no sign of wanting to interfere at all. Behind Juras Turlough could see the bank of screens. They showed the Gardsormr's ships. On one of them a door was opening. A figure emerged, walking onto the dry plain. It was humanoid – an elderly man. There was something disturbingly familiar about him. Something so disturbing that Turlough forgot the threat of Juras, and the unaccountable behaviour of The Magician.

The old man strolled slowly across to the Neutrinova. Turlough couldn't keep his eyes off him. When Juras leant past to double seal the hatch of the Neutrinova Turlough didn't know quite what to make of it. It was not until the girl's hands went firmly to his neck and began a good impression of attempting to strangle him did Turlough react. He pulled his arm forward and then pushed backwards with all his might. The elbow made contact directly with Juras's stomach, and she doubled up on the floor. Still with one eye on the screens Turlough turned slightly and grabbed the girl, punching her on the jaw with every gramme of strength he could muster. She fell and lay motionless. Turlough turned back to the screen and looked directly at the man now stationary outside the Neutrinova. He was now nearly at the little ship. What was it that was so oddly reminiscent?

The old man was waiting for the door to be opened. Juras lay still on the floor, no sign of life coming from her save erratic breathing. 'Go forth,' whispered The Magician, 'seek knowledge. Learn, do not hide.' The Magician's eyes moved from Turlough to the old man on the screen, gleaming with excitement. Whatever was going on, this was the moment he had been waiting for. Turlough released the locks and opened the door. He stepped out into the cool night air and stood facing his visitor.

'You can't be Gardsormr,' said Turlough. His voice was strained. It was hard to get the words out.

The old man looked back at him. He was tall and gaunt, his features thinned by age, but still showing a strength of character. The fair hair had been allowed to grow long and lay across his face and down onto his collar. The one-piece flight suit was incongruous in a man who, in other surroundings, would be seen as being of dignity and importance.

'Turlough!' The old man was content to just stare at the occupant of the Neutrinova. He had said the name. For a moment that seemed enough. He showed desire neither to enter the ship, nor to approach closer to Turlough.

Turlough struggled to free himself of the atmosphere that had developed around the meeting. It was cloying at his brain, stopping his thought process. 'What are you?' he demanded.

'You are wrong in your assumptions,' the old man told him. 'I *am* your Gardsormr. I am also Turlough.'

Turlough looked at The Magician who had come to his side. 'What is going on?' he demanded. The Time Lord refused to answer.

'I am Turlough,' repeated the old man. 'Do you not recognise yourself, even through the ravages of age? I am you!'

'It can't be!' shouted Turlough defiantly. 'None of this is possible.'

The old man sighed. 'How long have I waited for this moment – yet have I waited to be shouted at by my own youth? Turlough – I have heard a million people speak of me throughout the years. I hear what they say, and I have long since passed beyond any false modesty and personal doubts that used to cloud my judgement. Now in old age I have the luxury of others to do my work, others who are kind enough to recall what I was in youth – what you are becoming.

'Turlough, I was, you are, possessed of skills and abilities beyond the realm of most. And yet you, I, we are pulled all ways. You are not the material of heroes. You can be misled, misguided. You think of yourself, and then you are troubled by your wonderings. Let me gaze at you, Turlough

– let me gaze at my own youth, for I bring you a message of your potential future. A message that can save everything.'

Yet still Turlough was not convinced. 'Why should I believe anything you say?' he called urgently. 'What proof is there?'

'How do you prove to yourself that you are who you claim to be?' asked the old man. 'Do you look in a mirror and question your validity? Do you walk the streets and say, "Prove to me who I am"? Be patient, Turlough, and listen, and then take that step forward which can protect the galaxy from a disaster of such magnitude that even now I find it impossible to comprehend.'

'Very well,' said Turlough ungraciously. 'Say your piece, but I offer no guarantees to believe anything you say.'

But the old man did not begin, instead he continued to look at Turlough, muttering occasionally about the impetuosity of youth, and how long he had waited to meet it. Then at last he gathered his thoughts back together. He asked if he could step inside the Neutrinova and rest his weary legs. Reluctantly Turlough agreed. The Magician made room. Juras, a glazed look still in her eyes, remained flat out on the floor. The old man continued his exposition.

'You reject it now that I could be you, but you are fascinated by the concept – and rightly so. Yet what seeps into your mind more is the thought of saving some part of our civilisation. Oh, you are not philanthropic, I know, but you are quick, and devious, just as I have remained even in old age. And that mind of yours already knows that what I'm talking about means knowledge. Knowledge must always mean power if handled right. You are not a leader, Turlough, not in the sense of standing up and controlling men on the battlefield. But you can be a leader in the use of knowledge, using it in your own way for your own purpose. You will always retain something that could be a moral code lurking behind. You will act on what I say, for that reason: devious but moral. That is Vislor Turlough.'

Turlough remained dismissive. 'Like The Magician, you are form the future, so you know it will happen.' He disliked being used more than anything.

'You are young, Turlough,' said the old man, 'and you make the mistakes of youth of believing you know more than you do. I will give you one hint – you can go and solve the problem in detail at your leisure. The solution, if you get it right, can be your lasting testimonial. Time-space is a duality, not a singularity. It exists as a linear development – time passes, you grow older. With that you must not interfere. But it exists also – at the same time – in discontinuities. Put simply, I am from one timestream, but not necessarily from the one that you will move into. Ignore wht I say and you will increase the chances of entering my time-space. Take note of my words and life will be better for you.'

Turlough looked thoughtfully at the old man, and glanced once more across at The Magician. The old man caught the eye movement. 'You place too much belief in your Time Lord frinds. They like to believe themselves unique, but they are not. You will see.'

'Very well. Tell me what you have come to say. I will reserve judgement, and hear you in peace.'

The old man drew a deep breath and settled back further in his chair. 'In my timestream there was an authoritarian regime running Trion, a regime that was quite rightly abhorrent to anyone feeling for the legitimate activities of the Clans. The regime grew and developed and looked for allies beyond the natural sphere of influence of the Home Planet. Few systems wanted to know such a regime, although to their eternal discredit there were one or two whose own position on the rights of citizens were hardly wonderful. And meanwhile the citizens of Trion continued to support the regime using the vidcasts to caricature anyone who dared oppose their leader Rehctaht.'

'You are just telling me the history of my own time,' said Turlough.

The old man continued as if nothing had been said. 'In this situation Rehctaht grabbed any potential ally she could find, and so when the Gardsormr came along she accepted them even though she could not see them. They claimed to influence a wide area of support throughout much of the galaxy, but in reality the Gardsormr were her own kind – a small number of Clansmen from Trion opposed to her and all she stood for.

'We had no clear idea of what we would achieve, but it was a plan. Rehctaht, we discovered, was well aware of the political isolation that her fanaticism was developing. And in her growing madness came the idea that the Clans had betrayed the ordinary people of Trion. She believed that there were areas of science that they had deliberately kept from her, and she set up laboratories to discover those imagined new sciences.

'What could be done in such circumstances? Most Clansmen were exiled, some even killed. The few who remained worked for the madwoman. Thus it was, Turlough, that a small number of us formed a mysterious and supposedly alien force. We took the name from Earth, and called ourselves Gardsormr. The Gardsormr gave Rehctaht what she craved – allies – whilst seeking to undermine what she was doing, and to lessen the effects her madness was having on planets throughout the galaxy. The Gardsormr became the resistance.

'Eventually of course she was swept from power and the New Regime took over. Unfortunately, those who now found themselves in control, although massively preferable to Rehctaht, could not let go the reins themselves. Even those who had joined the Gardsormr felt that they too should have some sort of special recognition of what they had done. So the New Regime announced to an unsuspecting public that an alliance had been forged with the Gardsormr – which was a way of creating a myth which in turn would allow those in power to retain it. After all knowledge is power – as you well know.'

The old man paused and looked deeply at Juras lying on the floor. Turlough was dissatisfied.

'But if the Gardsormr really are allies, albeit rather twisted ones, who set up the prison planet, who caused the desolation on Earth, who tipped the island onto Trion, who controls the Land Snails? Your explanation is an excuse. It clears up nothing.'

'The ultimate answer to your problems is Rehctaht. Even New Trion was set up by her as a source of slave labour for some other wild scheme which she later forgot as crisis piled upon crisis. The Gardsormr have sought only to minimise the effects of her actions, and to rectify some of the damage. In your time continuum the mad woman still exists. Find her and you find all solutions. And that is my message to you, my own youth. Do not get diverted into the politics of the Home Planet, as I did. Until now in your confusion you have seen the Gardsormr as monsters. They are not. I played the political game for my own ends. My message to you is to ensure that your Turlough treads a straighter path. Find Rehctaht, destroy her. That will liberate Trion, secure your freedom and save the Clans. Nothing else will do.'

The old man stood, his hands behind his back helping him stretch. The speech seemed to have tired him – he was ready to return to his ship. But Turlough was still unsure.

'If I'm to believe your message, I need more information. Where do I find Rehctaht? How do I find her? And what about The Magician and Juras? What about the link with Earth – why choose a name from Earth for the Gardsormr? You must tell me more.'

But the old man was already half-way through the door. He looked back. 'Two more thoughs then,' he said. 'Take care of Juras Maateh, and believe all possibilities are probable.'

And with that he turned to his ship, and was gone.

11: KNAVE

No sooner had the old man disappeared into his ship than Juras came back to life. She opened her eyes, stared hard about her, looked curiously at Turlough, and then without a word moved across the room to the simple bunk, lay down and fell asleep. Meanwhile The Magician kept his gaze on Turlough, that annoying half-smile as always on his face.

Turlough turned and faced the screens disconsolantly watching the ring of ships around the Neutrinova take off in splendid formation. He stayed motionless as the exhaust jets switched off and the infinitely more powerful cold fusion took over, heaving the metal beyond the atmosphere and into the emptiness beyond. He could feel the eyes of the Time Lord still upon him once the screens had gone blank, but he refused to turn round. Instead he stayed staring at the scene outside, his mind turning over and over the ideas that the old man had put before him.

It did not take long to realise what his mind was trying to do – striving to find reasons for disbelieving that he had just met himself. It left him back at square one. Who, or what, was he chasing? Thinking he was after the Gardsormr, and having information about the nature of their ships it looked as if he at least had an identifiable quarry, even if he didn't quite know what to do with them when he found them. But now, told to chase the supposedly dead Rehctaht, he was left with more of a problem. It was that problem he was seeking to avoid by denying what his future self had told him.

Yet on the other hand he had gained one interesting piece of information. Time was not linear, as he had always presumed. And that made his heart beat a lot faster.

179

Without warning Turlough got up and faced The Magician. 'Stay and watch Juras,' he said as he walked out of the ship and started the trek across the plain towards the city.

Two hours later he entered the derelict house in which he had met David Swallow and Erica. There was no sign of either inhabitant. Turlough looked in each of the rooms but beyond the empty cans and eating utensils there was nothing. He turned to leave. As he did, an arm came round his neck and a knife blade pushed against his throat.

'No more trick talk,' came a voice from behind. 'Who are you, what are you?'

'Vislor Turlough, Clansman of Trion,' he replied automatically. 'If you know David Swallow you'll know more about me. I told him everything.'

'You told him a pack of lies,' was the reply. The man holding the knife clearly had no intention of letting go. 'You told him you were operating with your two pals. And what do we find? No sooner have you left here than you meet up with an entire fleet of ships. Now I ask myself, why should you keep that a secret? And I don't like the answer.'

'I had no idea they were coming,' said Turlough.

'Who were they?'

'You'd never believe me,' replied the young Clansman with a sigh.

'Try me.'

'My future self, come to warn me and offer advice,' replied Turlough. He knew what was coming next.

The grip on his neck tightened. 'You are right,' said the voice. 'I'll never believe you.' Without warning Turlough was pushed forward. He stumbled over some broken brick on the ground, but kept going. He was forced outside. Arms pinned behind his back Turlough was propelled through the dusty streets. After five minutes he saw two others come towards him. Strong men, unshaven, and dressed in the manner of David Swallow.

'I didn't have to go looking,' said the man holding one arm behind Turlough's back. 'He came back.' There was a moment's laughter and an exchange of words that Turlough could not fully catch, before Turlough was led round a corner and bundled into the back of a van. The door shut with a bang, and Turlough was left alone. He spent several moments rubbing his bruised arm before venturing to the tiny windows that looked out of the van. As he did there was a jerk and the vehicle moved forward across the disintegrating roadways.

They drove for twenty minutes through what must have once been the commercial centre of the city and then past waste land and the limits of the old town. All around was desert. Then the van stopped, the door was opened and Turlough was pulled onto rocky ground. To one side the land was as he had seen – desolate, bare, uninviting. But on the other side of the van was a total contrast. Behind a low wooden wall a large expanse of cultivated fields – an oasis of colour in the drab desert.

Turlough was roughly pushed through a small gap in the fence towards a group of huts that stood at the centre of the plantation. Inside he found the inevitable reception committee – four men and two women. Several had knives in their hands and left Turlough with little doubt of their ability to use them.

David Swallow stepped forward from the group. 'You are more than you would make out,' he said menacingly.

'I told you everything when we met yesterday,' Turlough replied. 'I've also told these two,' (he nodded towards his captors) 'how much I was surprised by events this morning. I seem to be dragged along in a series of happenings that I can't control and don't fully understand. My aim is, as I said, to gain revenge over those who destroyed my planet. And since whoever, or whatever, it was seems to also have an interest in Earth, I am here to find the link.'

'And just who, or what, do you think is responsible?' asked the leader.

'Until yesterday I believed it was an alien race called Gardsormr. Now I am not so sure. It may be the doing of the previous ruler of my Home Planet – a madwoman called Rehctaht.'

'How do you expect to find either of these alien creatures or this madwoman.'

'At present,' said Turlough evenly, 'I have no idea, although

I had rather hoped you would help me with that. There may be a connection with the Pharix telepaths that removed the Land Snails from the domes. The slugs, Pharix, the Slot that drives the trucks to and from the domes, those space ships that surrounded me last night – the result for you is one of benefit. Why set up a complex system to help you grow food?'

There was a silence. Members of the group looked from one to another. Whatever they had expected from Turlough it was not that. Emboldened, Turlough repeated his question.

David Swallow answered, quietly and uncertain lest he be reprimanded by one of the others. 'They bring the creatures to us; we don't know why. We bury them, they make the land grow fertile.'

'But it's more than fertility,' said Turlough. 'To have achieved such an abundance in the middle of the desert in the last three years means a rate of growth far beyond anything normal or natural. I lived on this planet before the nuclear war, and I know what used to happen here.'

There was another awkward silence. No one seemed willing to take the lead.

At last one of the men said, 'I might believe your story for the simple reason that it makes no sense.' Turlough looked puzzled, but the leader continued before he had time to interrupt. 'In not understanding the situation you share something in common with us. We have no idea why the Pharix telepaths come to us, why they leave us the Land Snails, or why they even go through their ritual slaughter every day. But they do, and without them we would have no Eden, no life. We post our guards at the south of the old town, and they watch and wait for any sign or clue that would actually report to us what is going on. We hoped at first that through the arrival of yourselves, then the second alien ship, and finally the whole fleet that we would be able to resolve matters. But I believe we cannot.'

'The transporter that drives the Land Snail to the telepaths: does it also then bring the cut-up pieces here?'

The leader agreed that was so; it happened every day. 'Then that is what I need to see,' said Turlough.

'There is no objection to seeing,' said the leader. 'We are, despite all our race has been through, still human beings. We still have a curiosity, a need to know. But we fear, and some of us fear more than others, that interference in these inexplicable actions by the Pharix and their alien drivers could lead to their stopping the deliveries. Our land would cease to be so abundant and we would suffer. Curiosity, if you know the old saying, killed the cat. And even the most curious of us does not intend to become a cat.'

'I'll be sure not to arouse suspicion,' said Turlough.

'The truck arrives in about twenty minutes. Observe it from behind the perimiter.'

Turlough was escorted from the central meeting room to the fence, and forced to sit on the lush grass. On time, and exactly as predicted, the truck arrived. Turlough peeped out over the fence, and saw several local inhabitants go out to meet the truck. They walked alongside it indicating where they wanted it parked. Turlough got to his feet and followed at a dicreet distance accompanied by the leader, David Swallow and several others from the reception committee. The truck, under instruction, swung in a wide arc around the edge of the settlement to a place on the far side where the barren desert met the lush grass. A huge pit had been dug close by. The driver stopped the vehicle, activated internal levers commanding the rear door to swing open. As it did the entire back section began to rise, tilting at an angle allowing the putrifying flesh to pour out into the ditch. As it went in so the residents set to work with spades filling in the whole area. Within thirty seconds the truck was empty as others came forward to rebuild the fencing to encompass the area where the Land Snail had been buried.

Whilst this was going on the rear of the truck was lowered as the driver prepared to return to the town. So engrossed had Turlough been in the way in which the snail was transferred from truck to ground that he had almost forgotten his main task of getting a close-up look of the driver. Suddenly he leapt up from his position behind a clump of trees and ran towards the truck. Even if he himself had not caught the driver's attention there was no doubt that the angry shouts of his captors would have brought the face of the driver around. Seeing him clearly, and suddenly remembering his promise, Turlough stopped, thus making himself even more exposed than before. The engine on the truck stopped. Slowly the cabin door opened and the driver got out. Those around Turlough ceased to work. Never before had there been such an event. All stood frozen in the no man's land of half-grass, half-desert just beyond the boundary of the village.

At his own pace the driver walked towards Turlough. There was no mistaking the long strides, the tallness of the frame. It was a Slot. And not any Slot, but *the* Slot. The Slot Turlough had met on the Home Planet. The Slot who had arrived so recently and talked to Turlough on the far side of the plain.

The alien stood in front of Turlough and looked down at him. 'You are still searching,' he said. Turlough said nothing. He could find no response. 'And you have met your older self. That is good. We are working to the same end, you and I. Do not forget. Time and gravity, here and now. That is the key.' And with that the creature returned to the truck and rapidly drove off back to the town, and presumably then on to the domes once more to keep up the macabre routine.

'So you do know more than us!' said the leader, hand on rifle, as he watched the dust storm created by the truck settle down.

Turlough turned to the man and looked at him. 'What I have told you is true,' said Turlough. 'Every event confuses me more. Especially that one. I met the alien on my planet when I was checking out the old ruins of past civilizations. I had a thought that since beings called Gardsormr existed both here and in relation to Trion maybe there was something in the myths of old civilizations on the two planets that linked them. He is a Slot – they are reputed to be much older than other inhabitants of Trion, older even than the Imperial Clans. Yet they are restricted to just one island. I had no idea they even had space travel, let alone time-travel and an interest in Earth. He certainly knows what is going on. What I need to know is why he won't tell me.'

There was no answer from the others as they walked back to the centre of the village. Apparently satisfied that Turlough was no immediate threat to them the group drifted away, leaving him in the company of David Swallow. The two men

184

sat on chairs by a crude wooden table in the shade of an oak. It looked as if it had been there for eighty years or more, but given the background of the village could not have been planted more than two or three years ago. It was yet another sign of the power of the nutrients that came from the Land Snails.

Somewhere, mused Turlough there was a key. A key, which the Slot, which The Magician and which his older self all confidently expected him to find. Ask the right question, he felt, and he would find that right answer. But what question? Not the obvious one about the whereabouts of Rehctaht. Apparently the name meant nothing to the Earthlings. But somewhere there was a clue. Somewhere. . .

Turlough looked across the village street. On the far side simple wooden buildings were adorned with flowers. Trees grew along the edge of the roadway. Despite the regular traffic of carts and human feet grass grew abundantly along the centre way. He could almost see it growing. The children loved it all of course. They played in the forest of plants – a beautiful environmemt to grow up in. For the first time Turlough really noticed the children. There were so many of them , aged up to four. Virtually none over that age though. And every man and woman not working in the fields or engaged in some other village activity carried a babe in arms. It was if life was replenishing itself a million times faster than it should to make up for the appalling destruction of the war. Turlough took a piece of paper from his pocket. On it he started making calculations. David Swallow looked over his shoulder in interest. Catching his gaze Turlough asked, 'Do you have any children, David?'

'Erica and I have five,' he said with pride. And then by way of further explanation added, 'Everyone joins together in the village in looking after the young.'

'And the truck comes here every day,' said Turlough with a sudden change of subject. 'Always with one full-size Land Snail.'

'Every day.'

'There are no other villages like yours?'

'None – although primitive, we still have a lot of the old

185

technology – including radio. We broadcast and listen. No one ever replies. Search parties go out from time to time, but find nothing . If there are other settlements they are across the seas in other countries. We are the United Kingdom, even without a king. We are Eden.'

'Right,' announced Turlough jumping up suddenly, with a manner he had learnt from the Doctor. 'I need to go back to the Neutrinova. Any chance of a lift?'

'I'm sure it can be arranged,' said David uncertainly. 'But I expect it will be ordered that someone go with you to keep an eye on you.'

'You?' said Turlough.

David reported back to the village leaders who agreed. Already Turlough seemed to have passed from their minds as a factor of major importance. David drove him back.

It was evening by the time they arrived. Ignoring the Neutrinova Turlough instructed David to park the van near the entrance to the first dome. 'I need to know the sizes,' said Turlough. 'And numbers. How many in each dome and how big. Count the full-grown versions that you get deposited in the village as size ten, and the smallest versions you find in the dome as size one, and chart up the number per dome. We'll just do the first four domes – you take the two on the left and I'll take the two on the right. I reckon we've got about twenty minutes to capture one before the truck arrives. And I want to be out before that happens.'

David was clearly impressed by the strength of Turlough's instructions, and showed no sign of recognising that much of it was pure bravado aimed at bolstering Turlough's own lack of desire to enter the dome again. However he forced himself in and completed the count that he had himself laid down. He then repeated it with the second dome and emerged to meet David just in time to see the collection truck making its way towards them. The truck went to the seventh dome this night, killing and collecting its cargo, before moving on. Turlough refused to explain his reasoning to David, but silently watched the truck move back towards the town. Asking David to return the next morning, and promising further explanations then, he bade the Earthman farewell and returned to the Neutrinova.

Turlough did not even bother to look and see the condition of Juras and The Magician inside the little ship. Instead he sat at the control panel and touched in a series of figures and mathematical conputations. The answers appeared at once on the screens. Turlough removed his hands from the controls. The figures had confirmed his suspicions. Tomorrow would, he feared, prove them right.

David arrived soon after sunrise. Turlough launched straight into his plans. 'I'll need a second view of the four domes we visited yesterday,' he said. 'Plus some analyses of what the Land Snails are made up of. When the Slot brings you the creature this afternoon can you get a bit – it doesn't have to be much – and bring it across to me, preferably in something like ethyl alcohol to stop it smelling too much.'

'No problem,' said David, 'but I'm still waiting for an explanation.'

'Speed,' said Turlough, 'the speed at which the Land Snails are growing, the speed at which the radiation disappeared, the speed at which your village is growing. That patch of land where the Land Snail was buried yesterday. What is it today?'

'Grassland of course,' said David.

'And tomorrow?'

'We'll sow seeds. Wheat, barley, – we're a growing population.'

'But that is it,' said Turlough. 'You are growing. Fast. Very fast. Too fast.'

'How can it be too fast? We exist in a land which used to house a population of sixty-five million,' argued David. 'And now we are under a thousand, although, as you say, growing fast.' David smiled. The thought seemed to please him. He left to collect the specimen Turlough had requested, leaving the Clansman in contemplation of the star charts of the Galaxy that the log of the Neutrinova carried. Somewhere amidst that cluster of a hundred billion stars the mad woman existed. Somewhere. . .

Turlough turned to The Magician. 'Do you know where Rehctaht is?' he said.

'Where is anything?' said The Magician. Turlough was surprised. The Magician had answered strangely and obliquiely

187

before, but never quite so philosophically. 'The uncertainty principle,' said the Time Lord by way of explanation. 'You cannot know if fundamental entities are particles or waves.'

'I know something of physics,' Turlough told him sarcastically.

'Then you know,' said The Magician, oblivious to the jibe, 'that when you make a measurement of any type the wave function breaks down and we discover a particle. But if we want to predict where the particle can be we have to use wave theory.' Turlough yawned, but still The Magician pressed on. 'So the question is, was the particle really there, or was it a figment of your imagination. Shouldn't it really have been spread out equally all over the wave.'

Turlough had had enough of the lecture which would have been primitive even for a nursery class on Trion. 'Everything is everywhere the wave allows it to be,' he said mechanically. It was a phrase he had learnt years before, repeated time and again as he learned his fundamental science.

'And have you never thought how that applies to real life?'

'All possibilities are probable,' said Turlough. Only after he had said it did he realise he had just quoted himself. There was a certain gleam in The Magician's eye that made him consider for a moment.

Turlough yawned again, stopped, thought and then repeated the phrase. He said it slowly, as if understanding each word for the first time.

Rephrasing it he said, 'Every option exists somewhere at sometime. *Every* option.' He stared wide eyed at The Magician for a full sixty seconds before turning back to the controls of the Neutrinova and touching in a mass of information. He was still at it when Juras came round from her latest bout of sleeping, and asked what he was up to. Turlough ignored her, and only finally stopped when David Swallow appeared in the late afternoon with his sample. Turlough immediately put the sample on the touch sensitive plate and waited. The results flashed up on the screen. Turlough took it all in and then turned back to David before going out to the domes and repeating yesterday's analysis of numbers and weights.

The job completed, Turlough spent some time in conversation with David before returning to the ship. David drove back to Eden in sombre mood. Turlough fed his final information into the Neutrinova's central intelligence system, and as ever, results came back immediately. Turlough cleared the machine, turned and looked hard at The Magician. He smiled back sweetly. They both then looked at Juras. She looked back, surprised to find them both staring at her. 'Juras,' said Turlough, 'what else was Rehctaht working on when you were involved in time research?'

'I don't know,' answered the girl defensively. 'There were other researchers, but we were all kept apart.'

'But you must have had some idea,' persisted Turlough. 'Some word would have crept out, perhaps some inadvertent comment or something. You weren't kept in total isolation for ever , were you?'

'Well, there was talk, but nothing very serious.'

'Talk about what?'

'The general research on the main areas. Others were on gravity as well as myself, and a few on ultimate unified theory, plus a couple on time-travel. We didn't know because Rehctaht was away most of the time. She even came to Earth once.'

'Her researchers seem to sum up most parts of the Universe,' said Turlough dryly.

'What do you mean?' asked Juras. She looked bewildered.

'Shall I show you?' said Turlough fiercely. 'Shall I take you out for a walk around this planet and show you the effects of all this madness. So you can then laugh at the way Vislor Turlough was used and twisted. I wasn't meant to find out, was I? I was supposed to be so dumb and self-centred that I would never take the trouble to work it out. Never bother to think about other people.' As he spoke Turlough grabbed Juras fiercely by the arm. She screamed and backed away, looking to The Magician for help. None came. Turlough hardened his grip. 'In your own arrogance you forgot that even devious self-seeking Turlough might still have some sort of feeling tucked away inside his head. Oh, how you must have laughed at the idea of using me. How funny. How very funny.' With a sudden jerk Turlough twisted Juras round and flung her across the room. In dismay and despair he sat down at the controls and buried his head in his hands. Rubbing her aching arm Juras walked unsteadily over to Turlough.

'What's happening?' she demanded, only just holding back the tears. 'I'm Juras Maateh. We've been friends for years. I know we differed in our views about what to do about Rehctaht, but I thought you accepted that fact. I didn't work for her. I just followed instructions biding my time.'

Turlough spun back to face Juras suddenly. 'Didn't work for her!' he mimicked. 'Of course you work for her. You *are* her. *You are Rehctaht!*'

Juras recoiled from Turlough in horror. 'You're mad,' she said. 'Quite mad. Something out there on this planet has affected your reasoning.'

'This planet gave me my reasoning,' replied Turlough bitterly. 'And you have just confirmed it. This planet was devastated by nuclear warfare. Now look at it. Where's the radiation gone, Juras?'

'Why don't you ask your friends, the Slots? They seem to know everything.' Now Juras was turning sarcastic.

'Oh, I should have done so long ago,' said Turlough. 'I really should, but I was put off by history and prejudice. They may look strange but I have more in common with them than I do with you.'

Juras tried to take the situation under control. 'Turlough,' she said pleadingly, 'tell me exactly what you think, and let me understand what has brought you to this conclusion. And then allow me to discuss it with you. I can help. I can tell you where you are wrong. Maybe there is some radiation left on this planet and it is affecting you. Perhaps that piece of the Land Snail David Swallow brought in has some strange properties that. . .'

'The last thing I shall do is talk with you,' said Turlough. 'I'm going to take the action I should have taken at the start of this whole affair if I hadn't been so blind. How stupid I've been, but not any more. Magician. . .' He looked at the Time Lord trying to judge which side he would come down on. 'You know what I am about to do. Will you help me restrain Juras, or are you about to side with her to restrain me?'

Still smiling The Magician grabbed Juras from behind, and took a long cord from his pocket and tied it around the girl. 'Gallifrey won't approve,' said Turlough wryly, relieved to have an ally on board. And then seeing Juras was safely restrained he said, 'Now we are going to change history.'

Juras attempted to rise. She seemed in a state of panic. 'You can't do that! You will destroy space-time. Once you start amending history entire sections of the continuum can just pop out of existence.'

Turlough touched several controls before turning back to Juras. 'Do me the honour of at least realising that I too have studied a little of ultimate unified theory. Shall I talk you through it just to show you?' Juras made no sign to contradict him. Turlough touched several more controls, and the ship lifted off. 'The ultimate theory of the universe, Juras. The ultimate goal. Put all the four forces of the universe into one melting pot – strong nuclear, weak nuclear, electro-magnetic and gravitational. Once you get that right you have the greatest single piece of knowledge that anyone could ever ask for. The knowledge of how the universe works.'

Turlough looked hard at Juras to see how she was taking his lecture, but she seemed to have sunk into a sullen silence. He decided to press on anyway. It would take several hours to make the journey he had in mind, and he needed something to pass the time.

'The first part of the theory was solved millenia ago – the two nuclear forces and the electro-magnetic. That was easy, they all fit together perfectly. But gravity is the problem. It is so easy to build a magnet, a light bulb, a nuclear bomb, a cold fission reactor. No problem at all. But how do you build an anti-gravity device? No Clansman knows because gravity just refuses to fit into the great scheme of things. And that was how it was when I left Trion. I pondered the problem – and I guess everyone did in the Institute, especially that hard centre; that one bit of difficulty that just won't go away. Everytime you try and solve the equations to get gravity to fit in with the other three forces in the universe you come out with the inevitable fact that the gravity on Trion should be getting less and less as the centuries go by. And the gravity on Earth too. But it isn't is it? Gravity stays the same. Now why? Why is that so?'

'You seem to know all the answers,' said Juras, 'you tell me.'

'I shall,' said Turlough with a gleam in his eye. 'Because someone is fiddling with reality.'

He stopped and looked at the controls on the little ship, checking that everything was in order. 'Rehctaht dreamt of total power. That is the one incontrovertible thing that everyone knows about her. And of course, now I have started to think straight it is clear that that means just one thing. Rehctaht wanted an ultimate unified theory that worked, so she could understand, and thus control all the forces in the universe. That is what you worked on, Juras. Gravity, yes, but gravity in terms of the ultimate theory. Yet no matter how hard you worked the theory wouldn't fit the facts, and all because gravity stood so resolutely still.

'Next you noticed something odd about gravity in this sector of the Galaxy. You prodded and probed but couldn't work it out. So in your total madness you started to experiment. If gravity wouldn't behave properly you thought there might be something wrong in the understanding of nuclear forces. So you arranged enormous nuclear explosions first on this planet, and then on new Trion and on Trion itself. You looked and measured but still the theory wouldn't hold together. The nuclear forces worked exactly as they should have done. Only gravity got it wrong. And you couldn't see why.'

Juras came back to life. 'Turlough, I acknowledge that you have a solid grasp of theoretical physics, that you have a brilliant understanding of temporal physics, and that by and large you are rather clever. But I am not Rehctaht. Any fool can see that.'

'But that is the central point,' said Turlough. 'Rehctaht is dead. Killed in the revolution that brought the Committee of Public Safety to power. And yet Rehctaht still exists with power to tip the island onto Trion and destroy it. How can that be?'

'Tell me,' said Juras reverting to a snear.

'Gravity should be changing over time just as the ultimate unified theory says,' repeated Turlough, 'but something, somewhere is actually stopping it happen. And that little act of stopping is using up tremendous energies. Find them, divert them from their task for just one second, and hey presto, the biggest outpouring of gravity waves the universe has seen since the Big Bang. In the ensuing chaos Rehctaht gains total knowledge and total power.'

'Turlough, how do you reach these wild conclusions?'

'Oh, it took a long time,' said Turlough. 'It was the Earthlink that brought it home to me. Earth – a pathetic little insignificant planet. Yet a battleground for endless conflicts between the Doctor and various renegade Time Lords. The scene of innumerable invasions from other planets, many of which the Doctor has witnessed, and diverted I might add. A place full of gravitational anomalies too. Now all the time I keep asking myself why. Why Earth? Why does everyone keep homing back on Earth?'

'Enlighten us all, said Juras.

'Because that is where the gravity control unit is. As yet I don't know why, but it is. And the forces involved are being used positively for once to speed up growth on this planet a millionfold. The Land Snails eat up the radiation, but power directed from the gravity generator is the source of the growth of the new world. There is no other explanation for the readings I've been taking.'

Juras looked tired and bored. 'All good fun, Turlough,' she said, 'but it doesn't add up to much does it? A lot of speculation and hunches, nothing more; no proof.'

But Turlough was not to be put off. 'Rehctaht as Juras made one error. When I said "G equals M to the power minus one by L cubed by T to the power of four", you corrected me. You said "to the power two". That was right – but you should never have known. That was an Earth theory of gravity worked out in the twentieth century whilst I was here. It was right then because the generator was working full strength on maintaining galactic gravity. Now it is wrong because a small percentage of power is being directed to help speed up evolution. You couldn't have thought that "minus four" was wrong. No one could unless they'd been to Earth. Juras Maateh never came here. But, as you just said, Rehctaht did.

'And then you made a second error. You got worried about

me changing time zones. Why? It won't affect us – we will still exist in any zone we move into. And even if it affects Trion it can't make matters any worse. So why worry? Only because a modified time zone might not involve the original Rehctaht and you might become trapped in Juras Maateh's body and mind for ever.

'Now it is time to resolve matters once and for all,' concluded Turlough brightly. 'If I am wrong nothing much will happen. But if I am right, all sorts of things will occur, and not many of them good for Rehctaht.'

He turned back to the controls and studied them carefully, bringing the ARTEMIS drive into full play as the little ship sped across space and moved backwards in time.

Eventually they arrived, exactly at the point Turlough wanted, in orbit around Trion, one month after the start of his exile on Earth.

'In a gravity-held universe,' Turlough announced, 'uncertainty rules totally. And a direct result of uncertainty is that all possible pasts and futures exist, because all particles exist in all locations of their potential wave patterns. We are in one potential. What we have to do now is to move towards another.'

'How?' asked Juras nervously.

Turlough looked mischevious. 'We know the past, don't we Juras? We know that I left Trion to exile on Earth. We know that I developed the ARTEMIS drive after the counter revolution. But what about a reality in which I developed ARTEMIS whilst Rehctaht was still in power. What if I broke exile on Earth and travelled to Trion with the drive unit?'

'It did not happen,' said the girl simply.

'But I am going to make it happen. Now. And that will put us automatically into a different continuity. One that does not condemn me to playing at being the Gardsormr, desperately arranging for life to resume itself at an impossibly fast speed on Earth, Trion and New Trion.'

'So illuminate me, Turlough,' said Juras with heavy sarcasm. 'Just how does revealing the secret of ARTEMIS to Rehctaht whilst you are still supposed to be on Earth stop all these things happening?'

'Because in this option, Rehctaht will die. I shall kill her.'

But Juras was not willing to let it happen. Unseen she had been working gently at the cord tying her hands behind her back. Gradually she had worked the bonds loose and chose this moment to charge at Turlough. Despite his awareness of the danger the girl posed he was caught off guard and fell to the floor, hitting the control panel as he went. Juras stood above him arms flying as she attacked viciously. As what was meant to be the killer blow came down, Turlough leaned back and touched the control panel behind him. In response the tiny craft tilted at an unlikely angle throwing them all off balance. It gave Turlough no more than a second's breathing space as Juras moved towards him again, this time holding the cord that had until recently kept her firmly secured. And from the way she was holding it there could be little doubt that she meant to put that rope around Turlough's neck. Backing off as far as he could in the tiny room Turlough called for help from The Magician.

'You must deal with this yourself,' came the unhelpful reply. 'My ethnics, you know. As a Time Lord I am powerless to influence you. You suspected the girl. Her actions prove you right. Now finish the job.'

'But if she gets me,' screamed Turlough, 'everyone will suffer. She'll do anything to get the Unified Theory.'

'And you have just confirmed to her the source of the problem,' said The Magician. 'It is up to you now. You must kill the girl. You must kill her.'

The Magician's voice seemed a million light years away. Turlough could not grasp what was being said. The words echoed in a long tunnel. Kill Juras Maateh? It seemed impossible. This was Juras. His friend since the days at the Institute. This wasn't Rehctaht. If only he could just talk with her everything could be resolved. There would be no problems.

Turlough relaxed his guard and looked for a chair. Someone was shouting at him. He couldn't quite put a face to the voice. In front was dear Juras. Her faced looked strained. He must ask her if she had been overdoing it. He ought to talk with her.

'Juras . . .' How strange his voice seemed. How distant. Was that really his voice? 'Juras . . .'

'Turlough . . .' She spoke. But, it too, was the wrong voice. That wasn't Juras. That was someone old. Much older. Turlough looked. There seemed to be some sort of fog in front of his eyes. He squinted and tried to peer through the haze. Turlough . . .' That voice. He knew it. And that person coming towards him. This woman walked with a limp. Who did he know with a limp. Not Juras. Not one of the girls from the Institute. Not one of the Doctor's companions.

The Doctor. Suddenly he thought of the Doctor. How was he these days? What was he doing, spinning around in that strange machine of his? What was it called? Turlough couldn't quite remember. He couldn't quite remember anything. Except a formula. One formula that was so important that he could recall it even now when everything else had gone. It was the formula for the gravity constant of the universe as seen from Earth. G equals M to the power minus one by L cubed by T to the power minus two. That formula could never give a dimensionless number for Earth scientists. And that was always their problem, because particle physics is full of formulae which give rise to dimensionless numbers. So how do you merge figures with dimensions with those without? Poor Earth. Poor Juras.

It was quite reasonable that Rehctaht would have known the formula. And with access to all the information on the unified theory she could have seen the connection. Yet Juras had said that she was kept apart from the workers on unified theory. There was only one person who could have known everything that was going on in the research bunkers . . .

With every remaining gramme of his strength Turlough hurled himself across the room. This time the girl was taken off guard and she hit the side of the craft with a sickening thump. As the fog in his brain began to clear Turlough looked at the figure he had knocked down. She was lying motionless on the floor. He had been right. It was not Juras. The woman was much older – maybe around sixty or so, with shorter hair, hardly reaching her neck, and the start of wrinkles on her face. Her hands too were gnarled and bony, more so than would have been normal in someone her age. Turlough put his hand to her jugular vein, and then removed it. Rehctaht was dead.

196

'She always knew her time would eventually be up,' said The Magician, walking over to Turlough. 'So she prepared for the event, ready to move into someone else's body. Word of your exploits with the Doctor had reached her even before the counter revolution. And she had the wit to realise that someone with your personality and your brains, combined with the experience of being with a Time Lord, would be likely to give rise to the very developments she needed. She didn't know you would go so far as to develop the ARTEMIS drive, but she certainly guessed you would discover the gravity generator on Earth.'

'Would Juras have known the reality?' asked Turlough looking at the corpse.

'I think not. To her it would have just been immediate death when Rehctaht entered her body. It would have been more tormenting for Rehctaht actually becoming Juras, until the self-imposed spike in her brain rang like an alarm bell and the real personna of Rehctaht took over briefly. If she was not fully mad beforehand she would have been after a few weeks of living in Juras Maateh's body and adopting Juras Maateh's personality.'

Together they carried Rehctaht to the disposal unit at one side of the Neutrinova. Then without a word Turlough returned to the controls and brought the ship back to his chosen location. As he did he had a sudden thought. 'You deliberately tied that cord so that she would get out,' he told The Magician

'I had to get you to kill her,' the Time Lord said. 'There was no other way. Only through her death would you take us to a new dimension.'

12: QUEEN

Turlough brought the ship into land on Trion without fuss. No one took much notice on the outlying airfield of what the pilot claimed was a tiny makeshift planet boat. In this time zone the Clans had not handed over the Neutrinova design to the Trions. Turlough bade farewell to The Magician and took the VT to his apartment. Holding his breath he checked the details of his situation. The autochart on the screen gave the year as 17,883. His other self would now be going through that living hell known as the English Public School. It also meant that he was still an exile, and Rehctaht still ruled Trion.

After a change of clothes and the donning of such disguises as he could find – which amounted to little – Turlough used the VT system to make his way towards the central government complex. From what Juras (or rather Rehctaht in Juras's personna) had told him, she had been recruited to work in the lowest levels of the bunkers under Government House, and that would be his goal.

Government House was, at least above ground level, a modest affair – a five-storey building dating back several hundred years, with a polished silver exterior that reflected back all light. Indeed such was the level of reflection that unless you knew where the actual entrance was it was often impossible to find any way in.

Turlough remembered the plan all too well for it was to this building that he had been brought for the inquisition that had led to his exile to Earth. No steps led to the entrance, and no doorway signs lit the way. One simply walked up to it and found that what appeared to be a continuation of the solid silver wall was actually a gap.

Inside four heavily armed youths encircled Turlough. Each

wore a helmet with miniature microphones in front. They were the eyes and ears of those below. These were Rehctaht's Volunteer Defence Squadrons – Rehctaht's Thugs as they were popularly known. They got time off their studies to help guard the mighty insane Empress. None of the boys could have been over fourteen years old. None of them was bright enough to recognise Turlough.

'I crave a meeting with the President Commissioner,' Turlough announced, using the language the empowered loved. The youths showed no sign of having heard, and continued their circling whilst endlessly prodding him with the butts of various armaments.

At last one stopped the fun. 'Name?' he drawled. He said it almost as if it were a trick question. Turlough told him, keeping his head straight forward as if these kids were senior officials. They liked that. Turlough knew the game and for once was willing to play it.

'Nature of business?' demanded another.

'Spacewarps,' said Turlough. It meant little, if anything to the youths, but sounded serious enough to warrant passing the message on. One thug spoke into his microphone, got a message back.

'You're in luck, Turlough,' said the boy. 'Follow.' Turlough followed. They walked across the large silver foyer and into a lift at the far end. It took them down. That, Turlough knew, meant he was getting closer to power.

Two floors below ground level the lift stopped, and Turlough was pushed unceremoniously into a small room. The door was locked behind him. There were two chairs. Turlough sat. A moment later he rose as a man walked in. Turlough swallowed a gasp. It was Naale Niairb. Turlough had never even considered that individuals this deeply involved in Rehctaht's regime could so rapidly extract themselves from its associations and become part of the subsequent Committee Of Public Safety. It explained a lot about the autocratic behaviour of the COPs. It also explained why he had never been able to get along with Niairb.

'Turlough the Runaway,' announced Niairb unpleasantly. 'Escaped from exile. What do you have to say before we get rid of you for good?' He too wore helmet and microphone, his every word transmitted back to Rehctaht. The woman trusted no one.

'Something to save my life,' replied Turlough purposefully. 'During my time away I have made a discovery of such moment that it made me not only return to Trion but also walk straight to you. Will you give me the time to speak?'

'Of course,' replied the repugnant inquisitor. 'Say away.'

'Condensed, the discovery is this: spacewarps are controlled by gravity waves. But throughout the galaxy the waves are not running true. There are extreme fluctuations in a certain segment. I have been there and measured them.'

'An interesting theoretical exercise,' said Niairb. 'What do you want – to prepare a paper on the subject which can be circulated to all the other Clansmen in exile?'

'The subject has massive implications practically,' replied Turlough, steadfastly refusing to rise to the bait. It was now that he would discover if his gamble in coming here would bear fruit. 'It leads to a much fuller comprehension of the nature of gravity and the development of the Ultimate Unified Theory.'

'You physicists are all the same,' drawled Niairb, clearly not comprehending a word of what Turlough was saying. 'Always so full of your theories that you never see that there is a real world out there. You are a criminal exile, Turlough, and none of your unreal waffle has suggested to me any reason why you should be treated otherwise. Therefore I . . . '

Interrupted in mid-sentence Niairb listened intently to the words pounding through the control phones directly into his ears. The slimy grin that had been ever present on his flabby face disappeared and a much graver aspect took over. When the instructions had evidently finished he looked back at Turlough and changed his approach. 'Nevertheless, as we all recognise that any theory, no matter how woolly or vague, and no matter who it is prepared by, can itself develop into practical applications, we shall take a moment to see just what your ideas lead to. If nowhere, you shall be dealt with as the runaway exile you clearly are. However, if there turns out to be something in your work, glorious Rehctaht may consider sparing you for a short time.'

Niairb spoke softly into his microphone, a door opened and two youths appeared, this time fully dressed in official uniform. With more respect than he had previously been shown Turlough was directed towards the lift and taken down another four floors. He was, quite literally, getting to the seat of power.

Rehctaht looked different, considerably younger, less strained, less insane, than the appearance she had adopted on the Neutrionva at the death of Juras. She held her head slightly to one side and put on a false, and to Turlough, disgusting smile. She sat behind a large desk, but at once got up, shook Turlough firmly by the hand and led him to a sofa where he sat beside her.

'And now, Vislor Turlough,' she announced immediately, 'you have something to say to me about spacewarps.' Her voice was soft, kindly, as if addressing a slightly wayward child who was about to confess to stealing a bag of sweets.

This was the moment Turlough had prepared for. He told the woman about his discovery of inequalities in gravity throughout the Galaxy, especially in the vicinity of an insignificant planet known as Earth. This localised disturbance had led him to make many measurements which in turn indicated that universal gravity was indeed growing less, rather than holding constant as contemporary measurements suggested. This at last opened the way to the formulation of the ultimate unified theory. 'That would mean,' he concluded, 'the development of a theory of all forces which in turn must lead to the ability to control all factors in the Universe – to control the destiny of the Universe itself.

The smile on the face remained. 'And why do you bring this news to me, after you threw yourself into exile? When your case came up you said one or two unpleasant things, Clansman.'

'Being away frompm the mother planet gives one a chance to think,' Turlough told the woman. 'One meets beings with totally different conceptions of reality. It helps formulate thought and ideas. I had already reached the conclusion that I had been wrong to leave Trion before making my discovery on Earth, but at that stage I had nothing with which to barter my return. Now I ask that I may be allowed to live on Trion, and in return I offer myself as a worker on gravitation and the ultimate unified theory.'

'And how long do you need to develop your work?'

'Hardly any time at all, ma'am, given the right computational equipment and formulational aids. A few days at most to come up with an initial working model. Thirty days perhaps to develop that into a full scale practical design that will allow manipulation of all our universe forces. I did much preliminary work on my way here.'

'Very well,' said Rehctaht, standing. 'You shall have what you require, and your own workshop. I shall appoint an assistant and receive a full report daily. Stick to your timetable.'

Guards entered the room and escorted Turlough from the presence of the leader. He was taken straight to a workroom containing a single desk covered in touch controls which gave him access to the full computational powers of Trion. He sat down to work.

After two hours he called for food. It came and was surprisingly good. After five hours he grew weary and lay down to rest. He awoke an indeterminate time later, called for breakfast and carried on with his work. Later that day he finished the preliminaries and sent a message to Rehctaht that the model was concluded. She did not ask to see Turlough but instead had his computations transmitted to her quarters. Only then did she call him in.

'An interesting set of proposals, Clansman,' she said. 'Talk me through the approach.'

Turlough did as he was bid, speaking of the four fundamental forces of nature, the historical struggle to link gravity in with the other three and so on. She nodded from time to time, asked the occasional question, and seemed happy with the outcome. Finally she said, 'Return to your room and rest. I shall inform you tomorrow on my decision concerning the development of your most interesting work.'

Turlough deliberately refrained from taking food or drink that night, knowing for certain that it would be drugged. He forced himself to stay awake and alert, and was finally rewarded for his persistence by the arrival of guards in the early hours. Appearing heavily asleep he allowed them to carry him back to Rehctaht's rooms. Keeping his eyes firmly closed Turlough listened to the woman's ranting as he slumped uncomfortably in a chair.

Yet his thought that the leader was going to make her move then, was wrong. After little more than a cursory glance in his direction Rehctaht told the guards to proceed which they duly did by picking Turlough up as if he were a sack, and bundling him on an electric cart. He was dropped half an hour later in a pitch black area of indeterminate size. His actions of avoiding the drugging had merely left him tired and hungry, and given him, as yet, no appreciable advantage. He gave up the struggle and fell asleep.

Turlough awoke to find himself in a square room. The walls were painted with converging and diverging brown and blue lines. A dull cream light from the ceiling gave illumination. Midway along each wall was a door. The room itself contained no bed, no chair. Turlough picked himself up and approached one wall carefully. It gave no signs of any power source around it, but he had grown cautious. Stepping back to the centre of the room he removed one boot and threw it at the door. Boot hit door. Nothing else happened. The boot fell to the floor. Turlough repeated the exercise with all four doors and then the walls between them. In each case the result was the same.

Turlough put his boot back on, removed his jacket, wrapped part of it around his hand and then cautiously pushed a door. Still there was no throw-back of power or electricity. The door opened into a winding corridor decorated in the same style as the square room and illuminated with the same dull cream light. In the distance could be heard an unpleasant sound – part scream part roar . . .

Turlough walked slowly forward into the tunnel, and as he did so the door swung back and closed firmly behind him. The sound grew louder. Moving back he tried to open it again, but it refused to swing forwards and it was impossible to get a grip on the smooth surface in order to pull it back. He now had no option but to walk the corridor.

The corridor continued in its curved way for a short distance –

no more than one hundred metres. Every few paces.
Turlough turned and looked back, but each time the tunnel stretched in each direction in the same monotonous style. At the far end was a door of the same description as the one he had so recently walked through. This one gave inwards. He pushed, and found himself once more in a square room with brown and blue lines covering four walls, ceiling and floor. A dull cream light from the ceiling gave illumination. Midway along each wall was a door.

Turlough walked into the middle of the floor and heard the dull thud of the door closing behind him. Sounds continued from afar. It began to seem as if the scream and the roar came from separate sources. The scream was a scream of fear and pain.

He walked back to the door and pushed, but it would not give. Keeping his back to the door he stood and thought, before moving across the room to the exit opposite. It gave readily and led into another curving corridor of brown and blue. He walked backwards into the room until he bumped into the door he had recently come through. That still would not give. He tried the door on the left – a corridor – and on the right – the same. He took the left and walked just under one hundred metres until he came to another door, leading into a square room decorated in brown and blue. Each room was the exact image of the one just left.

Turlough searched his pockets for something that would allow him to hold the door open. He found a pebble from Earth, thin enough at one end to act as a doorstop. As before he tried the other three doors. Each opened on command. Finally, bemused, and not a little scared he returned to the centre of the room and thought.

Every room had three doors that would open and one – the one he came through – that would not. Added to which he knew that each tunnel he had seen always bore to the right, but never far enough to bring him back to where he started.

He went through the process once more, but the exercise only served to confirm his feelings except that now he could hear the cries of help and screams of pain more clearly. He was in a maze without food or water, and lacking any notion of how

204

to get out. Somewhere in the distance was a creature, or creatures that from the sound at least were bigger and stronger than Turlough, even when he was feeling at his best. And at this stage he was not feeling his best. Rehctaht was trying to drive him insane.

Turlough sat on the floor in the centre of the room and marked out imaginary lines on the ground trying to construct a plan of the whole blue and brown complex. Within seconds he realised that the system, as he had observed it, was impossible. For there to be three doors out and only one back into each room the complex could not be constructed in an essentially two-dimensional field. And as he was certain he had not moved up or downhill. What there ought to be was an extra entrance and an exit on each of the walls – two doors per wall, one allowing him into the room, and one out. Unless . . .

Turlough walked a journey between two rooms once more, this time pausing just before reaching the final door back into a room. He then set about exploring the walls of the tunnel, and was able to make out with his fingers (but not with his eyes in the dim light) the edge of an alternative tunnel door. There was a way in and out of each tunnel, and someone or something activated controls which decided which would be open to him once he had started a journey down the corridor. Probably some action of opening a door, or maybe merely the pressure of his feet in the room itself did it. He entered the next chamber. The cries for help were louder still. He was getting closer to the danger.

His second logical deduction was that, given that all tunnels turned right, and since each corridor appeared to bend through ninety degrees, repeating the operation he should achieve the shortest route of coming back to where he started. To check, he used his stone to scratch a mark on the door. He then ran at full speed through the door on his right along the corridor, into the next room and then right again, and back. The door he came through was marked. His model was accurate. The screams and roars were louder than ever.

He paused again and drew another diagram. And then another. And then a third. No matter how he used his knowledge one thing became clear. This was not a closed system.

There was no way of drawing the plan such that if he constantly took the doors on the left he would end up back where he started. If there were a way out it would be found by sticking constantly to one option in each and every room. He turned left, away from the screams.

By the fifteenth room Turlough was getting tired and thirsty. Panic edged his movements. By the twentieth he was starting to find his vision slightly blurred, and by the thirty-second room he walked straight into a wall that contained no door. The Clansman stood there looking at it, unable to understand why it did not open. Only when he cleared his head by closing his eyes for several moments did he realise he had come to one edge of the maze without finding a way out. Simply, he had come to a room with no left door.

Turlough walked straight ahead. He did that ten times before coming to a room that had no straight ahead door. It was a dead stop leaving only the option of turning right. Yet a right turn, as he knew only too well, would take him back into the heart of the maze. The maze was closed; there was no escape. Turlough started to shout. And then cry. He sobbed uncontrollably. In the distance he could hear someone screaming.

It was a good half hour before Turlough regained his self control. 'I am an Imperial Clansman,' he said aloud to anyone who cared to listen, shaking his head and adjusting his jacket to make it more presentable. Then he sat cross-legged in the centre of the room and started to seriously apply his brain, rather than his leg muscles to the problem. He had worked out a plan of the maze. He had tested that plan in several ways and found each time his plan had been vindicated. But unfortunately that gave him neither a way our nor an insight into why he had been put there. He looked at the ceiling. It was just possible that the roof of the room he had first found himself in offered some sort of entrance and exit, but the chance of finding that room again in such a massive construction was too slim to contemplate. Added to which the rooms contained no furniture which might allow him to climb up, and nothing which might be thrown. Turlough stayed seated.

He thought of why Rehctaht should want to put him in a maze such as this. He thought of what the woman had done to Juras. He thought of how it could have been possible to disorientate Juras sufficiently to enable Rehctaht to take over the girl's mind. And through his befuddled brain, that one idea began to take hold. Outside, the counter-revolution was now brewing. And where better to achieve disorientation than in an endless stream of rooms where occupants would start with logic, but end up screaming for release in pure despair?

The lack of food or drink meant that the desired effect anticipated by Rehctaht was achieved fairly rapidly. Any long term deterioration in his body functioning was exactly what Rehctaht would not want. Rapid panic was the order of the day. Somewhere, either in one of the tunnels or else in one of the chambers, there had to be the way in and out, yet the chances of finding it were so slim as to make the search pointless. Most inmates would go halfways mad before getting a quarter of the way through.

On the other hand, the calculations Turlough had made to discover the exact nature of the maze were not so complex that they would not be achieved by most people subjected to the torture. Perhaps he was meant to find out. Maybe knowing the impossibility of finding a solution was just as punishing as endlessly running from room to room without any real awareness of how the maze was constructed. Either way was torture.

Turlough began walking along the edge of the room hitting the wall with no door, his eyes on the ground, concentrating totally on the sound. He didn't expect much, but there was always the chance.

He first took the door in front of him then in the next room the door on the left. This he knew from his plan would take him around the outer perimeter of the maze. The wall gave back the same dull thud. After two rooms Turlough's fist began to ache, but the ache served a purpose. Even when the first signs of blood appeared, he stayed on course. The pain was keeping his mind focused on something other than the appalling futility of what he was doing. When the moment came he had to be ready.

He had progressed through nineteen chambers before his befuddled brain told him that he had gone past a location in which the sound of the wall changed. With delicate gentle movements he turned himself around and started retracing his steps all the while punching the wall with his other hand. If this time the sound did not change he would know that he was close to breaking. But in the fourth room back he found he was right. The wall was hollow. He had found a way out.

Turlough kicked at the obstruction with his foot. It gave way and led into a darkened passage. The Clansman stood staring at it. He felt he couldn't enter. It wasn't safe. How could it be? It wasn't brown and blue. He was still standing there staring along the emergency exit tunnel, saliva gently dripping from his mouth, blood streaming from the fist of his left hand when the wardens came and removed him ten minutes later.

They put the unconscious Turlough on a bunk in a well-appointed private hospital suite. His damaged hand was treated for extensive bruising and bandaged. His temperature was checked, along with his pulse, EEG readings and blood pressure. When all was deemed normal the leader was called to inspect the work. Rehctaht declared herself pleased with the outcome as she lay down on the bed by Turlough's side.

'Awaken him gently,' she proclaimed. The top ranking hospital staff, all dedicated followers of the Rehctaht seizure of power, and the sum total of Trion life who knew what was happening to the leader, moved to obey. For the transfer to work they had to have both parties conscious.

The simple machine that stood between the two beds belied the complexity of what was to happen. Rehctaht would not only take her mind into Turlough, she would also take her own physical existence. It would hide, out of phase, ready to be repossessed when her dedicated followers had organised the situation such that it was possible for the woman to rule once more. They would also install an emergency cut out, known as a spike, which would activate Rehctaht's original personna in time of great emergency.

The transfer experience could result in shock for the host, so the Clansman needed to be awake, but mentally disorientated. He would see the invasion as another psychological disorder, and sit there debating the problem with himself whilst the invading mind slipped in and took over.

'Double check,' commanded Rehctaht. Everything had already been proven, balanced, run and rerun ten times but the staff jumped to obey. Rehctaht ruled through the personality of fear and even here, linked to machinery on a hospital bed her voice could cause panic.

All was reported to be ready as Rehctaht gave the word. Slowly, stage by stage her body phased out of existence. Ripples could be seen on Turlough's face, and beneath his clothing. The injured fist clenched and unclenched, and twice a yell came from his tortured mouth. That was unusual and caused the medical team to make further calculations, but all was proclaimed in order. Then the activities subsided, the body of Turlough collapsed from exhaustion and moved into the deepest of sleeps. Transference was over.

The body of Rehctaht-Turlough was kept under guard as the counter-revolution gathered momentum, as the inevitable fighting ranged outside the headquarters of the now discredited Rehctaht revolutionaries. Ten hours after transference the medics, satisfied that their glorious leader was now safely housed in the body of the Clansman, left the building by a variety of secret exits and mingled with the crowd anxious now to show their hatred of the regime that had sought to wipe out the Imperial Clans. The cry for the return of their benign influence was heard all around.

When discovered by a group of counter-revolutionaries making their way through the catacombs of the council chambers Turlough was at first mistakenly believed to be a supporter of the missing Rehctaht. Later, when correctly identified as a Clansman, believed exiled, the medics were called in to investigate the strange marks on his forehead and the more easily understood bruising in his first.

Amid commotion Turlough woke. His body shook violently, and he had to be supported as he went through a long stream of spasms. Whilst slowly regaining coherence he said little, and saw no one save the hospital team tending him. They were, they had to admit, unsure of what was ailing the young man, but as they watched his body and constitution grow stronger they felt sure that even if the hero of the counter revolution (and any Clansman who had suffered under Rehctaht was a hero) could never be returned to full mental health he would at least be able to be shown to the populace. The revolution had its figurehead.

Demands to see Turlough were, of course, enormous. All were refused, including one (unnoticed amid the general rebuff of enquiries) from a Time Lord. As the newly-formed Committee Of Public Safety agreed, anyone getting too close to Turlough would realise that, at least at present, he did not quite fit into the popular image of a Clansman as intellectual giant.

For the Time Lord the days since Turlough had ventured into Rehctaht's inner sanctum had been ones of quiet contemplation and occasional sightseeing. There was, he knew, as yet nothing that could be done, nothing that could speed up events that had to take their natural course. At least until the appointed time.

Visitors from Gallifrey were hardly usual on Trion, but they were not unknown, and although a lot of people struggled to get a good look at the strangely dressed Time Lord with his eternal smile, white robe, blue sash, red cloak, white stick and figure-of-eight hat they were, by and large, far too polite to stare openly. That he visited the Giants' Drop in the Charlottenlund ruins was understandable. Most visitors from other worlds did that. And besides, conjectured the guide, who in another time plain three months before had recognised Turlough in the same caves, it was just possible that the Gallifreyan knew a thing or two about the Giants' Drop which no one else knew. He certainly spent more time than most looking at the inscriptions. She didn't want to disturb him of course, but orders were orders and she had to keep the party moving once she'd got them all across the magnetic ramp. Besides moving him along gave her a chance to speak to the Time Lord. And as she well knew, that would make her the centre of attention of her friends for months to come. She edged back across the cavern and moved behind him, coughing politely to gain his attention.

The being from Gallifrey drew himself up to his full height

and smiled benignly at the girl. 'A fascinating feature,' he said. 'More to it than meets the eyes! Unique in the galaxy. A memorable sight,' and he moved slowly across the Drop.

Together guide and Time Lord rejoined the rest of the tourists, The Magician talking politely all the while about the magnificent way in which Charlottenlund had been preserved and the remarkable clarity of the Guide's eloquence. In the last gallery, he turned to the guide. 'Has anyone been to the very bottom of the Drop?' he asked.

'Only during the original archaelogical work,' answered the girl. 'Not recently.'

'Interesting and significant,' said the Time Lord enigmatically, but would be drawn no further. He walked out into the sunlight, and headed for the VT station.

The Magician's TARDIS suitably disguised as undergrowth near Turlough's house sat deep in the rain forest. He entered and immediately set the co-ordinates for the central government hospital. The rangefinder found Turlough instantly, and within seconds the TARDIS rematerialised, disguised this time as a large medicine locker within two metres of Turlough's bedside. The Time Lord exited from the rear and peeped round the construction. The Clansman was alone, peering at a vidtransmission, a glazed look on his face. The Magician walked up to the bed and greeted him like a long lost friend.

Turlough looked perplexed but said nothing. 'Come on, old chap,' prompted the Time Lord, 'you recall me, don't you? All those times together! Great battles! Seeking out Gardsormr. Land Snails, the ARTEMIS drives, worlds seen, history recounted, future plans laid . . .'

'Can't say I do,' said Turlough at first. Then suddenly he brightened saying, 'Ah yes, The Magician. We travelled together, you and I.' And then less certainly, he added, 'Didn't we?'

'Spot on, total recall in one,' enthused The Magician. 'Right first go. Time for a mite more travelling now, eh? Places to go, deeds to do, the Galaxy awaits and time must be put to rights,' and with that he put a hand forward to help Turlough out of bed.

But Turlough seemed decidedly unsure of what he actually wanted to do at this stage. He withdrew from the outstretched hand and shrank back below the sheets. The Magician sought to calm him. 'Come now,' he said sweetly. 'A little ride, some open air, get colour back into your cheeks. You know the sort of thing. Let your mind wander; discover who you really are. See the world, expand the brain, as the old saying goes. People to see, history to make.'

But still Turlough was having none of it. As The Magician laid a hand on Turlough's arm and began to pull him forward so the Clansman began to call for the nursing staff. They were not long in coming. The anticipated shouts of 'who are you?' and 'get away from that bed' mingled with calls for armed orderlies to be brought in. The Magician however showed not the slightest sign of either letting go or speeding himself up. Carefully he used hidden strength to pull the Clansman forward and over his shoulder. The timing seemed perfect, the result to an outsider would have looked like a ballet. As medics moved one way, so precisely and accurately the Time Lord moved the other. As nurses lunged onto the bed so The Magician picked up Turlough. With his captive safely over his shoulder he walked behind the large medicine cabinet, unnoticed by hospital staff in the rush, and popped in through the door behind, closing it securely as he did so. Pursuing him from both sides the medical teams, now joined by armed orderlies approached from left and right and collided with one another. As they picked themselves up they witnessed the hitherto unknown effect of a medicine cabinet disappearing into thin air.

Inside the machine Turlough looked about him, half accepting, half recoiling from what he saw. The TARDIS of The Magician was very similar to that of the Doctor but this control room was more crowded being used as a repository for a variety of chairs of all shapes and sizes. Turlough was left to find one that suited him, and he collapsed into it. For a few moments the Time Lord attended to the controls surrounding the rising and falling column, but finally turned back and gazed benignly at his captive.

'Where are you taking me? demanded Turlough as soon as

he saw The Magician turn round.

'Not a very original remark,' replied the Time Lord, 'but not to worry. We are going to see an old acquaintance. One whom you will remember joyously. My friend your great adventure, one in which I have been most privileged to have shared, is coming to an end. Triumph is assured, conclusion inevitable.' He gave Turlough a lily.

'Who are we seeing?' Turlough's voice sounded scared.

'You will recognise him in just one moment,' replied the Time Lord, as he turned on the viewing scanner. 'Be patient – just a few seconds more and all will come to light.' Outside, the world was in shadow. To left and right huge walls towered above them; in front a single column. In Turlough's befuddled brain the image meant something. But he couldn't make out the detail . . .

The Magician opened the main door and beckoned Turlough to follow. The Clansman did so, his feet dragging slowly on the dusty ground as he made his way outside. The TARDIS was now a pillar of stone, dwarfed by a sheer rockface standing close by. On either side rocks were drilled with holes – windows and doors at all levels. The area was deserted, save for one tall creature who came forward. A creature Turlough had met before on Earth, and again once before that in this very location. A Slot. *The* Slot – the one he always met.

The Magician waved the Slot into the TARDIS, grabbed Turlough (who was in danger of drifting away to look at the sights) back in. Immediately he set co-ordinates. Turlough returned to a chair. The Slot sat next to him. They dematerialised and moved into temporal suspension. Time Lord and Slot looked at the Clansman. Turlough felt uneasy and tried to wriggle back from their gaze. The Magician put out a restraining hand.

'What is your name?' asked The Magician formally.

'Vislor Turlough,' came the reply.

'Race?'

'Imperial Clansman of Total Science Knowledge of the Forty-Second Dynasty, Masters of Trion and the Eighteen Suns, Physical Rulers of the Galactic Core.'

213

'Impressive,' said The Magician with a smile, and he returned to the controls.

Turlough looked confused, but asked no question, feeling certain that he would get little in the way of meaningful reply.

The TARDIS rematerialised. Outside was near total darkness — perhaps a narrow walled cave. Nothing was visible through the scanner. The Magician opened the door and ushered Turlough into the blackness. The Clansman looked out, and then up. High above, almost invisible, was a pinpont of light. Or rather a string of lights moving across the sky. Yet it could not be the sky for they were the only lights. One tiny band straight above, and nothing else.

Turlough looked down at the floor. It was a highly polished silver which even in this blackness picked up the faint reflection of the lights above. So bemused was he by his surroundings that he hardly noticed that The Magician and the Slot were no longer with him. He turned back to the TARDIS, but as he put out his hand to touch it it disappeared. He was alone.

Unsure, bemused, his mind fragmented, Turlough wandered along the narrow passageway, glancing occasionally at the lights dancing far above his head. The tunnel narrowed and split. He looked up again. He was about to lose sight of the dancing lights. It seemed important that he didn't. Turlough turned and walked back the way he had come, past the position previously occupied by The Magician's TARDIS. Ahead the channel narrowed, but this time instead of splitting it came to a dead end. Turlough turned and walked the fifteen hundred metres back to the centre of the passageway. Directly above tiny lights still danced. He walked on another fifteen hundred metres and turned left. The tunnel petered out after a short distance. He retraced his steps and took the right fork. That too lasted but a little way before coming to a dead halt. There was no doubt. There was no way out.

Turlough retracted his steps to the centre. He knew he was trapped. Yet he had been imprisoned before, and escaped. In a maze. He remembered the maze. Things were different then. He had been faced with a logical problem and solved it. But here he was confined. For the twentieth time he looked up above him.

The little lights. He was somewhere normally seen from on high.

Turlough kept walking, not knowing why but feeling movement was better than stagnation. He gained an insight yet couldn't quite grasp why The Magician and the Slot should have taken the trouble to put him at the bottom of the Giants' Drop. Above were the tiny lights of the magnetic bridge. He really was enguled. Totally, utterly.

He walked. He knew he was trapped. He walked and turned. He became aware of a dull pain in his left arm. No, not in his arm. At the end of his arm. In his fist. He looked down. It was covered in blood. How could that be? He started walking, but the pain grew more intense. He looked again. As he walked his hand was hitting the side of the wall. Blood was flowly freely. And he couldn't stop hitting the uneven rock.

'Do something!' Turlough looked around in surprise at the shout. There was no one. He continued walking. Another shout. He heard his name. The sound was in his head.

'They've trapped you, you fool. They have left you here to die.'

Turlough put his hands to his ears. He didn't want to hear. Blood smeared his face. He resumed walking, banging the wall all the time. The shouting in his head continued. He spoke for himself. 'I am Turlough,' he said. It sounded soft. He repeated it louder. He said it again with greater tenacity. Now he was shrieking. The voice in his head tried to shout back. It was telling him he was *not* Turlough. It told him he was Rehctaht. But that was impossible. He was Turlough. He shouted again. Banging hard on the wall he marched up and down. The voice in his head argued. He shouted. He screeched. He moaned at the pain. And he stopped.

There was nothing. The voice in his mind had vanished. He marched again and started shouting just to make sure. He was still shouting when The Magician and the Slot rematerialised and pulled Turlough inside the TARDIS shaped like a fallen rock.

13: KING

The Magician worked hard bandaging Turlough's hand. It took the young Clansman twenty minutes to calm down and look afresh at his rescuers. He had no idea where he was, or what they were doing.

'It was Rechctaht,' said Turlough at last. He emphasised the word, as if it could have been someone else inside his mind. 'I had no idea . . .'

'No idea it would be like that?' asked The Magician kindly. 'You risked your life to defeat that woman.' He patted Turlough on the shoulder. 'If nothing else, that shows that the exile Turlough has grown up into a full-blooded Clansman worthy of Total Science Knowledge.'

Turlough managed a brief smile and then looked back at the Slot. He wanted to ask what he was doing there, but memories from the brain of Rehctaht which had resided in him came flooding in. They triggered recollections of his own suspicions. The Magician saw the look and took the opportunity to explain. 'You guessed that for Rehctaht to take you over she would need your brain disorientated. That was true, but you were wrong to think it would be a simple drug. That woman was beyond evil and devious far above anyone that has gone before. To disorientate in a maze was a much subtler approach because it left your body free of any physical interference from drugs as she prepared to take over. What we had to do was to expose you to another hopeless situation and get you to fight the presence of her in your robust, devious, stubbborn, mind. I am glad to say you fought so brilliantly. Vislor Turlough, you are all I ever claimed, and more. Far more.'

Turlough remembered the experiences vividly. 'The Giants' Drop,' he said. He turned to the Slot. 'Your people built it.' The Slot nodded. 'Do you still know why?'

'A focusing point for our psychological powers before most of our kind – known as The Laima – left this universe for ever. We built Charlottenlund.'

'And because you originally treated the Trions as food you must have been around when we were still evolving from the jungle.'

'After that period of barbarianism when we did, as you said, treat other beings as food, we concentrated on the psychological approach. Our knowledge and power were great, greater even than the Imperial Clans of today.'

'But the Laima did discover the ultimate unified theory?'

'That, and the realisation that the gravity constant of the universe was running down in a way that was unhelpful for their planned move into the next universe. So the Laima set up the gravity control unit on what you call Earth, leaving a few – known as the Slots – behind on Trion to monitor its progress. However, physical science was never our forte. Our ancestors tended to solve physical problems with whatever theory was needed to get by, without any real detailed thought. As time passed we Slots conveniently forgot about the gravity generator, tending instead the central column at the heart of our island – our one way of communicating with our lost bretheren, now in a new universe forever. And finally we realised that your race was emerging and that the section you now call the Clans, would gave great scientific potential. We named the planet Trion after the three great civilisations related to the planet – Laima, Slots, and Clansfolk. We imagined one day you would take care of the gravity unit, and so the image faded. We failed to notice life on Earth until it was too late.'

'Then it is no surprise that every race in the galaxy wants to go to Earth and inspect such a curious civilisation,' said Turlough. 'Every measurement of space time, every theory of the universe there is influenced by an artifact. They cannot even discover the correct nature of the speed of light!' It was, for all three, rather an amusing thought.

'Yet we try to make up for such an event,' continued the Slot. 'In another time dimension, where Earth, Trion and even New Trion are destroyed by the wildness of Rehctaht, we devised, with your older self, a way of aiding survival. And there for once the gravity generator helped the people of Earth.'

'And those deformed telepaths – the Pharix. Where did they come from?'

'Each year a few Laima come back – their curiosity dominating them to such a degree that they have to see what life has come to in this, their original universe. We find they had developed a very high moral stance, but have declined physically beyond belief. In the time zone you saw, three had elected to spend their time undertaking work to help out the Earthlings. As one said to you, it was their penance.'

The Magician coughed. 'Although this is a most interesting conversation,' he said deferentially, 'and indeed a truly historic meeting of our three races – a time to be recalled in all official histories of reality – there are nevertheless other matters to be resolved.'

Turlough looked at the Time Lord curiously. 'I can see,' he said as The Magician moved to the central control panel, 'how the Slots are involved in the question of Earth. I can also see why the Time Lords in general are interested in Earth . . .'

'. . . to see how a race makes out when they find themselves in the one part of the universe where the natural laws of gravity are twisted. Yes, a fascinating study.'

'But why are you, a Time Lord, following me around?' continued Turlough. 'Surely not just to rescue me from Rehctaht.'

'In reality my role only starts now,' replied The Magician ambiguously. There was a grinding sound at the TARDIS dematerialised. 'Have you thought of what you will do now you have defeated that woman for a second time?'

'Live on Trion for a while . . .' suggested Turlough hopefully, although even as he said it he knew that it was a forlorn belief.

'And what will you do when your other half returns?' Turlough looked puzzled. 'The other half,' continued The

Magician, 'that is currently hopping around the galaxy with the Doctor, will soon be arriving on a rather nasty planet with a very active volcano, only to be told that there has been a second revolution and that Imperial Clansmen may come home. He (that is you) will be surprised to meet his (your) double to say the least. Expecting to be a hero, he (you) might take exception to sharing the honours. Mightn't you (he)?'

Turlough conceded the difficulty. 'Besides which,' added The Magician, 'Juras might find it hard to pick between you. Remember, on this world she was never taken over by Rehctaht.'

'But that implies I have to go back to my previous space-time where Juras is dead – killed by me – and Trion is little more than rubble, caused by the space island which I piloted. Neither of those factors are likely to make me much of a galactic hero.'

'There is another way,' said the Time Lord, 'with your help and that of our friend,' he pointed to the Slot. 'I once more moved you out of your space-time continuum when I picked you up from the hospital bed. What originally happened in that continuum is that you remained there another week, were released, and, still half unsure of who you really were, started wandering around the historic monuments of the planet, metaphorically looking for your own past. You began to realise your brain was not your own. A violent struggle took place within yourself, and you succeeded in turning the magnetic bridge off as you plunged to your death down the Giants' Drop in order to rid Trion of Rehctaht forever.'

'Thank you for rescuing me from yet another disasterous scenario,' said Turlough. 'Where does that get me?'

'A TARDIS remains in its own space-time continuum, jumping sideways in space but only forwards and back in time. However, with the help of this gentleman's psychological powers,' (he waved at the Slot graciously) 'we can actually move back into the time stream that I interrupted.' Turlough moved to ask further questions, but the Magician held up an arm as the Slot put his hands on the central column of the TARDIS and concentrated hard.

It was all over in a matter of seconds. Turlough looked

around. Nothing had changed. There were still the three in the same crowded control room. The TARDIS had materialised; The Magician opened the door, and the three trooped outside.

The sight that met their eyes was not pleasant. Turlough, having plunged to his death was splattered around the silver floor. Blood, bones, flesh were everywhere. Turlough rushed back inside the TARDIS.

When he emerged, his stomach empty and feeling still very sensitive, he found the Time Lord and the Slot almost finished as they collected the remains into bags secured away in the depths of the TARDIS. They had even contrived somehow to clean the silver floor. 'Turlough is dead,' said The Magician, 'long live Turlough.'

Turlough looked bemused. The Time Lord tried to help him out. 'You have just escaped from exile and are system-wide hero. You have taken on surrogate Rehctaht and killed her, but in so doing have now fallen down The Giants' Drop. Many saw you fall. They will be down here soon with magnocranes.

'Now my friend and I must be going. We have shared a stupendous adventure Clansman Turlough; I am indebted to you. We shall meet again.' Adjusting his figure-of-eight hat the Time Lord handed Turlough a rose before edging back towards the Slot in the entrance of the TARDIS. Turlough was about to say farewell when a thought struck. 'How do I explain being alive after that fall?' he said.

'Up to you, old boy,' replied The Magician. 'But I wouldn't advise too much detail about Slots and Time Lords. Once people start realising their reality is being manipulated, they get anxious, forget about heroes and that sort of thing and then blame you for playing with their lives. And one other thing: I should keep rather quiet about gravity units – at least at first. Don't want to upset life on Earth too much, do we?'

'And what will you do?' asked Turlough, anxious to keep his companions with him for as long as possible.

'There is still a reality anomaly concerning the Mobile Castle,' said The Magician. 'We have to do a spot of temporal manoeuvering to get it in exactly the right place at the right time.'

And with that the two aliens disappeared, quickly followed by the TARDIS.

Moments later the magnocrane hit the bottom of the Drop and Turlough walked across to a totally bemused technician and an even more disturbed medical team. By the time they reached the top level a crowd had gathered. There were astonished gasps as Turlough stepped out unhurt. Juras Maateh was there. Alerted by the news of the disaster she had rushed to the caves at once.

Turlough put his arms around the girl and hugged her closed to him. She broke free from Turlough's embrace. 'Turlough!' she shouted. 'How?'

'A bit difficult to explain,' he replied as he walked away with the girl to the VT station, pursued by a crowd of astonished onlookers.

'When I saw you in hospital,' Juras continued, 'you could hardly remember who I was.'

'Indeed,' said Turlough, 'I think I lost my memory for a while. But now . . . Have you ever heard of an ARTEMIS drive?'

Juras shook her head, her arm linked with Turlough's.

'It's just an idea I've had. Let me tell you . . .'

DOCTOR WHO

	TERRANCE DICKS	
0426114558	Doctor Who and The Abominable Snowmen	£1.35
0426200373	Doctor Who and The Android Invasion	£1.25
0426201086	Doctor Who and The Androids of Tara	£1.35
	IAN MARTER	
0426116313	Doctor Who and The Ark in Space	£1.35
	TERRANCE DICKS	
0426201043	Doctor Who and The Armageddon Factor	£1.50
0426112954	Doctor Who and The Auton Invasion	£1.50
0426116747	Doctor Who and The Brain of Morbius	£1.35
0426110250	Doctor Who and The Carnival of Monsters	£1.35
	MALCOLM HULKE	
042611471X	Doctor Who and The Cave Monsters	£1.50
	TERRANCE DICKS	
0426117034	Doctor Who and The Claws of Axos	£1.35
	DAVID FISHER	
042620123X	Doctor Who and The Creature from the Pit	£1.35
	DAVID WHITAKER	
0426113160	Doctor Who and The Crusaders	£1.50
	BRIAN HAYLES	
0426200616	Doctor Who and The Curse of Peladon	£1.50
	GERRY DAVIS	
0426114639	Doctor Who and The Cybermen	£1.50
	BARRY LETTS	
0426113322	Doctor Who and The Daemons	£1.50

Prices are subject to alteration

DOCTOR WHO

0426101103	**DAVID WHITAKER** Doctor Who and The Daleks	£1.50
042611244X	**TERRANCE DICKS** Doctor Who and The Dalek Invasion of Earth	£1.50
0426103807	Doctor Who and The Day of the Daleks	£1.35
042620042X	Doctor Who—Death to the Daleks	£1.35
0426119657	Doctor Who and The Deadly Assassin	£1.50
0426200969	Doctor Who and The Destiny of the Daleks	£1.35
0426108744	**MALCOLM HULKE** Doctor Who and The Dinosaur Invasion	£1.35
0426103726	Doctor Who and The Doomsday Weapon	£1.50
0426201464	**IAN MARTER** Doctor Who and The Enemy of the World	£1.50
0426200063	**TERRANCE DICKS** Doctor Who and The Face of Evil	£1.50
0426201507	**ANDREW SMITH** Doctor Who—Full Circle	£1.50
0426112601	**TERRANCE DICKS** Doctor Who and The Genesis of the Daleks	£1.35
0426112792	Doctor Who and The Giant Robot	£1.35
0426115430	**MALCOLM HULKE** Doctor Who and The Green Death	£1.35
0426113322	**BARRY LETTS** Doctor Who and The Daemons	£1.50

R Books are obtainable from many booksellers newsagents. If you have any difficulty please send chase price plus postage on the scale below to:

Star Cash Sales
P.O. Box 11
Falmouth
Cornwall

OR

Star Book Service,
G.P.O. Box 29,
Douglas
Isle of Man,
British Isles.

While every effort is made to keep prices low, it is sometimes necessary to increase prices at short notice. Star Books reserve the right to show new retail prices on covers which may differ from those advertised in the text or elsewhere.

Postage and Packing Rate

UK: 55p for the first book, 22p for the second book and 14p for each additional book ordered to a maximum charge of £1.75p. BFPO and EIRE: 55p for the first book, 22p for the second book, 14p per copy for the next 7 books, thereafter 8p per book. Overseas: £1.00 for the first book and 25p per copy for each additional book.